# ADVANCED PRAISE

Xicanxfuturism is much more than an anthology—it is a set of principles, an invitation to dialogue, a teaching tool, a literary intervention, a call and response, and most importantly it is an act of resistance against the continual attempts at erasure and ethnic cleansing of Mexican and Latinx communities in the US through its powerful insistence on our futures. As a "codex," the literal meaning of which is "tree trunk," the authors and editors assert Xicanx roots in the survival of colonial/ imperial attempts at annihilation while also imagining different liberatory spaces and forms of expression. From Pedro Iniguez's speculative poetics that take us to galaxies far far away to the bilingual "cyber chamacos" in the poetry of Erika Said Izaguirre; to essays on the origins of Xicanx mythology as a call for liberatory action by Ernesto Ayala to fictional works that blend cultures, languages, and worlds like that of Ricardo Tavarez or the aftermaths of dystopian wars in the case of Dante Olivas' short story, "Come los ricos. Eat the Rich" or severe climate change in Frederick Luis Aldama's graphic short story "Chupacabra Charlie"; this is a volume of Xicanx steadfastness in the land, in our cultures, and in our dreams. Composed of four thematic sections and various writings styles and forms, these two dozen contributors defy borders, genres to break new boundaries in Xicanx literature, Fantasy, Visual Art, Science Fiction, Comics, Poetry and more along the way. It is a volume full of hope in dark times, as poet Osmani Ochoa asserts, it is an "everlasting prayer/ of what we've always deserved/...reborn/ from the last of borders." AMEN.

—Melissa Castillo-Garsow, Associate Professor of English, Lehman College & Graduate Center, CUNY.

*Xicanxfuturism Gritos for Tomorrow Codex I,* reimagines the past, present and future of La Raza through the most intriguing stories, art and political theory. The Indigenous knowledge and Xicanx history transcends everything we've ever known as we board starships leaving planet Genesis as refugees, grab a burger with a Chicanonaut or memorialize our forgotten names through recipes. This codex is so much more than an anthology but a view into the possibilities of tomorrow; a tomorrow of outcomes. What will the world look like when we finally resist as a people? Will the universe remember our struggles? This codex dares to imagine what that future may look like.

—Robert Ramirez, Chicano Poet & Activist, Founder of The Brown Book Club

# XICANXFUTURISM

## GRITOS FOR TOMORROW

# XICANXFUTURISM
## GRITOS FOR TOMORROW

## CODEX I

Edited by

Scott Russell Duncan and Jenny Irizary

**RIOT OF ROSES**
PUBLISHING HOUSE
SEJATNGA
UNCEDED TONGVA TERRITORY
SOUTH WHITTIER, CALIFORNIA

XICANXFUTURISM
GRITOS FOR TOMORROW

CODEX I

# DEDICATION

# CONTENTS



•
CE:
MIGRANTFUTURISM

●●

## OME:
## TIERRA Y LIBERTAD

●●●

## YEI:
## MOTHER EARH AWAKENS

••••
## NAHUI:
## YES, WE WILL

## EDITORS' NOTE:

Questions of standardized demarcation in text, such as nomenclature or the italicization and spelling of words, can be contentious. The languages used by Xicanx people, including Chicano English, Spanglish, Caló, and various forms of Spanish, are often mixed, colloquial, and fluid. In this codex, the editors have generally deferred to each author's voice, leaving such decisions to be resolved within each piece.

# PREFACE

## E.G. CONDÉ

Peering down over the wasteland of colonial decimation, the figure of the Xicanx looms above, spun from the magic of song and dance. Xicanx is the immortal legacy of indigenous ancestors who survive into the future in blood and story. This anthology asks what is the shape of that future for Xicanx people? In poems, stories, and dreamlike artwork, it explores what it means to embrace the rubble, the residues of decimation that messily make us into something in-between. Neither wholly white nor indigenous, American nor Mexican, the Xicanx is the cyborg that inhabits the frontera, where the seams of multiple realities are rifting like tectonic plates in subduction.

In the stories that follow from this marvelous collection (Codex I and Codex II), glimpses of the futures are conjured by the sorcery of storytelling, a weave of narrative threads that embrace the marginal, conjuring worlds without borders, where the mythscapes of ancestral Mexica, Pueblo, and Apache entangle with the Virgen de Guadalupe and the big black eyes of extraterrestrials from faraway galaxies. Xicanxfuturism is a myth cycle that celebrates mutation. Uttered in Spanglish, this symphony of multilingual tales is like a plunge into a wormhole of colorfully feathered possibilities; where interstellar "taco stand oases" (Pedro Iniguez) dock with obsidian spacecraft (elindiocopyright1985), where "cosmic-bronze emissaries" (Juan Manuel Pérez) declare with unflinching certainty, their "declaration of...belonging anywhere, everywhere" (Osmani Ochoa). This is a palimpsest of "migrant futures" that takes the shape of the jaguar (M.M. Olivas), that is itself a kind of quantum sorcery (Joe Menchaca) of imagination, a persistent brujería (Irene Blea) that remakes Aztlán (Ernesto Mireles), shifting the "horizon" (Luis Valderas) of intergenerational oppression to something that is limitless and ever-expansive.

Through the rich traditions of Afrofuturism, Africanfuturism, and Indigenous futurisms, marginalized people are imagining futures for themselves, writing against attempts to erase them from history and our precarious present. Xicanxfuturisms joins this literary lineage of liberatory imaginative practice to build worlds beyond the violent limits of borders. While readers with a strong connection to the Xicanx world will find many personal resonances in these dazzling tales, I am certain that those outside of the community, like myself, will walk away from this tale feeling inspired and energized about what tomorrow could become.

# INTRODUCTION

## SCOTT RUSSELL DUNCAN

Xicanxfuturism has been an anthology that brought transformation: ending of old ways and beginnings of new friendships, as a book on the future should. It brings to my mind the Call to Revive Our Native Minds that I read before the events I host. As Dr. Ernesto Mireles, who is a contributor to this anthology, has previously pointed out, we have lost the land, but we have our minds, but just barely. For 500 years settler-colonialism has attacked our culture, identity, history, our unity...the list goes. We need our minds, we need each other:

**Call to Revive Our Native Minds**
Disengage with exploitation
Refuse erasure
Honor Indigenous spaces
Restore the environment
Represent liberation
Organize our community

This is Xicanxfuturism. A short call for the future, a belief in Xicanx people, Native people, Raza (a term used decades and decades before Vasconcelos got to it). Xicanx people are the no-spacesuit-needing mutants of the land that have survived disasters and will thrive in the disasters that await us until the next cycle.

This *Xicanxfuturism* is not an anthology. *Xicanxfuturism* follows the tradition of a codex, a mix of images and words presented for discussions. One of the many discussions our community needs to have is about having a future, about restoring stewardship of the planet and ourselves. I've spoken to many contributors in this codex about the future, on Xicanismo, and I'm hoping to speak more and speak to more of them. I'm name dropping to give a sense that you are a part of this time-frozen conversation...meaning, these words, images, and ideas are now leaping-off points for your discussions. And this conversation, as many do, went longer than expected and so we have made two separate publications, *Xicanxfuturism Codex I,* which continues into *Xicanxfuturism Codex II.*

You might have noticed the term Xicanx. Xicanx and its forms is the only label we chose for ourselves that looks to our Native heritage and resistance to settler-colonialism. Granted, we got problems, is it Chicano, Chicana, Chicane or Xicanx? I'm using the X at the end to be inclusive to all our people and the first X because I'm down with the Brown, with our Native selves. Xicanx doesn't collaborate with our own oppression. The end X, along with inclusivity for our siblings, is a Xicanxfuturist labeling, an emblem of capacity to transform and change after connecting with each other and knowing how to better reflect each other's humanity, whether this is the final form or not (after all there is also Raza).

The writer Joel Flores recently told me a great Xicanxfuturist idea on the initial X and it became his flash essay. Check out "The X in Xicanismo" in the upcoming Codex II for more on the X.

There are many ways to scry the future, to prepare for it and break down the present and cook up a better tasting what's to come. Of course, not everyone sees the future in this codex, or the world outside it, in the same way, as it should be.

We are ever evolving, anticipating the next cycle, the new mutation we need for the current generation to survive. We are ever shedding our skin, as the Commander of Project:MASA, Luis Valderas has told me. We have been shedding skins dealing with apocalypses and wastelands, tired of them or not, for 500 years.

And recently the wasteland came home to the place I was born, where some ancestors had been for millennia (Luiseño). Other ancestors (Mexican Californio) built a city and forms of oppression there, then others (Anglo) stole it and oppressed land and people to an unimaginable, but very real, degree. Los Angeles burned unlike it had burned before, tearing down structures mismanaged and built in the settlers' past, billowing poison in the air like a kaiju Mother Earth telling us the abuse is enough. As a teenager, a SoCal Mountain across from where I lived burned; my friends and I stood in amazement as we turned around and saw giant flames, just long enough to be doused in pink fire retardant from a low-flying old bomber. The land is drier, angrier now than last century. Fire is our future.

The fire rages even as we put this codex out for production with state violence conducted by ICE and other forces against the people of Los Angeles and this man-made disaster is spreading to other areas. The elimination of due process means ICE's acts are ethnic cleansing, and the irony is that we are targeted for our Native features that come from this continent. It is not the first or second time US forces have terrorized the Raza of Los Angeles. The land is occupied, as are we.

There is hope in ourselves and in our ability to combat exploitation of the environment and our own bodies. Our stories, art, and essays demand it.

Of course, the pieces contained within and without this codex are part of this hopeful conversation. E.C.-Dukes and Ronnie Dukes's graphic novels inspire us to chase clean energy, to slam the accelerator and run like hell from those who would stop it as it powers us on in our task of healing the planet.

Many aspects are uncertain, as the many attacks on our identity and personhood have made us a community of fear, inaction and have caged, policed, and devalued us continually at the threat of being erased and gaslighted into believing we don't belong to the land where we might have local tribal affiliations or that our ancestors crossed for millennia. We are figuring out ourselves and the future. Attack us, detract from us, label us with words meant to control us from other continents like Hispanic or Latinx, we can still go into our households, whether of migrants who crossed from Jalisco or of those who were crossed over by two colonizations, and see the shared lifestyle, memories, kitsch and kitchens.

These are many varied angles on the gem of Xicanxfuturism. To me, Xicanxfuturism is the hope for a literature (artsy or otherwise) mired in the spinning wheels of representation, backwards-looking traditions no longer operable, and worldviews that support the settler-colonial status quo, its imposed borders, and the lie that we have not always been around, rooted here yet on the move for thousands of years. Speculative fiction for Xicanx peoples remains a place unfettered by the narratives stuck on repeat because our conditions haven't changed and because speculative fiction remains the realm of imagination and possibility beyond what is real, with solutions that may not be quite possible. For example, *Xicanxfuturism* has stories about ejecting our problematic castes, billionaires and their wannabes, to other worlds. Or migrating with the same kind of street vendor hustle on the rings of Saturn or Mars, such as the taco truck on the cover by elindiocopyright1985.

But Xicanxfuturism and the speculative imagination are also nonfiction...where are we going wrong, where can we go now? Fiction, non-fiction, poetry, and the visual all have necessary visions to convey. Ernesto Ayala has spoken about loving your Raza, a Xicanxfuturist act, meaning, we will develop, we will be nurtured. Dr. Ernesto Mireles often speaks of Xicanx not living our own history, but the settlers' and that a reconnection with our history will create ourselves as a people who can determine their destiny, their future.

Questions are part of Xicanxfuturism. Dr. Juan G. Berumen had asked in a presentation, where do your Indigenous roots come from? And opened Pre-Cuauhtémoc maps and showed migrations happen over time, all discussions that weigh in on the future, where our migrations might pause. In another presentation, Tainofuturist author E.G. Condé had all us Mexicans in tears when he asked, "How did you crawl out of your last wreckage?" How we answer is Xicanxfuturism. Another Boricua and assistant editor on *Xicanxfuturism,* Jenny Irizary, has talked to me on authenticity and trauma. How do we engage with a culture sometimes hidden from us, a culture of survival, to get us here, when trauma silences so much? Our answers, how we walk the present and the future is finding our own futurism.

There are things to fear in the future, blundering into tomorrow and putting all our efforts into a system that feeds on our humanity, as we have before. Xicanxfuturism is an attempt to imagine something else, at least, to imagine how the path our feet might hit will look and feel and where we might walk elsewhere.

At each section title you'll find introductions on the art and writing it contains. At the end of each section there are short study guides called Obsidian Visions with questions to help the discussion so desperately needed for the future.

While many folks seem to think carving out a rightful place for Xicanx writers and artists precludes connections, the opposite is true, a strengthened and cohesive Raza is better able to aid and thank others. While our community is fragmented and blurry, I can push through the fog to thank Bill Campbell for *Mothership,* Ytasha L. Womack for *Afrofuturism,* as well as to Shane Hawk for *Never Whistle at Night,* Grace L. Dillion for *Walking the Clouds,* and Joshua Whitehead for *Love After The End.* I'd also like to thank the editors Alex Hernandez, Matthew David Goodwin, and Sarah Rafael García for editing and creating speculative anthologies such as *Speculative Fiction for Dreamers,* and Cathryn Josefina Merla-Watson and B. V. Olguin for editing and creating *Altermundos.* The artist Catherine S. Ramírez, who originated Chicanafuturism, gets a big thank you for pioneering art and thoughts on our conditions and tomorrows. These connected and interconnected futurisms have kept us dreaming and knowing our dreams matter and inspired the creation or helped endure the birth pangs of *Xicanxfuturism: Gritos for Tomorrow.*

Jenny Irizary, assistant editor, has my deepest gratitude for the keen insights, thoughtful questions, and the many ideas that strengthened this codex, as well as our volatile arguments over vampires vs. robots. (Also thanks to Yellow Kitty for his vociferous opinions.) Their contributions were essential. Thanks also to Luz Schweig (visionary editor of *Somos Xicanas*) for her support of this project and my work. And thanks to the publisher, Riot of Roses and its head, the wonderful poet Brenda Vaca, who took on this codex on top of a busy schedule. All of you have been incredible friends, and I am grateful for your camaraderie throughout the journey of creating the codex.

Before I leave, I'd like to recognize a quartet of contributors to this anthology, the fathers of Xicanx sci-fi R. Ch. Garcia and Ernest Hogan, the Commander of Project:MASA, Luis Valderas, and scholar, author and editor Frederick Luis Aldama. Their work has greatly inspired many Xicanxfuturists and sci-fi writers and artists of all backgrounds.

# TENETS OF XICANXFUTURISM

## INDIVIDUAL XICANXFUTURISM TENETS

- (M.M. Olivas) Xicanxfuturism is the modality for which to create a newer, more diverse cultural consciousness that is queer, feminine, adaptive, and accepting, unbound from physical and social border walls.

- (Angela Acosta) Xicanxfuturism puts forth ways of existing, not always that different from those of the present day, and being as individuals whose languages, cultures, and lives have been shaped by (neo)colonialism and (neo)imperialism.

- (Ernest Hogan) Xicanx is a science fiction state of being.
    - We are new life and new civilizations, boldly crossing all borders.
    - Xicanxfuturism dreaming rasquache futures, using aesthetic terrorism, creative blasphemy, and guerrilla worldbuilding in the face of those who would have us exterminated.

- (Pedro Iniguez) Science-Fiction subgenre incorporating near- or far-future Chicano subculture, struggles, music, food, as well as the feeling of "In-between-ess," caught between national identities and mixed-race heritage, along with the use of Spanglish, among many other aspects.

- (Scott Russell Duncan) Xicanxfuturism is a decolonial, resistive speculative cast into the possibility of existing in the future as a culture for a people who have not only migrated but been crossed over, and reconnecting to Indigenous practices, land stewardship, and driving destinies. Xicanxfuturism is a how-to for La Raza to build a rocket ship to ourselves.

- (Anonymous) Xicanxfuturism is the extension of Chicano identity and culture into the infinites of possibility. It is physical, emotional, and spiritual. It is who we always were and can be.

- (Luis Valderas) Xicanxfuturism is using both serious and satirical approaches to contemporary events dealing with immigration, identity, social and environmental justice, as they relate to "Chican@ Space" at a national and cosmic level. This makes itself evident within the narrative and conceptual aesthetics used by the artist. This includes visual, music, performance and theater arts.

- (Luis Valderas) Xicanxfuturism is our gente and our culture giving ourselves permission to be present in the future as cosmic citizens.

- (Luis Valderas) The purpose of the Project:MASA Series was to present the visual aesthetics and concepts of chican@ futurism as they grew out of Chicano art. These exhibits featured iconography, imagery and narrative visual art that presented and defined the visual aesthetic.

- (Luis Valderas) Acknowledgment of Responsibilities of a Cosmic Citizen
    1. You are responsible to yourself—Your actions affect you and your wellbeing.
    2. You are responsible to others—Your actions affect others and their wellbeing.
    3. You are responsible to your community as a whole—Your actions affect the wellbeing of the community.
    4. You are responsible to the earth—Your actions affect the wellbeing of the earth and all living thing on it.
    5. You are responsible to the cosmos—Your actions affect the balance of the cosmos.

- (Sendy Tapia) Xicanxfuturism is ancestral guidance in all its purest forms: breathing, being, living, thriving, and persevering beyond all tethers to a colonized Western world.

- (Dr. E.C.-Dukes) Oftentimes, Xicanxfuturism is discussed alongside Afrofuturism as evidenced by Ytasha L. Womack (2013). In Latinx studies, according to Aldama and González (2018) Latinofuturism is "science fiction that rises to the level of meaningful literature always reflects or refracts some crucial issue within society" (108). Aldama and González assert Latinofuturism "is concerned with imagining Latinxs in alternate spaces" (106). Specifically, Catherine S. Ramírez (2008) theorized Chicanafuturism to envision Chicanas in the future. The use of the letter x in Xicanx centers Indigeneity and is gender-inclusive. Xicanx recalls the work of Ana Castillo (1994) and her use of the word Xicana to assert our Indigenous roots. We may also consider the work of José Esteban Muñoz (2009) whose work on queerness calls on us to do, not just be, for a better future. Muñoz discusses queerness as resistance, an ideology, an art form, and what we collectively hope for in the future. "We must dream and enact new and better pleasures, other ways of being in the world, and ultimately new worlds," argues Muñoz (1). The work of these previous scholars may help to form the definition and tenets of Xicanxfuturism.

**References:**

Aldama, Frederick, and Christopher González. *Latinx Studies: The key concepts.* Routledge, 2018.
Ramírez, Catherine S. "Afrofuturism/Chicanafuturism: fictive kin." *Aztlán: A Journal of Chicano Studies* 33, no. 1 (2008): 185-194.
Womack, Ytasha L. *Afrofuturism: The World of Black Sci-fi and Fantasy Culture.* Chicago Review Press, 2013.

- (Dr. E.C.-Dukes) Inspired by the work of previous BIPOC scholars in Afrofuturism, Latinofuturism, and Chicanafuturism, a new word Xicanxfuturism is a science fiction genre that centers Xicanx people and envisions a new and better future for them. Xicanxfuturism features an empowered Xicanx community creating complicated solutions to complicated problems in our society. Xicanxfuturism resists current oppressive systems and visualizes new ones that are rooted in collective liberation. Xicanxfuturism rejects white supremacy, bigotry, xenophobia, and genocide. Xicanxfuturism embraces revolution to fight against apartheid, assaults on civil liberties, and to protect the environment. Xicanxfuturism is an artistic tool used to fight for the liberation of all oppressed peoples and features our commitment to justice. The role of Xicanxfuturism is to free our people from colonial and imperialist propaganda. The goal of Xicanxfuturism is to envision a world that is anti-capitalist and anti-imperialism. Xicanxfuturism aims to release us from our chains to one-dimensional thinking that makes us believe there is only one way to success and instead puts forward other ways of living, being, and thinking. The purpose of Xicanxfuturism is to expose our physical and mental enslavement by white Euro-centric dominant ideology, to expose our subaltern status to each other and not for the benefit of the oppressor. Xicanxfuturism is by, for, and about Xicanx people.

- (Patrick Fontes) Chicano Futurism explores the manifold, imaginative possibilities of the Chicano experience through the lens of speculative, science fiction. Strolling through porticos leading to varied dimensions in time and space, Chicano protagonists refashion science fiction into fantastic realities adorned with familiar touch, smell and sights.

- (W.O. Torres) Xicanxfuturism is more than Mexicans in the future. It's announcing our presence as dreamers and imagineers of what a future can look like. And it's unlike anything that's been handed to us.

- (Victoria Bañales) Xicanxfuturism is centering Xicane peoples and cultures, imagining a future where we are agents of transformation, where pasts, presents, and futures are bridged and collapsed, giving rise to new representations, where metal, magic, and materiality are fused, creating space and ships as we navigate yesterday, today, and tomorrow, in this plane or another.

# XICANXFUTURIST TENETS

## COMPILED BY DR. E.C.-DUKES

- **Revolutionize through Genre:** Approach critical issues in speculative science fiction narratives that center Xicanx people and envisions a new and better future for them at a national and cosmic level. Imagine new life, new civilizations, and new technologies boldly crossing all borders, for, with, and about Xicanx people.

- **Unrestrained Modality:** Create cultural consciousness that is queer, feminine, adaptive, and accepting, unbound from physical and social border walls, fusing various modes and materials to refashion the Xicanx experience using visual and aural diverse artistic tools for production.

- **Ideology that Resists:** Reject all forms of oppression, announce our presence, and accept ancestral guidance. Be responsible to ourselves and others, the community, the earth, and the cosmos. Reconnect to Indigenous practices, land stewardship, and driving destinies. Center Indigeneity and be gender-inclusive. Protect the environment. Expose colonial and imperialist propaganda. Envision a world that releases us from physical and mental enslavement. Redefine being.

- **Xicanx Expression:** Center Xicanx peoples and cultures, imagining a future where we are agents of transformation giving rise to new representations. Produce iconography, imagery and narrative visual art in the future with infinites of possibility that is an extension of Xicanx identity and culture. Build a physical, emotional, and spiritual how-to for la raza to build up ourselves. Transfer the feeling of "in-between-ess" caught between national identities and mixed-race heritage, along with the use of Spanglish, a rasquache aesthetic, and creative worldbuilding.

- **Liberating Space:** Visualize and form spaces of collective liberation that persevere beyond all tethers to a colonized imperialistic world. Imagine Xicanx in future spaces.

- **Unite Future with Fantastic Reality:** Imagine ourselves in a new world adorned with familiar touch, smell and sights remembering who we were and depicting what we can be. Invent complicated solutions to complicated problems.

# CE:
# MIGRANTFUTURISM

Migrantfuturism, though not coined by Osmani Ochoa, was applied by them to the condition of our gente, drawing on themes of travel, migration, immigrant rights, and continuing the walk all ancestors have made on Turtle Island / Cemanahuac, crossing roads of the past, present and future, retaking paths and looking for new ways.

# RE: <MIGRANT>FUTURISM

## OSMANI OCHOA

<migrant>futurism
blooms from the ruins
and ashes of racial capitalism

sprout
ing
from
the
decom
posed
flesh
left
behind by
the monstr
osities
of
(nuclea
r)
genoci
de &
empire

Our bodies are starships.
Our vision, our star map
Of future utopias that emerge from our own hands.
We steer our bodies past moons and asteroids
Until we land        on a new world
Of our own creation.

Our starship's rooted
In radical migrant / refugee lineages
To be en route means
Conceiving a future where everyone
Is liberated, without:

borders /

      walls /

  displacement /

            immigration status /
exploitation /

        occupation /

  surveillance /

     white supremacy /

          transphobia /
xenophobia /

           misogyny /

     machismo /

imprisonment /

        deportations /

<migrant>futurism
defies/threatens the status quo
and dominant paradigms
it produces a fear of an alien planet
and all its possibilities
we stir a panic of the change we might birth
or the current world we may begin
to crack and upend.


Cuauhtemoc

prophesized          that     after

An age of      darkness        our sun     will shine

again.          We are        carriers   of


DNA braids
        of ancient
memories. Centuries
        pass. Our
bioluminescent skin
        lowly brightens
and flickers.
        We are the
quasar light
        of cosmic
night-
        fall.

<Migrant>futurism     is          proletariat

                                        fist
defiantly pointing

          towards the        opening      sky

cascaded       by         the    sunlight

      of
      a      red         horizon.

It is    ours
            yesterday,       today,       to-

morrow.          <Migrant>futurism          is

     unheard,      everlasting       prayer

   of    what we've         always     deserved.

It's     in              motion

      It    will  land
              and will be here to stay     & depart
              >>>return
      built and reborn
              from the last of borders
      a renaissance
A declaration of we are
                  as   we     are
      anywhere    nowhere      everywhere

<Migrant>futurism is us

          here

            now.

# COYOTE AND PLANET GENESIS

## OSMANI OCHOA

*"Es posible que Dios exista, pero con todo
  lo que nos ha pasado, ¿podría importar?*
—Mario Vargas Llosa

*Part 1.*
They call him Coyote.
Mom and me are waiting
For him and dad.
They arrive
to get us out
before we'd be swallowed
by the sun.
Our oceans evaporated.
Coyote's spaceship,
a giant seashell,
is our ticket out of Planet Genesis.

*Part 2.*
The ramp lifts,
sealing the entrance.
With a low hum,
the spaceship ascends,
leaving behind
rocky red, scorching surface
and the sky ablaze
in orange, cackling flames.
Coyote has a map
of galaxy wormholes
to get us to refuge, Planet Kepler

Five-hundred light years away
We will get there in one
By his tricks.

*Part 3.*
One year passes
when we arrive.
A colossal structure hovers,
mid-air.
Coyote directs us, "Get your codes ready.
We need them to cross Moon Checkpoint."
Armed robots, the Planetary Patrols
Are gatekeepers to safety.
"Mom, they look scary."
She holds me tightly.
Dad's hands tremble.

*Part 4.*
Planetary Patrol Robot: *via communication device* Unidentified spacecraft, state your purpose and identity.
Coyote: We are Alienites from Planet Genesis, seeking refuge, as our planet was swallowed by our sun.
Planetary Patrol Robot: You will need clearance and authorization to proceed. Submit your identification codes for verification.
*Coyote complies, sending off everyone's codes. The Planetary Patrols analyze the data with scrutiny and suspicion.*
Planetary Patrol Robot: Your identification codes are not recognized in our database. You are *not* authorized to land!
Coyote: Please, we come peacefully. We just need to find refuge in a new planet. We can't possibly go back!
Planetary Patrol Robot: No. We stopped admitting Alienites, you must turn back now!
My dad: Captain, is there any way we can communicate with Planet Kepler's Leadership Council to resolve this issue?
*pause, robot analyzes the entire crew and spaceship closely*

Planetary Patrol Robot: Okay, we will send the details of your petition to our superiors. You may try again after receiving official authorization.
*The pink energy field of the Moon Checkpoint began to glow brighter, barring the spaceship from advancing further.*
My mom: *nods* Thank you for your understanding. We'll wait for further instruction.


*Part 5.*
Our spaceship hovers
near the Moon Checkpoint,
trembles forcefully
to the rhythm
of a loud explosion.
A fellow Alienite spaceship
is in flames,
bombed by the Planetary Patrols.
"Mom! Dad! We need to get out of here!"
A wailing siren
echoes in space.
Our spaceship screen flickers,
a message from the Leadership Council:
"We regret to inform you
that your request for passage
has been denied
due to security reasons.
You are welcome
to try again in the future
when we are no longer under planetary lock-down.
Safe travels."


*Part 6.*
Coyote swiftly
maneuvers the spaceship
to another wormhole.
752 other Alienite spaceships follow us,

1,000 light-years away
towards another planet
with enough water for everyone.
My mom laments:
"I hope the next planet,
doesn't have armed guards
or checkpoints or walls
that keep us out.
We never had that in Planet Genesis."

Coyote informs us:
"We'll get to Planet Earth
In no time."

*Part 7.*
*Nothing in any universe stays the same, forever.*
*This is what world-building looks like.*
*We've traveled from stars, genesis, death, birth, end of worlds to new beginnings*
*In spirals, cycles upon cycles.*
*Vulnerability created the cosmos.*
*We are making our way*
*through every corner*
*of space and time*
*to restore much-needed balance.*
*We bring*
*faint rumblings*
*of interstellar revolutions*
*happening now*
*but light years away*
*where you will see*
*what was once unfathomable.*
*There's a spiral*
*of no beginning and no end.*
*And here we are.*

*We've always existed.*
*You just didn't have*
*the technology*
*or the will*
*to hear us.*

# EPÍLOGO: GUERRA DE LAS GALAXIAS (UN CORRIDO TUMBADO)

## OSMANI OCHOA

Les cuento una historia
Que nace en otro planeta
En una galaxia lejana
Su propio universo crearon
Algo difícil de entender:

Un extraterrestre.
Coyote, lo llamaban
Con sus miles de naves
Viajaba por todas

las galaxias.
Allá no había racismo
Ni colonización

No tenían fronteras
Fue un héroe, un embajador
Ayudando a su raza escapar

de su planeta.
Coyote con su mapa
Viajaba por portales espaciales
Para poder transportar
Alienígenas a mundos mejores.

Esta historia concluye
Con un viaje intergaláctico

Cuando llegarían a su destino
No se imaginarían
Que tristemente lanzarían
una guerra de galaxias.
Y nuevos mundos construirían.

Murió jefe de jefes
por burlarse de las
                    fronteras
y defender a su raza
que venía de las estrellas.

# THE HORIZON

## LUIS VALDERAS

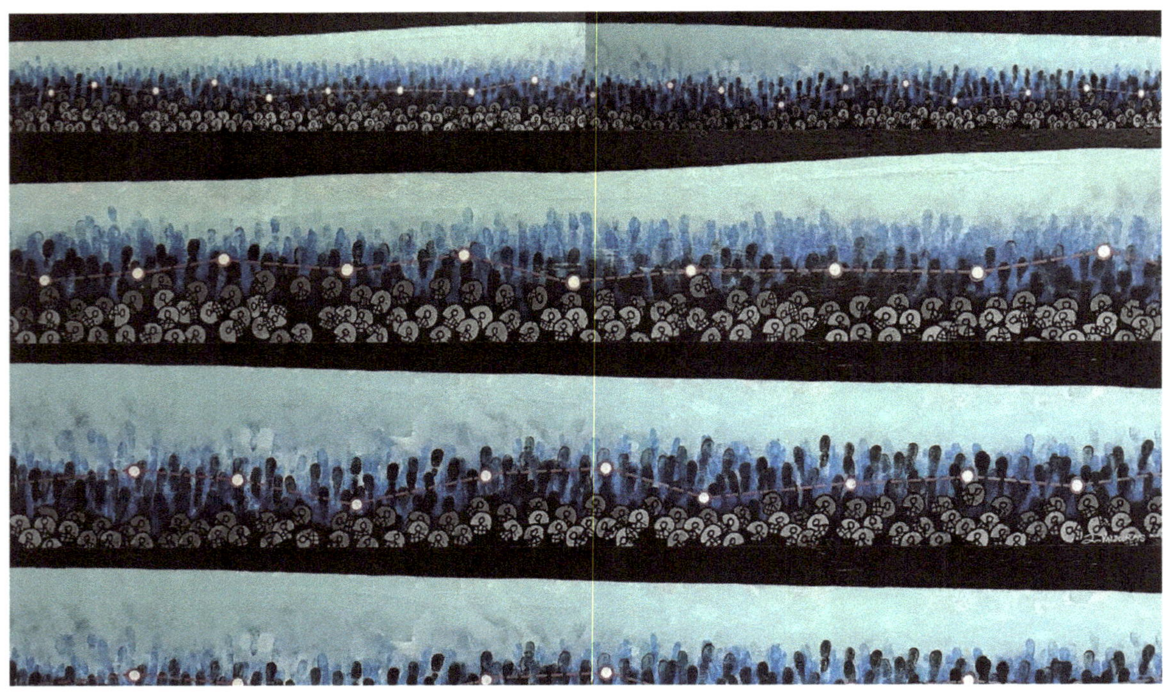

*Image of the full diptych*

*The Horizon*
Mixed media
12'x1'x2"—diptych
Luis Valderas 2007

This piece is a part of a series where I addressed issues around mass immigration and the fear it induces. My long-glance interpretation of the view from a space capsule during re-entry, and how that idea relates to crossing the Rio Grande River when re-entering the United States, the land of my ancestors, acts as a futurist metaphor. My family has had a generational relationship with this border—southern or northern depending on which generation and who was in political power. In my case el norte is home. I used the dashes and points, used on maps, to mark cities on the frontera that stretches across the horizon. My fingerprints allude to the masses approaching the border which is cobbled with calaveras in remembrance of those that came before. Together these icons harken to the xenophobic rhetoric and propaganda warning of the onslaught of masses of immigrants into the United States. From a distance this can be seen as a landscape but on closer examination the humanity, reaching for freedom, is revealed.

# LOW (ORBIT) RIDER

## PEDRO INIGUEZ

He pulls down his Locs
as the sun's last glimmer vanishes
behind the Earth,
shrouding that great blue marble
in twilight.
His spray-painted delta wing craft
cruises glacially above the atmosphere,
just above the grasp of its gravity well.
He hasn't been planetside
since his youth. Since the Great Migration.
The world he inhabits now is frigid,
its soil, the color of rust,
of ground coffee.
To those born there,
he's on OG, a Chicanonaut.
A brown man as alien as the little green men
in movies of old.
On occasion he takes
these voyages to glimpse Earth's azure beauty.
To remember its warmth.
He recalls the homies he lost here:
Some shredded by space debris.
Others burned up on reentry;
illegal hypersonic drag races gone awry.
A blip lights up his control panel.
Space Force comms him,
tells him to disperse.
Sighing, he hits the switch
and the jets fire up.

He decides he'll grab a burger
at a local fly-through space station
before he heads to a house
that doesn't feel like home.

# IRON ORE WASTELAND

PEDRO INIGUEZ

iron ore wasteland
a taco stand oasis
lunar miners smile

# NORTE

## MARTIN HILL ORTIZ

Luis had been told that at the north pole every direction was south. Now, standing on a sheet of ice at the top of the world, he discovered that was not true. Left, right, front and back were south. But there was also "up."

Above him, just beyond his outstretched fingertips was a swirling disc with spirals of yellow and gray. It was barely the width of his shoulders.

Luis thought of the hole in the ozone but immediately chided himself. This phenomenon was too tiny. And why so near the ground? And why exactly above the northernmost point of the world?

He thought of the aurora borealis. But he had seen auroras and this minuscule disc was nothing like them.

And why had no explorer before him ever mentioned such a wondrous floating disc?

So small and tight and beautiful. It was like a miniature spiraling galaxy, stars as fine as gold dust.

He stood in the early winter's shadow. The sun below the horizon made a half circle of light promising a dawn that would not come for months. On the other side, the icescape was dark with night.

Many before him had journeyed solo here. He liked to believe he was the first Chicano, but the records he scanned said nothing of that. He thought of Matthew Henson, a black man who, with Robert Peary, were the first to bestride the northernmost point to the world.

He thought of his childhood in Sonora. His mother spoke to him of el Norte where they would go someday. An unattainable goal.

He remembered trekking with his mother across the badlands of Texas. And then the concentration camp where he stayed for a year, never expecting to see his mother again. The tears of reunion. The years afterwards when he isolated himself, afraid of the world.

For so much of his life dreams, like rainbows, always lurched further away when he approached. And here he stood below some strange object just beyond his reach.

He felt the heaviness of his coats, his boots, his crampons. And yet, when he leaped, he touched the spiral, forever changing his life.

# LAS RAÍCES DE AZTLAN

## ERNESTO AYALA

In my everyday life I have worked various jobs including landscaping, factory assembly line, hauling, setting and cutting Christmas trees and I got a Class B License so I could drive a small passenger bus for a senior center. Driving the bus gave me at certain moments time to think and see the city. I would pick up elderly people in the San Fernando Valley to take to this Senior Center in Panorama City. Panorama City is an area of the San Fernando Valley, California that I compared to a smaller version of the neighborhoods surrounding MacArthur Park (Pico Union) in Los Angeles proper. It is the area with a larger population of recently arrived Raza. There are also many Central Americans in this area. On any given day you can drive around that part of the Valle and you will see many street vendors selling pupusas and other Central American foods. This neighborhood is in contrast to the older Chicano-Mexicano neighborhoods of Pacoima, San Fernando and parts of Sylmar where there are multi-generational families and Mexicano families that have been here for quite some time already. On one day driving my usual route I began noting how hidden in everyday life are tell-tale signs of a reality that has been in formation for thousands of years that totally contradicts the "American" narrative we are told every single day of our lives.

At that point in time, a store had opened near the Senior Center called "La Tapachulteca" that caters to the growing Central American population in the area, specifically people from El Salvador. Up the street from there on my route there were two separate murals. One of them, a tattoo shop adorned with Chicano gang-style calligraphy and artwork all around, on the side has a huge "AZTLAN" written in "Cali-Graffiti" style and a Mesoamerican-style skull with a headdress by its side, up the street and, unfortunately gone by now, a much older mural depicting the founding of Tenochtitlan when the people found the eagle on the nopal devouring a snake in the middle of Lake Texcoco. Instead of "Tenochtitlan" it said "Aztlan" in large plain letters in the foreground of the scene. Three separate locations in the same area with a word in Nahuatl telling a story as old as time in this part of the world. Two of those use the place name of Aztlan, one to show a sense of Chicano cultural pride in our Mesoamerican roots and the other depicting the ancient myth which continues being retold to this day of the migration from Aztlan to Tenochtitlan.

What do I mean by this story as old as time or the "American" narrative we are told every single day of our lives? Well, it goes like this, the USA is usually depicted as a country much like all others that came about through a war of independence and then through a Civil War that helped end the brutal practice of chattel slavery practiced against African people. The original inhabitants are painted as folkloric relics of a distant past which unfortunately somehow disappeared with the "advancement of civilization." Anything outside of that is considered "foreign" and anyone not a part of that picture is labeled an "immigrant" the liberal slogan usually goes "We are a nation of immigrants!" Yet, there is another story, one that has been in the process of unearthing by the Chicano and Native peoples, in particular those of the now "Southwestern" states of the USA.

What is this story? It is one emerging from every corner of what today many have chosen to call Aztlan. The story I like to call a little story that could derail an empire is told frequently, although not as much anymore by Chicanos and Raza here in the USA. The story basically retells the origin story of Mexico in regard to the founding of Mexico-Tenochtitlan. It has served many Mexicanos and Chicanos to feel a sense of pride in still being at home here despite the many injustices and atrocities meted out to our people. But we are not here necessarily to only retell this ancient myth. What we should try to do is understand why after thousands of years this myth which is one amongst so many that our ancestors held... Why does this myth continue to be recounted whether with a sense of pride and nationalist fervor or out of fear and repudiation?

Well, first of all, is there even any basis for this myth? It is a known fact that 5000 years ago Mesolithic peoples in Aridoamerica spoke a language that has been named "Proto-Uto-Nahuatl." This ancient language is what birthed dozens of indigenous languages spoken today or that at one point were spoken from an area as far as Idaho and Utah in the present-day USA to Guatemala, Nicaragua, El Salvador and, obviously, throughout Mexico as well. The specific areas where this language originated long ago has been debated, but it is undeniably believed to have been in today's "Southwest" States of the United States. A recent study by David L. Shaul published as *A Prehistory of Western North America* concludes through the study of linguistics that the homeland of Proto-Uto-Nahuatl was none other than the Southern San Joaquin Valley of California, an area heavily Chicano-Mexicano today. It is then known that speakers of Proto-Uto-Nahuatl spread out and thus came the family of languages known as "Uto-Nahuatl." The name was given to describe the (farthest geographically) speakers of these languages from the Ute of Utah/Idaho to the Nahuatl speakers, which spoke it as far south as Central America. Some notable Uto-Nahuatl languages are Tongva/Kizh of today's Los Angeles, Tataviam of my dearest Valle de San Fernando which is also part of Los Angeles. Other well-known Uto-Nahuatl languages are Comanche, Hopi-Pueblo, Wixarika (Huichol), O'odham, Tarahumara, and Shoshoni.

The language spread by migrating peoples who went north and for the most part south and then eventually these similarities in languages helped the migration of Maize up north. Maize, that all-too-common staple in our diets, not only connects the Chicano to the Mexicano and traditional Indigenous peoples in both Aztlan and Mexico but connects us to Centro America and connects us to Northern Native tribal nations and as far south as South America. Quoting Guillermo Bonfil Batalla, the late and very esteemed Chicano author and journalist Roberto "Cintli" Rodriguez stated, "As Mexican anthropologist Guillermo Bonfil Batalla (1996) argued, maiz itself is the civilizational impulse or seed (xinachtli) that triggered the development of what is today known as Mesoamerica. Traces of that impulse can be seen beyond Mesoamerica, throughout virtually all the maiz-based cultures of Turtle Island or the Americas" (Rodriguez 4).

Certainly, several maize-based cultures of nuestra America shared creation stories; one example is that of the "Hero Twins": which are spoken of in the ancient *Popul Vuh* (Tedlock) of the Maya as Hunahpu and Xbalanque they are represented among the Diné (Navajo) of Nuevo Mexico, Arizona and Utah as Naayéé'neizghání and Tóbájíshchíní. Further on the same creation story has been found in the ancient city of Cahokia in the present-day state of Illinois. Directly across the great Mississippi River a culture that left a massive pre-Columbian abandoned city of huge temple mounds held the belief in the hero twins as well based on archaeological evidence. Cultural links show up throughout Aztlan and Mesoamerica in various other ways as well. The veneration of Tlaloc, the deity of precipitation and giver of life to the Mexica and other Nahuatlaca, is directly linked to the Hopi and Pueblo Kachina cult. The Kachina are spiritual beings in Hopi culture; it is believed that they bring the rains and thus life. One such being also represented as a Kachina is Masaw (Maasaw, Masau'u) guardian spirit of the fourth world who assumes Tlaloc's role within the Hopi peoples. This is not even to mention the appearance of Tlaloc in ancient Mimbres and Jornada Mogollon ceramics and rock art dated A.D. 1000. Both Mimbres and Jornada Mogollon are "mother cultures" of the Southwest/Aztlan (*Popol Vuh*; Rodríguez; Riley; Shaul).

Speaking of the Hopi peoples, they are composed of several clans that at one point came together and after time developed into who today we know as Hopi. Of these clans several are of Mesoamerican origin, in fact one of them is even named the Kyarwungwa. Kyarwungwa is "Parrot." Parrots are not native to the Southwest. Parrots, in particular Scarlet

Macaws, were imported into the region, bred and raised there. For example, evidence of Macaw aviaries has been found at Chaco Canyon in Nuevo Mexico (Fisher). The Chaco culture is an ancient Puebloan culture which precedes the Hopi-Pueblo peoples of today. Chaco Canyon is believed to have been functioning around AD 900 to 1150. Notable discoveries among the ancient ruins include vessels made for drinking cacao and cacao residue in them (Fisher). Cacao is also not native to the so-called Southwestern desert regions, it is a small tropical tree originally from Mexico and Centro America brought in through trade networks that expanded for thousands of miles in which several other products such as copper, turquoise and specific types of shells were traded from North to South and vice versa.

Knowing this should describe to us a world that prior to colonization was connected far beyond what we have been told in today's classrooms that reduce the history of Chicanos to "Mexican-Americans" if they even learn even that at all and it also serves to tear us apart from our nearest of kin and from whom many Chicanos naturally descend from the Native peoples of the so-called Southwest. Many have wondered what might have been of this dynamic reality that existed prior to the invasion and subjugation by the Spanish crown. This I don't say because I feel it's necessary to ponder or spend ridiculous amounts of time navel gazing at what could have been (coulda shoulda), but reframing our origins in this way paints a much deeper and broader historical picture that is negated to us the Chicanos from day one. It is a fundamental paradigm shift necessary to understand who we are. It lets us know that migration to and fro over this vast region is something that precedes not only Spain, but the present occupation of the United States on this land. It should help us erode the borders that they have placed on our very understanding of ourselves. Borders placed psychologically that keep us perpetually feeling as outsiders, foreigners and immigrants in our own land. This is not to say being an immigrant is a bad thing, but can you really consider someone that migrates on a land that reflects them as well an "immigrant"?

And so, we begin noting not only that we had our own historical timeline which may have led to many "what ifs" but that our timeline, our very own historical path and process as Chicanos was not only intercepted once, but twice. First came the Spanish crown and then later the United States. Both came to colonize, and colonize they did, they reshaped our entire existence to fit their own needs. Here we can think of Bissau-Guinean and Cape Verdean agricultural engineer, revolutionary, anti-colonial, nationalist poet and leader Amilcar Cabral who clarified in speaking of colonization in general that, "The principal characteristic, common to every kind of imperialist domination, is the negation of the historical process of the dominated people by means of violently usurping the free operation of the process of development of the productive forces" (Cabral).

The ancient myth of the migration from Aztlan by the then Azteca who became Mexica begins taking on a more factual basis. But we should again ask ourselves why out of so many ancient myths that not only the Mexica held, but that so many other indigenous cultures had and continue to have, should the story of Aztlan continue to be propagated as many thousands of years later? In *Insurgent Aztlan: The Liberating Power of Cultural Resistance* Dr. Ernesto Mireles clarifies that,

> The only known fact about Aztlan is that the homeland of the Mexica was located somewhere to the north of Central Mexico. Where exactly is unimportant; what is important is the belief in nation, entitlement and indigeneity. I wonder why this story should survive, of the countless that have perished. Even more astonishing, mainstream Anglo scholars, politicians, and political pundits of the late twentieth century and early twenty-first century have awarded this myth some recognition...
>
> This story survived because at its root it creates a future escape from and promise of indigenous resurgence in the face of domination and control of first the Spaniards and later the twentieth century United States (Mireles 74).

It is here where we begin to understand why this myth has punched through thousands of years of history to resurface once again. You have in essence a massive chunk of land which like the rest of our continent was undergoing its own timeline, its Pre-Columbian past was deeply intertwined with that of Mesoamerica. The linguistic, cultural, economic, religious and geographical proximity it held were so a part of everyday life that the Spanish invasion taking advantage of the Aztlan myth and trade routes was able to penetrate what later on became Northern Mexico after a war of independence. The people that valiantly fought to remove the Spanish crown a short twenty plus years later came under the Yanqui Boot. This massive chunk of land was then severed again from its timeline as now a territory of the USA.

The story of Aztlan now goes from a cultural myth to a description of a developing nation. But what might shock many is that the story of Aztlan, as the story of nations developing out of others, is absolutely nothing new. The revolutionary socialist and nationalist anti-colonial struggles of the last century are perfect examples of this. Many nations were formed out of colonial domination and a reordering of the world to benefit European colonialism. Nevertheless, that reordering did not stop the historical process of those peoples; it merely caused it to develop in new ways under new conditions. The United States fought a long and costly war in a land once called "French Indochina," the people of that land ardently fought to expel the French colonizers, but they were only able to do that once consolidated as "Vietnamese" with a specific homeland now named "Vietnam." This did not exist prior to colonization, there was no Vietnam, there was no Vietnamese, the land obviously was there and the ancestors of the Vietnamese people who were from different ethnic groups obviously also there. But are we to deny the Vietnamese people any legitimacy? No! Over a million lives lost in their heroic wars of national liberation to even make that a point (against France and then the USA) and loudly proclaim that Vietnam and the Vietnamese are a people and nation and they will fight to the end to prove it.

On the minds of the entire world today is the name of Palestine, these heroic people who as of now lost over 30,000 people to the US-funded onslaught by the settler state of Israel are a perfect example of this very point. Palestine as a nation did not exist prior to the Zionist interjection. A territory called "historical Palestine" did exist but as we know of it today or as we hear our Palestinian brothers, sisters, and siblings proclaim, there was not. The Palestinian people obviously know this very well. The Palestinian National Charter, a founding document of the Palestinian Liberation Organization and a type of Palestinian Declaration of Independence, clearly states this in Article 2: "Palestine, with the boundaries it had during the British Mandate, is an indivisible territorial unit" (*Palestinian National Charter*). Who gave the British any legitimacy to carve anything out of that territory? Well, themselves. Nevertheless, out of this colonial restructuring of that part of the world are we to deny that a legitimate nation with the full right to self-determination did not arise? Only a Zionist would deny that. In fact, this cohesive nationalist pride, this sense of self that they are Palestinian no matter what, is what keeps the Palestinian people moving forwards despite the genocidal onslaught of the US-funded Zionist death machine.

The Materialist conception of history helps us understand history as not a series of unrelated events or a random, tangled mess, as the US educational system teaches us, but how everything is interconnected and related and what is here now withers away, but not before its contradictions help something else develop anew. As I have stated earlier, when the USA (and Spain) arrived here it imposed itself on a region with a prior existing dynamic human interrelation. Understanding that will give a basis for understanding the development for the contemporary understanding of an "Aztlan." The idea does not come out of nowhere for Chicanos, it develops out of a material reality of land theft and colonization. It was in 1962 that this was first put on paper by Jack D. Forbes in *The Mexican Heritage of Aztlan,*

> The Aztecas del norte (an Azteca is a person of Aztlán or the Southwest) compose the largest single tribe or nation of Anishinaabeg (Indians) found in the United States today. Like other Native American groups, the Aztecas of Aztlán are not completely unified or homogeneous people. Some call themselves Chicanos and see themselves as people whose true homeland is Aztlán (Forbes).

Years later, Chicano poet Alurista in the "Plan Espiritual de Aztlán" would be the second person to put the idea of the formerly Mexican territories annexed by the USA in the invasion of 1848 as a Chicano homeland named "Aztlan" *(Plan Espiritual de Aztlán).*

Now back to the materialist conception of history, which at times seems to be a challenge for many even on the left when examining the USA. To understand Aztlan one must not only understand Mexican history, but the United States itself. The USA as a nation state did not develop organically from the ground-up like many or most other nations. There was never one unified whole, instead the USA developed from the East and devoured its way to the West. Landgrab after landgrab, genocide after genocide. The USA, in other words, is formed from the imprisoning of different groups it has subjugated. Our First Nations, Africans, Boricuas, Hawaiians, and finally the remaining Native peoples including the Mexicano of the "Southwest" fell victim to the US imperialist monster.

But while it subjugated the Mexicano, the Empire needed a source of quick, cheap and plentiful labor to build up the immense and rich territory it had just acquired. The USA then, contrary to its racialized "anti-immigrant" rhetoric it slings at Mexicanos (and CentroAmericanos now) in times of economic crisis, also hypocritically needs and has relied on the labor of Chicano-Mexicanos and La Raza in general. In its need to fulfill its capitalist necessities internally the USA has allowed migration while criminalizing the migrant. It has allowed the occupied territories of Aztlan to become re-browned once again. Entire cities of the so-called "Southwest" have been built by brown hands. By amassing an entire group of people in the form of wage workers with a historical attachment to these territories the USA has helped create Aztlan, out of its own contradictions the notion of an actual, physical territory of Aztlan looms over its head. Many a Marxist will describe the process of one mode of production replacing another gradually. For example, the centralization of labor in the factory system by the industrial revolution laid the foundations for workers to be able to become concentrated in mass numbers and thus the seed of socialist thought and action developed as a mass of workers now labored next to each other in the same place under the same conditions. Of course, workers would organize themselves en masse based on their class interests as proletarians in contradiction to the interests of their bosses, the capitalist class. Of course, labor unions and socialist and communist political organizations would develop in those conditions. In the same sense in a society such as that of the United States, where its class stratification is highly racialized because of its colonial history, at least among the Chicano and Raza peoples where colonialism is the main contradiction, will the seed of "Aztlan" develop and an ancient myth thrust through thousands of years of history to be reborn as a future hope of nation, of independence, of development for an oppressed and colonized class and with a political organization developing around the struggle to build towards that goal as well.

We can see these ideas amongst the Chicano people throughout their history. The Chicano Power Period (1965-1975) was just the most recent active period where the blinds came off, but notions of nationalism and national liberation have existed before and continue to be written about decades after. Prior to the Chicano Power Period right after the US invasion and colonization several regional attempts were made by Chicanos-Mexicanos to defend their land and people using armed resistance. Juan Nepomuceno Cortina and Los Cortinistas who waged guerrilla warfare in Texas, Tiburcio Vasquez and Joaquin Murrieta of California and Las Gorras Blancas of Nuevo Mexico are but a notable few.

During and after the Chicano Power Period Several organizations among the Chicano-Mexicano population have in their time organized around the question of the land (Aztlan) and written on this matter such as (but not limited to) the August Twenty-Ninth Movement (ATM), Centro de Acción Social Autónoma (CASA), Union Del Barrio (UDB) and consistently since 1970 La Raza Unida now Partido Nacional de La Raza Unida (PNLRU). In a PNLRU document titled "Study and scenario on the Chicano National Question" under "Program for Chicano Mexicano Liberation," point one reads:

THE RIGHT FOR SELF DETERMINATION OF THE CHICANO MEXICANO NATION: At the Second National Convention of El Partido the position was taken that we constitute a nation, based on the criteria of internal colonialism. As Chicanos/Mexicanos, we claim the southwestern states as our nation: California, Arizona, New Mexico, Colorado and Texas. We also take the position that those Chicano/Mexicanos living outside of the Southwest must be guaranteed democratic rights and regional autonomy ("Study and Scenario on the Chicano National Question").

The Chicano struggle for a homeland (Aztlan) has also been recognized by other peoples including Indigenous peoples. The work of El Partido Nacional de La Raza Unida with the traditional Native Nations of the Southwest/Aztlan in particular shows this. During the 1980s the PNLRU maintained a significant working relationship with the International Indian Treaty Council. In a letter written by then Director of the IITC William "Bill" Wahpepah to Xenaro Ayala (my father) then Chairman of the PNLRU, Mr. Wahpepah says, "I wish to express our commitment to an ongoing relationship of mutual solidarity with LRUP. AIM and the IITC wholeheartedly support the Chicano struggle for self-determination which the LRUP represents. We see it as one of the indigenous struggles for sovereignty and self-determination in this hemisphere" (Wahpepah). Four years later in a one-page document titled "Treaty of Guadalupe Hidalgo Liaisons, Friends and Supporters" the IITC clearly states,

In recent years the IITC has sought a means to bridge relations to include the Chicano Indigenous people among the family of nations. The utilization of the TGHP as a catalyst for reunification has helped toward this purpose. The TGHP is an ongoing research and development component of the IITC since 1980 in Fort Belnap, Montana, at the Sixth IITC Conference. At that time the General Assembly of the International Indian Treaty Conference unanimously acknowledged the Chicano Indigenous peoples, and the spiritual land of Aztlan ("Treaty of Guadalupe Hidalgo").

Many others have expressed solidarity with the Chicano struggle for self-determination, which Aztlan embodies both nationally and internationally.

My father used to say how sometimes people would do something that was recommended they do but only after they heard it elsewhere and not after they had already heard the same suggestion at home. Could it be a consequence of colonization that we don't trust ourselves until we hear those that occupy our homeland state what we have been telling ourselves over and over? Many might be surprised to hear that those in power the ruling class, the colonizer, the imperialists, capitalists all know very well the inherent threat that Chicano self-determination (i.e. Aztlan) represents to the stability of the USA. Perhaps then many more will listen and give the same sense of urgency and attentiveness to this question.

In a 1978 *Playboy Magazine* interview of then Director of the Central Intelligence Agency, William Colby, had quite the answer when asked what was the "greatest threat to America today," he responded,

> [T]he most obvious threat is that there are 60,000,000 Mexicans today and there are going to be 120,000,000 of them by the end of the century... There are 7,000,000 or 8,000,000 Mexicans who live in the United States today and of the extra 60,000,000 who will be around by the end of the century, there is no way to keep a good 20,000,000 of them from living in the country. We can reinforce the Border Patrol and they don't have enough bullets to stop them all" (Gonzales 69).

Then in a declassified snippet of a *Intelligence Digest* magazine available for agents of spy agencies internationally, a page in the June 1981 edition explicitly states in a highly censored page "We have for some considerable time now, warned about the politicizing of the Mexicans within the US and the claims for 'lost and stolen' Mexican lands... (*Intelligence Digest* 1).

"Alarming" should be the words ringing out when one reads these words.

It doesn't end there; the explosion in our population in the past 20-30 years specifically in the physical territories Chicanos have named Aztlan, doesn't go by unnoticed by the ruling class. In a document that is said to have inspired the present-day Trump movement, Samuel Huntington a political scientist, adviser, and co-founder of the *Foreign Policy* magazine wrote, "The Hispanic Challenge" in which he says almost verbatim but in a negative light what the Chicano Movement has been saying for decades,

> No other immigrant group in U.S. history has asserted or could assert a historical claim to U.S. territory. Mexicans and Mexican Americans can and do make that claim. Almost all of Texas, New Mexico, Arizona, California, Nevada, and Utah was part of Mexico until Mexico lost them as a result of the Texan War of Independence in 1835-1836 and the Mexican-American War of 1846-1848. Mexico is the only country that the United States has invaded, occupied its capital—placing the Marines in the 'halls of Montezuma'—and then annexed half its territory. Mexicans do not forget these events. Quite understandably, they feel that they have special rights in these territories. 'Unlike other immigrants,' Boston College political scientist Peter Skerry notes, 'Mexicans arrive here from a neighboring nation that has suffered military defeat at the hands of the United States; and they settle predominantly in a region that was once part of their homeland... Mexican Americans enjoy a sense of being on their own turf that is not shared by other immigrants (Huntington).

If the previous quotes weren't enough to drive the point home, while keeping in mind the present genocide taking place in Gaza of Occupied Palestine, Prime Minister of Israel, Benjamin Netanyahu himself, has drawn the parallels between Aztlan and Palestine without saying "Aztlan" in *A Durable Peace,*

> The United States is not exempt from this potential nightmare. In a decade or two the southwestern region of America is likely to be predominately Hispanic, mainly as a result of continuous emigration from Mexico. It is not inconceivable that in this community champions of the Palestinian Principle could emerge. These would demand not merely equality before the law, or naturalization, or even Spanish as a first language. Instead they would say that since they form a local majority in the territory (which was forcibly taken from Mexico in the war of 1848), they deserve a state of their own. 'But you already have a state—it's called Mexico,' would come the response. 'You have every right to demand civil rights in the United States, but you have no right to

demand a second Mexico.' This hypothetical exchange may sound far-fetched today. But it will not necessarily appear that way tomorrow, especially if the Palestinian Principle is allowed to continue to spread, which it surely will if a new Palestinian state comes into being (Netanyahu 164-165).

To further dig the knife in a study on the GDP of "Latinos" in the USA by the California Lutheran University and the UCLA Center for the study of Latino Health and Culture in 2023 concluded that, "The total economic output (or GDP) of Latinos living in the United States in 2021 was $3.2 trillion, up from $2.8 trillion in 2020, $2.1 trillion in 2015, and $1.7 trillion in 2010. If Latinos living in the United States were an independent country, the U.S. Latino GDP would be the fifth largest GDP in the world, larger than the GDPs of India, the United Kingdom, or France" *(2023 U.S. Latino GDP Report* 3). Not only is La Raza an economic powerhouse by their own accounts, numerically we are quickly becoming or already the majority in every single state in the contested territories of Aztlan.

The territories that were once Mexico and have always been Native, the territories that have a unique history apart from the rest of the United States are exponentially returning to a timeline denied them long ago. The roots to this story go back thousands of years and may in the not-so-distant future blossom into the full potential of a liberated Chicano-Indigenous people but this can only happen with the proper guidance of a well-organized political party to act as a weapon to guide La Raza into victory over their perpetrators and form together with the rest of humanity a new world... Starting with our very own Aztlan Libre!

## Works Cited

Bonfil Batalla, Guillermo. *México Profundo: Reclaiming a Civilization.* Translated by Philip A. Dennis, University of Texas Press, 1996.

Cabral, Amílcar. *Unity and Struggle: Speeches and Writings.* Monthly Review Press, 2016.

Colby, William. "Interview with William Colby." *Playboy,* July 1978, pp. 69–80.

Fisher, R. D. "Paquimé: The Anasazi Rosetta Stone." Digital Teamworks, June 2004, https:// digitalteamworks.com/canyons/fisher/site.htm. Accessed 3 March 2023.

Forbes, Jack D. *The Mexican Heritage of Aztlán.* El Grito del Norte Press, 1962.

"Foreign Policy Options: Terrorism." *Intelligence Digest*, 1981.

Guadarrama, Bernardo. *El Códice Boturini o Tira de la Peregrinación*. Fondo de Cultura Económica, 2023.

Hamilton, David, et al. *2023 U.S. Latino GDP Report*. Center for the Study of Latino Health and Culture, 2023.

Huntington, Samuel P. "The Hispanic Challenge." Foreign Policy, no. 141, 2004, pp. 30-45. JSTOR, https://doi.org/10.2307/4147547

Masuku, M. M., and V. H. Mlambo. "Tribalism and Ethnophobia Among Black South Africans." *Journal of Ethnic and Cultural Studies*, vol. 10, no. 1, 2023, pp. 125-140, https://www.jstor.org/stable/48718238

Mireles, Ernesto Todd. *Insurgent Aztlan: The Liberating Power of Cultural Resistance*. Somos en Escrito Foundation Press, 2020.

Mukhopadhyay, Tirtha Prasad, and Alan Philip Garfinkel. *Iconicity of the Uto-Aztecans*. Berghahn Books, 2023.

Netanyahu, Benjamin. *A Durable Peace: Israel and Its Place Among the Nations*. Warner Books, 2000.

*The Palestinian National Charter: Resolutions of the Palestine National Council July 1-17, 1968*. The Avalon Project, Yale Law School, https://avalon.law.yale.edu/20th_century/plocov.asp, Accessed 5 Feb. 2023.

*Plan Espiritual de Aztlán*. 1969. Reprinted in *Aztlán: Essays on the Chicano Homeland*, edited by Rudolfo Anaya and Francisco Lomelí, University of New Mexico Press, 1989, pp. 1-5.

*Popol Vuh: The Mayan Book of the Dawn of Life*. Translated by Dennis Tedlock, Revised ed., Simon & Schuster, 1996.

*Program for Chicano Mexicano Liberation*. El Partido Nacional de La Raza Unida, 1985. Personal archive.

Riley, Carroll L. *Becoming Aztlan: Mesoamerican Influence in the Greater Southwest, A.D. 1200–1500*. University of Utah Press, 2005.

Rodríguez, Roberto Cintli. *Our Sacred Maíz Is Our Mother: Indigeneity and Belonging in the Americas*. University of Arizona Press, 2014.

Shaul, David Leedom. *A Prehistory of Western North America*. University of New Mexico Press, 2014.

*Study and Scenario on the Chicano National Question*. El Partido Nacional de La Raza Unida, 1985. Personal archive.

*Treaty of Guadalupe Hidalgo Liaisons, Friends and Supporters*. International Indian Treaty Council, ca. 1980s. Personal archive.

Wahpepah, William. Letter to Xenaro Ayala. 25 Jan. 1984. International Indian Treaty Council.

# #00201

## ELINDIOCOPYRIGHT1985

# MAY WE BE NAMED

## ANGELA ACOSTA

Humanity's voyagers always came in ships, back when Sol was the closest star and home stayed within the ecliptic. They came from places no longer shown on star charts that now guided them towards lands where Terra would be but a distant memory. With skin colored from equatorial sunbeams and languages forged from centuries of cultural contact and strife, they were ready when the Exodus finally occurred, and generation ships whisked them away across a sea wider than the Atlantic.

Marcela tore her eyes from the screen that displayed the full weight of generations of ship-born ancestors when a thin stream of light coming from the hallway alerted her to Zamora's presence.

"¿Tienes chisme?" Zamora asked, sauntering into the room like only a little sister could.

Marcela relaxed her stiff shoulders and let out a breath she didn't realize she was holding in. She'd tracked enough of the gamma lineage for this wake cycle. With the lights back on, she started reshuffling the notes she printed out on carbon copies that littered her desk.

"Yeah, turns out they meant to put you on the Calabaza ship and got the paperwork mixed up," Marcela smirked, waving one of her notes in the air.

"No way! You know I can't even cook frijoles right; I don't belong on a restaurant ship. Unless, you know, I got to be the engineer and eat up all those delicacies."

"You wish!" Marcela nudged Zamora with her elbow.

"So, made any progress today?"

"Five generations of lineage gamma from three centuries ago found in the data sent by laser from the Prerromano ship, no está mal," Marcela shrugged and looked back at the data in front of her.

She continued, "It's strange, really. There seem to be fewer lineages than active ships. I can't find *us* in all the data. You know even Tía Flora gave up ages ago on this project."

"¿A qué te refieres con lo de 'find us'? I thought this was about the ancestry of the whole fleet. What do *we* have to do with anything? What does our ship's history matter?"

"It means everything! I know I'm supposed to be collaborating on this project for the good of the fleet, but you know I've been doing some research on the side."

"But they're always telling us that we're all siblings, and that race doesn't exist anymore, that we're all homo sapiens. Somos de la raza…"

"Cósmica, literalmente. Pues ya lo sé, pero es un mito, uno de esos que vinieron con los primeros cohetes."

Having just finished her own school lessons for the day, including a lecture on how the old ways no longer applied, Zamora was utterly perplexed. She perched herself on a free corner of Marcela's desk and took a closer look at the branches of the family tree, thinning out as they got closer to the present moment of year 534 of the Exodus.

"Mira Zamora, where is our family in this?" Marcela zoomed into a patch only a few years removed from Zamora's birth in year 523.

"It doesn't matter…"

"Humor me."

"¿A quién le importa?"

"Pues a nosotras, a todos los del Arbolito. Look, before I crunched in the data for gamma lineage, I already noticed some irregularities from the beginning. They're telling us we're doing something meaningful by putting together these lineages, that it's for the good of the fleet and our history. It's just busy work, Zamora."

"Fine. I don't know who all our family is, but Marcela, tengo haaaaambrreeee. Can we pleaseeeee go to the mess hall now? I heard Tío José is making pupusas, and I want one that isn't spicy."

"Ya vamos, but I still want to learn more about this. Maybe I can bug Tía Flora about the genealogy research after dinner."

Sure enough, Zamora piled her plate high with pupusas and maíz, freshly made from their onboard hydroponics garden. Marcela, ever apprehensive about her research, took a smaller portion of food and joined the other kids and teenagers huddled around a game of dominos made from scrap cardboard. Marcela enjoyed the camaraderie but couldn't wait to finally talk to some adults. For some reason they always stayed quiet about what they knew of their families and though they praised her for her research, they never asked many questions or gave her any good leads. She always had to look elsewhere, like taking chances asking the Prerromano ship with a complicated array of laser networks to reach them five lightyears away.

Tía Flora was watching her favorite zero g handball game and knitting. *Approach with caution,* Marcela thought to herself. She sat herself next to her only biological aunt and engaged in the requisite small talk. By the second half of the game, Marcela had steeled herself for the conversation.

"Tía, you know I've been doing a lot of work on the lineage, and I don't need to bore you with it, but..."

"Mi'ja, I'm glad you're doing that research project, but it doesn't interest me anymore. What are you doing, hunting down lineage omega or something?"

"I'm working on lineage gamma now, actually; I have five more generations worked out. In fact, I've already sorted out adopted and biological parents and have some diagrams for the research team I'm going to send by laser tomorrow..." Marcela needed to stop herself before she lost sight of what she came to talk to her aunt about. Tía Flora had already focused back on the game, the clinking of the knitting needles in sync with the pace of the game.

"Sorry, force of habit. Tía Flora, I want you to tell me about us. ¿Quiénes somos los del Arbolito? ¿De dónde venimos?"

Tía Flora finally perked up and cracked a smile. "It took you 17 years to ask me that, eh? It took my friend Adriana over 20, and she quickly became disinterested again."

Marcela relaxed in her chair and tucked herself into the story Tía Flora was inevitably going to launch into. Tía Flora switched to Spanish, as she was wont to do when talking about the past, but her tone of voice changed and it was as if she saw herself somewhere else. The youth proudly tout the fact that the past is light minutes away and wholly unreachable while elders grieve that chasm of memories.

"Hace ya 30 años que Adriana me preguntó sobre nuestros antepasados. Y, a pesar de la falta de información que tenía, yo sabía que había que compartirla con cualquier persona que tenía el mismísimo deseo. Me imagino que hasta la Zamorita sabe recitar las historias oficiales de quienes somos, ¿cierto?"

Marcela smiled. "Justamente me las estaba contando según lo que iba aprendiendo en la escuela."

"Pues, la Adriana me dijo una frase que nunca jamás saldrá de mi mente. Me dijo basta con esas historias del Éxodo con las ramas de los árboles y que 'I don't want your tender history, give me the truth.' So I did."

"Tender history, huh? Is it, though? Now that I really think about it, es un cuento de hadas. I've always wondered about how the data was received on these family trees and why I couldn't ever find myself on them. You know, I always thought I was different for asking about my own heritage. Pero, there's something they're not telling us, and it's going to be bittersweet."

"Yes, but I have no doubt you are as ready as you'll ever be to hear it. Éramos muchos durante los primeros cohetes y hemos venido desde zonas muy lejanas de la tierra. Había gente de los ríos, de la selva llamada la selva amazónica, de islas y grandes continentes. Había de todo."

"Pero nos han dicho que han venido todos de la península de Florida y que allí empezó la migración."

"Que no, que la península solo tenía las bases de lanzamiento."

Marcela muttered to herself, "That sure does make more sense..."

Tía Flora stared at the screen transfixed in thought, as if recalling the very thread of the ancestors she was to spring forth from her mind like Athena.

She continued in English, "I found...a packet of data. I was going through some of the earliest data sent about the different lineages and I found a diary. It was a real book, too, scanned, of course, but I hope somewhere those pages are still preserved. I had half a mind not to tell anyone about it and keep minding my business, especially since it's not mentioned anywhere in the ever-expanding literature on Exodus genealogy. It was the diary of someone named Hortensia from the beginning of the exodus. She talked about several ships we still have in the fleet, la Calabaza, el Ateneo, el Dominicano, however there was something greater I learned that day. People who couldn't afford passage on the Exodus fleet sold the only thing they had left. It confused me, because I know those people were so connected to their plastic items and chucherías." The clicking of her knitting needles reminded Marcela of the noise of plastic toys her sister played with.

"But you figured it out, right?"

"Mi'ja, they had nothing left to give, no currency or valuable metals, and they could barely even secure a kilo in the bulkhead, so they sold their names."

"¿Qué dices? Ya tenemos todos los nombres. Nos han nombrado a todos nosotros."

"Pero tú y yo solo tenemos un solo nombre, la María Victoria tiene dos, pero así son todas las Marías."

"But we each have a name, Tía. I still don't understand."

Tía Flora put down her knitting needles and beckoned Marcela closer. Parting her wavy dark hair, she began making a large braid.

"Nos han dicho que nosotros del Arbolito somos latinos. Somos de distintas regiones del continente de las Américas y todos hablamos español e inglés. There are at least five other ships like us with slightly different accents and facial features, and they make us believe we're all the same."

"We come from Terra, there's no difference, is there? The skin color is just from the different melanin produced in sunnier, warmer places compared to colder ones."

"Eres muy inteligente; you know there's more than that. Yes, these colors used to define us and now we think more logically, but the Exodus took away our names and our culture. We had special foods, and, while I know most aren't religious anymore, there were special ceremonies and festivals just for us. We gave that up the moment we named ourselves part of the fleet."

Left, right, middle, Tía Flora's fingers made quick work of Marcela's hair. Marcela thought the braid felt odd, a bit lopsided, but she didn't want to criticize her aunt. It'd be easy enough to readjust later.

Tía Flora secured the bottom of the braid with an elastic band, and Marcela went in search of a mirror and finally saw what her aunt had so lovingly knitted into her hair. Her thick hair had been carefully sectioned into different braids, all coming together to form a larger braid that ran down the right side of her head.

"Mira, ¡qué bonita!" Tía Flora exclaimed, admiring her work.

"Thank you, tía. It's your best creation yet. Where'd you learn to do something like this? We almost never wear our hair in braids. We're supposed to keep it tied neatly away from our face with a ponytail or bun."

"I got the idea from our ancestors. Thousands of years ago, our ancestors, the ones with wavy hair, textured hair, and hair dark as the hulls of our ships, wore braids as a source of cultural identity. They wove patterns into braids to chart maps towards the homes they left behind, just as we leave drawings as marks of each ship in the fleet."

"That's really beautiful," Marcela reflected. She felt a tightness welling up in her chest, and a newfound appreciation for the ancestors from Terra bloomed within her. Not even when conducting her research did she ever truly feel the full weight of the bygone generations who attempted to pass their knowledge to her. She was the product of dozens, if not hundreds of generations of sentient homo sapiens who kept humanity moving forward without forgetting their roots.

"It suits you well. Your ancestors would be proud of you."

"Thank you, Tía. I have to ask; did you ever figure out any of the names they gave away?" Marcela was suddenly anxious, knowing she'd remember this moment for years to come. This was to be the moment when everything clicked, when she no longer was one of a multicultural fleet, but the daughter of people from countries she could find on the old globe.

Tía Flora harrumphed, ostensibly at the terrible play that had finally ended the handball game, but Marcela knew it was really meant for her.

"Pues, ya te lo conté, we gave them up centuries ago. We tucked our braids into our helmets and some of us were smart enough to use the braids to spell our histories in Nahuatl, like the Calabaza ship. They're the Xolapa from México. But we weren't so lucky."

"But couldn't we take a DNA test? Contact other ships for information that might've been overlooked in the existing lineage? We could…"

"It's too late for that. We're never going to have their names or the certainty of knowing who our ancestors truly were, but I do have something you might want to see." Tía Flora turned off the projector and sent her off to find Zamora. She needed to see this, too.

The chefs had already gone off duty, and the sisters and Tía Flora huddled under the dimmed light of the mess hall. Zamora looked unsure of herself as she shuffled her feet in place, and Marcela wished the photons from the nearest star system could illuminate the dark portholes, but they were once again too far in the black.

Tía Flora flipped through a few recipe books and finally settled on the one that looked the most battered and full of stains from centuries of moles and salsa.

"Pues mira. Ni el dedo de Colón podría apuntar a lo que está escrito aquí. Zamora, can you read for us?" Tía Flora put her hand on her shoulder in encouragement.

Zamora twisted her face like she'd just eaten a lime. "It's in Spanish?"

"Claro, mi'ja. Así fueron escritos todos los libros de nuestros antepasados."

"Pero solo hay una lengua escrita, el inglés," Marcela chimed in.

"Pues me parece otra ridiculez de esa escuela…obvio que todos los seres humanos podían escribir con pluma. ¿Creen que los latinos iban a escribir sus historias en el idioma de otro continente? Sound it out, you'll figure out what it says pretty quickly."

Zamora began, "Las galletas de Elisa. Se preparan con…con sus ingredientes favoritos. A ella…le gustaba hornearlas para días festivos como…como los cumpleaños y las quinceañeras."

Looking over Zamora's shoulder, Marcela read the recipe to herself and said, "It's a cookie recipe, but it's telling us about someone named Elisa. And the one on the page next to it says, 'Los pasteles de tío Oswaldo.' What is this, Tía?"

"Girls, when they sold their names and left Terra with the Exodus, they made these recipe books to share their favorite dishes. They turned recipe books into the ancestors they couldn't take with them. These are their obituaries."

"But there's hardly anything about Elisa in this..." Marcela protested.

"You must read the whole book; each recipe gives you a little more about each person's story. I've been piecing together when people were born and that sort of thing."

"So we can finally put together this lineage?"

"No, so we can read about their lives. We can honor them even without the branches on the Arbolito all filled out. Many of these people likely aren't related to us, anyway."

"Marcela, basta con your research. Tía, have you ever made these recipes?" Zamora interrupted.

"We still make some of them, but without the animal products they had access to on Terra, they probably don't taste the same."

"Can we still try?"

Tía Flora chuckled to herself, "I'd thought I'd never see the day when you'd want to try to bake something. Sure, tomorrow morning you don't have any lessons so why don't you bring some of your friends to the kitchen and we'll whip something up."

The next day, Zamora and a few of her friends were busily churning out cookies under the careful watch of Tía Flora, using ingredients rationed for those who weren't on the team of cooks. Notwithstanding Zamora's occasional clumsiness and trepidation around the oven, the lunch rush was ecstatic to try something new. A few of the adults even petitioned to add the sugar cookies to the dessert menu, the highest honor for the young bakers. Zamora later tearfully told Marcela that it was all her fault if they shipped her off to the Calabaza ship now that she can properly bake.

Marcela sometimes wished she were as capricious as her younger sister, but age and her research kept her curious. She wanted to beam to everyone else on the research team that it was just a project to keep people busy. They were fed packets of data and crunched the numbers all day long so the ships with the most resources could continue chasing after habitable planets and build new spaceports. Those very families must have taken her own ancestors' names hostage centuries ago.

Indignant, Marcela clenched her hands and closed her eyes. She breathed deeply, imagining a warmth spreading through her body as if she were spirited away to her ancestors' hot and humid homelands.

She closed out some of the programs she had been running with the ancestry data and set aside a data packet for herself to send to a few trusted friends she had on the Arbolito and other ships. Speaking clearly into the monitor in front of her, she spoke a language she hoped to one day be able to write.

"Soy Marcela, del Arbolito. Créanme cuando les explico que nuestros antepasados tenían nombres para sus familias. Mi tía me dice que sus nombres fueron vendidos a los que controlaron el Éxodo y que fueron tirados como basura de plástico. Ya no quiero repetir esa historia, así que quiero que nos nombren. Hasta que tengamos anclados a los linajes todos los nombres, me llamaré Marcela Nombremos. Puede que parezca contra los deseos de la flotilla, pero quiero identificarme como persona con una historia. Cualquier interesado puede usar este nombre. No lo daré a mis hijos si los tenga. Es un nombre a alquiler, un nombre que declara su intención. Espero que les sirva."

# TEXCANOCÓSMICOS: EL CHICANOFUTURISMO

## JUAN MANUEL PÉREZ

•

they are survivors
migrants since far, ancient times
flowing here and there

••

they have persisted
in the face of constant death
in deep ides of days

•••

they have been rulers
at their feet, every known realm
every dominion

••••

they have been servants
providing for many needs
in so many ways

———

they have been poets
fierce warriors and crimson priests
they have done it all

———

throughout every life
cosmic-bronze emissaries
flowers of today

●●

———

space is their mother
her planets, their sacred wombs
seeding tomorrow

# CHICANAUTOPIA

## ERIKA SAID IZAGUIRRE

when solar panels are
installed in every house
of this old tierra Americana
and Madre Earth is in
danger no more

when every person has
a microchip ID under the
skin brown, yellow, white

when every social class
shares bionic organs
robotic prosthetics
scanning AI eyes
manufactured by the same
cheap 3D printer

[ no name brand or
Capitalist interest, but
communality and unión
del pueblo entero ]

when driverless cars
are flying over
long gone borders
no passports required
speed limit 700 MPH
no customs, no walls

when the internet becomes
global by law, a birthright
and plastic is as obsolete
as racismo

when language barriers are
an issue centuries old
'cause the AI implanted in our
non-binary brains will
universalize
all human connections

when the Spanish is considered
a classical language, and the
Spanglish so alive
taught and preserved
as the cradle of world culture
in the post-modern
civilization

when we Chicanx are all
over U.S. History books:
the people who dared to
leave behind narco wars
and poverty and violence

the people who swapped
countries in a time
when that was mortal task

the people who refused
to stay and die in those places
where the rich and the white
were stealing land resources

exploiting our brown bodies
for their own enrichment

our people is the people who
woke up from a nightmare of
migration into the Empire
and turned it into a dream
and survived against all odds
against all cops
against all migras
against all laws made
by hate and white supremacy

our people is the people who
had been fighting
for this since
the times of yanqui invasions
to our territories

our people as in our
grandparents, grandmothers

our people as in our
sacerdotisas, curanderxs
brujxs, santerxs

our people who's fighting
for this now so
in the future
we will look back at 2025:
the dark ages
for the dark-skinned
the migrant hunting like
the inquisition

the border wall, an American
Berliner Mauer:
muro de la vergüenza
a babel tower that
fell from grace

when mother nature, mother
Virgen de Guadalupe
are no longer "la chingada"
but a kiss in a wound
that is finally closing
healed the land of the
original ancestors
peace restored among our
Latin American countries

we will be able to
say that all
the death
all the love
all the Spanglish spoken
without shame
and without auto-translators
was worth it

Ay, mis hermanxs
it will be
all
worth it

# CYBER AZTLÁN

## ERIKA SAID IZAGUIRRE

1

I cyber talked with my
cyber ex-boyfriend
he said that we should
give up the cyber fight

we cyber argued and
cyber discussed the
cyber custody of our
cyber chamacos:
who is going to keep the
old cyber tejido
we brought back from our
cyber trip to México?

when we were trying to
go cyber back to
the origins, remembering
where our non-
cyberselves came from

I don't wanna give up the
cyber fight
I wanna cyber dance
ritmos latinos
matachines
cyber sing sacred chants
cyber speak in my English

with Spanish accent
cyber protest in my
cyber Spanglish tongue
so sweet and so raw
spicy for things that
are not cyber related

I wanna cyber travel
back to my cyber hometown
with no stops from no
cyber customs officers
no cyber passports
needed to cross
through non existent
cyber borders

I wanna cyber ride
around my cyber barrio
talk to the cyber cholas
and the cyber vatos
so I can cyber move on
and forget the real wounds
in my real brown body

2

sí, that's right
my wounds
are not cyber

3

there are
two

kinds of
wounds
in my
cyber
heart

they cross the
cyberspace's
border
and hurt
me in
real time:

     a) the wounds left by my ex
     'cause we were young and
     human and
     real
     [ it's part of the experience
     of non-cyber life ]

     b) the wounds left by a patriarchal
     system that digged in me
     trauma through
     racism and capitalism
     [ this should not be a part of any
     human experience ]

I'm not talking
about something
cyber when
I speak about
this wounds
even though
it's cyber

important to
mention them:
inequality
is material
and is wrong
and is real


4


sometimes me, like my ex
forget that we have a body

it's easier to picture all the
evil in the world
as something cyber
rather than something
that is taking innocent lives
real lives of
innocent real (some)bodies
like my exe's real (some)body
and my chamacos' real (some)bodies
and my own real brown (some)body

[ Everybody is a body and
every body is somebody ]


5


when I'm cyber me
my physical body
the space it takes
the geographical spot
it stands at
the skin dark

and luxurious
to me
as it resembles
the golden aura of a
foundational goddess
makes it hard to
believe that
this skin can be so
undesirable to
racist folks
to the point of hate
and domination
eradication
but, really
it ain't matter
'cause
cyber me
do not carry a body
and
cyber them
don't even exist here

6

my cyber friends on
the other hand
they speak all languages
and come in
all colors
they go to cyber churches
cyber mosques
cyber synagogues
or have cyber altars to
deities such as Elegua

Yemayá, Pomba Gira, Babalú
Aye, Brahma, Parvati
Shiva, Santa Muerte o el Santo
Niño de Atocha

my cyber friends don't
have pronouns and don't care
if I have or don't have any money

their cyber jobs are unimportant
their cyber houses all the same

I know it sounds like
communism
but in the cyber world
we don't even follow
a political system

it's not cyber needed

the only thing we cyber
care about
is to live simple
unbothered
cyber lives

7

what if I clone my
cyber ex?

I can cyber date
a bot
and cyber reproduce

like Cipactónal &
Oxomoco
[ the first woman &
man ever created
on non-cyber Earth ]

I can cyber reproduce
and birth
a new
cyber brown era

7

I am the cyber ancestor
of future cyber children
that will break the fourth wall
of the cyber world
and cross and immigrate
out there where there are
physical bodies
they will show to their
cyber Oxomoco father
that we
don't call him Adam
and that we
cyber brown people
don't give up
the fight
easily

# UBER X FRONTERA

E.C.-DUKES AND RONNIE DUKES

El Chuco
Hop on, ese!

Juárez, Chihuahua.
On the other side...
¡Súbete! ¡Súbete!
<Hop on! Hop on!>

Back to Chuco...

Wassup, primos? Any passengers yet?

No riders yet, Prima.

¿Qué venden?<What are you selling?>
Agua. ¿Quieres? <Water. Want some?>
NO.
Joven, ¿vendes paseos? <Young man. Are you giving rides?>

¿Por qué? ¿Quieres uno? <Why? Do you want one?>
Sí. <Yes.>

Pero, ¿y si no tengo pasaporte? <But, what if I don't have a passport?>
No se preocupe. <Don't you worry.>
Súbase, tía. <Hop on, Auntie.>

Amarrése. <Buckle up.>
Ey, Daizee. Este es UberX Frontera. Próxima parada, El Chuco. <Hey, Daizee. This is UberX Frontera. Next stop, El Chuco.>

Primo Tury, estamos listos para la rampa. <Cousin Tury, we're ready for the ramp.>
Bueno. Listo. <Okay. Ready.>

¡Órale, Primos!
U.S. BORDER GUARD
235 days with no illegal crossings. Woo-hoo!
Scratch that. 235 days crossing with dignity, Chuco-style!
DUKEScomics.com
4

# OBSIDIAN VISIONS: MIGRANTFUTURISM

1. What are the ramifications for gente in the future, when it comes to migration, such as in Pedro Iniguez's poems, and elindiocopyright1985's image of the migrant sign on the rings of Saturn? The continuation of culture? "Life goes on" no matter where you might stop and live, what planet or time?

2. Many of the stories in this section meld sci-fi pop and Xicanx culture, how do you see the sci-fi change as it pairs with the cultural item and vice versa? For example, the coyote in "Migrant (futurism) / poetic (economics)" by Osmani Ochoa.

3. Are speculative elements (technology) freeing for migrants or are they a hindrance?

4. What do the fiction, non-fiction, poetry and visual pieces on migration seem to agree on or what connects them? How does the idea of movement factor?

5. How does the land and landscape affect these stories? Such as the polar caps in Martin Hill Ortiz's "Norte" and the desert in "Uber X Frontera" by E.C.-Dukes and Ronnie Dukes, or any of the other pieces?

# ŌME:
# TIERRA Y LIBERTAD

Raza belong to the land, work the land, whether imaginary national lines crossed us or we migrated as we always have. The call of "Tierra y Libertad" from Emiliano Zapata for land rights, for self-determination, rings down the ages into Xicanxfuturism, from liberation from patriarchy to freedom from land barons and state control of oligarchs who seek others to step on. Xicanxfuturism aspires to the state of being of Tierra y Libertad.

# #00202

ELINDIOCOPYRIGHT1985

# ROYAL WEDDING

## CATRIÓNA RUEDA ESQUIBEL

Newsbrief from the Intergalactic News Network, INN, your "in" on what's happening, around the galaxy, around the clock!

The video feed features a woman with silver gilt hair, Glory Chastain, and a man with the bluest eyes in Newscasting, Chase DeGloria.

Thank you for tuning in to the Royal Wedding of the ViceRoy of Hispaniola to the Ivelisse, Princess, I mean Heiress, to the Planet Azteque, which was discovered by Hispaniola a generation ago.

Let's go back eighteen years, when Planet Azteque was first discovered. A subsistence-level planet, acquired by the colonial force of Hispaniola. [Cut to a montage of a pastoral scene, rippling water, music]

[Off-screen: Would that happen today? Primitive lands colonized by a greater technological force?]

[Off screen, voice 2: It's difficult to say what would have happened a generation ago. Those were different people. Different times.]

[Off screen, first voice: Isn't oppression in an unequal power relationship always wrong?]

[Pastoral scene] Looking back a generation ago, we see the parents of Ivelisse, the Great King Moctezuma and his wife the Princess Malintzin of the mountain Kingdom. Their marriage had united the Valley and the Mountain, bringing the peoples together in one united Kingdom.

[Images of a starkly handsome bronze warrior king, and an extremely beautiful dark woman, clasped in a romantic embrace]

[Off screen: Isn't it true that there has never been a "united" mountain kingdom? That Princess Malintzín's title was just a fiction concocted for political expediency?]

And when that kingdom faced invaders of clearly advanced technological and genetic makeup, that kingdom was doomed!

[Off screen: Isn't it true that King Moctezuma attempted to murder his infant daughter?]

Alas, we don't know the details of the death of the king and queen, that bloody scene. All we know is that there emerged one survivor, the Child Ivelisse, covered with her parents' blood and with a flower painted crudely on her forehead.

[Off screen: Isn't it true that Princess Malintzín left a record telling of her husband's attempts to murder their child to protect her from disgrace?]

Princess Malintzin defended her child, indeed killing her husband, her lord, her true love, because "a people's future cannot come at the cost of their children's lives." What a spokesperson for non-violence! How beautiful, how Tragic! Princess Malintzin took her own life, you know, after being forced to choose between her husband's life and her daughter's. Heartbroken at having killed the Lord of her Heart, she cut her own throat. But what courage she showed! How that courage must have come down through her daughter!

Fortunately, the soldiers of Hispaniola were there to rescue the baby.

[Off screen: weren't those same soldiers the cause of her parents' death?]

Who was raised up as the flower of her people! Guarded by the Soldiers of Hispaniola, protected by the ViceRoy himself.

The ViceRoy, now the Royal Groom of today's wedding.

[Off screen: doesn't that make him like twenty years older than his child bride? Doesn't that imply that he's taken sexual advantage of a child under his care?]

Ivelisse is no Child Bride! She is an adult, 19 years old, legally able to wed now. Today!

Let's take a look at her wedding gown, made up of 376 separate lace flowers, each one representing one of the native tribes.

[Off screen: It's amazing the girl can move in that dress!]

Glory, can you tell us some of the unique characteristics of this Royal Wedding?

Of course, Chase! Today's Royal Wedding will unite the Planet Azteque with the Ruling Family of Hispaniola. The Princess has been treasured by the Hispaniola royals, and her safety has been entrusted to the Hispaniola ViceRoy, who has served as guardian over Ivelisse until she obtained her majority, today.

Glory, doesn't that mean the ViceRoy is marrying his former ward?

Yes, Chase, in what will go down as a romance for the ages, the older ViceRoy of course fell in love with the beautiful Princess! What is so amazing is that she loved him back! He's a worldly figure, who represents the technological advances that Hispaniola has brought to the Planet Azteque. Perhaps he is like her lost father, the King Moctezuma!

Glory, what are some other unique characteristics of this wedding?

I'm glad you asked that Chase! The ceremony is unique in that there are no children present today. Mainly that's because the tickets are so limited in number that no adult would waste a ticket on a child! All the children of the ruling class are safely protected within the City's walls in the Royal Creche, guarded by Hispaniola security forces.

So no Children at all, Glory?

That's right, Chase! But that doesn't mean that tailors were not working overtime to prepare the wardrobes for the scions of the aristocracy! Each child made an appearance with their family when they disembarked from the jeweled carriages! Then the parents entered the Templo Mayor, and the children entered the Royal Creche.

[Off-screen: Safe from kidnappers! The rebels in the city have become quite bold at kidnapping!]

Such a beautiful showing, Glory! And we couldn't ask for a more beautiful day! The sun is shining over Planeta Azteque. The Ruling Class is packed in the Templo Mayor, shoulder to shoulder for this ceremony!

That's right, Chase! And the technology of Hispaniola is always visible! Even invisible! For instance, did you know that all the children in the kingdom have cerebral implants, so they can be tracked anywhere on the planet?

[Laughing] But Glory, surely there's no risk of the children running off unsupervised!

[Laughing] No, Chase! This is just one of the many security features that the technology has brought! Peace of Mind!

[Off screen: from fear of kidnappers!]

Chase, security is extra tight around the wedding today! The Interplanetary Council is in attendance, to Witness that the Bride is entering into this marriage with no coercion or threat, that she's truly in love with her groom.

Glory, many cynics say that this wedding will make the Hispaniola Conquest of Planeta Azteque complete, joining the Princess's legitimate bloodline with that of the Colonizer ViceRoy!

Chase, there are always nay-sayers who deny the power of True Love to conquer obstacles, and to unite people of different backgrounds. In fact, the Princess Ivelisse will declare her love for her groom before the Interplanetary Council, demonstrating the legitimacy of this marriage and giving truth to the old adage that Love Conquers All!

That's right, Glory! That's another unique characteristic of today's wedding: The interrogation of the Bride! It will be beamed live to over nine hundred galaxies! [Laughing] I wish the Interplanetary News Network had an exclusive right to broadcast, but the truth is that all the networks are covering this wedding!

And that's another reason security is so tight, Chase! They are to protect the Princess from any threat to her safety before the Declaration!

Here we go, Glory, with the ViceRoy's entrance into the temple, followed by the Princess's procession!

Cameras are rolling, capturing the beautiful, elaborate clothing of the nobles. It is long, slow, and ceremonial.

And here we go, Chase! The moment of the Declaration! The marriage rite will be performed by the President of the Interplanetary Council!

He steps forward. "Congratulations to you, Ivelisse, Heiress to the Planeta Azteque, on attaining your majority of Nineteen Years. Pardon me, as I must ask, as a formality, do you enter into this marriage of your own free will?"

Many microphones swivel towards her, a dark-skinned girl, rather plain, but beautifully attired! She smiles brilliantly and approaches the microphone. She announces, with what appears to be a great deal of Pride, "I am a whore."

What did she say, Glory?

I think she said, Chase, I think she declared herself to be a whore!

That can't be right, Glory! Was there some glitch in transmission? Or translation?

"Excuse me, Princess Ivelisse, but..."

"I am a whore," she declares again. "By the laws of my people, that means that any marriage I enter into, either before or after this declaration, is null and void. Also, any future children I may bear are by definition illegitimate and cannot inherit."

The Princess is pulled back from the microphones by her dazed guards.

The ViceRoy, the Groom is blustering, he's turning red! He's turning purple!

The Heiress's security force, which had been focusing on protecting her from assassination and preventing any attempts at escape, are absolutely unprepared for the heiress's outburst!  The temple is in an uproar. The groom is bellowing, but you can tell he has no idea what is actually happening. His cultural advisors, however, are scrolling through their data and beginning to realize the full implications of the heiress's words.

That's right, Chase! According to the patriarchal Valley laws, if a woman confesses or is judged to be a whore, her marriage is immediately nullified and all present and future children are declared illegitimate. Meaning, she can have no "legitimate" heir.

Chase [laughing] Those old Valley patriarchs were sticklers on the whole legitimacy thing.

I'll say, Chase! So this means that the Heiress has effectively overturned her marriage and prevented any future child of her body from being used in a similar fashion.

Video footage continues to roll, depicting chaos and confusion within the temple, with lawyers and counselors shouting and the media transmitting it to an interPlanetary audience, with commentators and statistics.

Glory, we haven't seen a coup like this since—

At that moment, a deafening explosion rips across the Temple. It takes a few moments, because everyone is sure that the rebels have bombed the Templo Mayor, but there seems to be no damage to the Templo Mayor itself.

"The Creche!" Someone calls. "The children!"

Outside among the rubble, a newscaster describes the scene: The building that housed the nursery has been completely demolished. The wealthy parents are rushing out of the Templo Mayor and attempting to dig through the rubble to reach their children.

Glory, can you give us an update on what's happening?

The gilt-hair woman now wears an orange coverall. Her face and hair are covered in ash. Chase, it's been hours of chaos here at the site of the Royal Creche! Teams having been digging for bodies, hoping to find the children, the nannies, but so far, nothing.

Nothing, Glory? No bodies recovered?

That's right, Chase! So far the Royal Creche appears empty of bodies. No one at all. This has led to the fear that the children have all been kidnapped!

Let's cut now to our team with the security force. Is there a fear that the children have been kidnapped, Generalissimo?

No, of course not! As we've said, we have the latest in cerebral implants in all of the children of the aristocracy. Let's go now to our digital map, which will light up, showing the location of each child.

The cameras show the digital map, which remains dark. There are no lights indicating locations of the missing children.

And that's the latest, Chase, from the Planeta Azteque, where today, Princess Ivelisse gave her Declaración Putanesca—that is, she declared herself to be a whore—right before the explosions took place.

Glory, what's the status of the Princess after her strange Declaración Putanesca?

That's the funny thing, Chase! She hasn't been seen since! There's this footage from one of our camera crews, which, as you see, clearly shows the ViceRoy attempting to murder her in three separate attempts. Here you see him wielding his sword, then grabbing a rifle off of one the soldiers, and finally trying to strangle her with his bare hands. Each time he is pushed back by the Royal Guard. Then they swept from the chamber just as the explosion took place. No word yet on her location. No word from anyone in the Hispaniola Regency on the declaración or the disappearance of the Princess Ivelisse!

The chiron shows a headline of MURDER OF THE INNOCENTS NEVER TOOK PLACE! NO BODIES FOUND IN DESTRUCTION OF ROYAL CRECHE AT AZTEQUE. MASS KIDNAPPING FEARED.

Chase, we'll continue to monitor this developing story of the Whore Princess who Disappeared and the Explosion at the Royal Creche! Back to you, Chase!

Well, thank you for tuning in today for our coverage of the Royal Wedding. This developing story is now the Explosion at the Royal Creche and the Whore Princess who Disappeared. We'll continue to bring you updates, around the galaxy, around the clock.

# COME LOS RICOS. EAT THE RICH

## DANTE OLIVAS

*Kleptocracy: (noun) a type of government whose corrupt leaders use their political power to exploit the wealth of the people and the land they govern by embezzling or misappropriating government funds at the expense of the governed population.*

As the family writer, I'll tell you the story of my uncle Abundito, named after Abundito David Florez/Ortiz X. This is how he changed the rural areas of the Republic of Denver.

The land had been dying for a long time. After the Second Civil War, the former United States broke into regions. The Republic of Denver included the Rocky Mountain Region on the border with *Mexico.* What was once the four-corner states was now the Republic of Denver. Many lived in elite wealth to the north, as Old Denver was an urbanite space that became gentrified over time, and the demand for cannabis became lucrative in the state. Racial disparities had grown to extreme proportions in the Second Civil War of the 2060s, leaving many people of color to deal with the fallout of an equitable system built in the years prior. Conservative leaders pushed for restrictive legislation that caused agriculture maintenance prices to skyrocket. Access to clean water became a luxury, and many farmers could not afford to keep their farms going. As their lands sat neglected and unworked, the soil turned to dirt. Even small-scale farms that relied on snow and rainfall were struggling with the ever-present climate change of the world.

The Second Civil War taught young Raza never to learn how to organize. An entire generation of elders passed, and their organizational skills went with them. While this generation retained its history in mandated American ethnic studies programs, they did not learn that *la lucha sigue.*

Anything south of Old Denver was considered a rural area. People in these areas were more likely to suffer from chronic illnesses like diabetes, heart disease, obesity, and cancer. The Health Department of the Southwest Region, the HD for short, supplied these communities with medical supplies and medicine to manage these diseases. Still, the supplies were cheap and only addressed symptoms. They could not be called treatments, just things that prolonged the inevitable and painful deaths of many people who could not afford them outside of the HD. The HD had markets where you would buy essentials: highly processed cheap foods made of chuchería and flour and generic medicines that might as well have been sugar water.

With the rising cost of living and the stagnancy of wage increases, many people needed help to afford to travel to Old Denver for fresh food. Instead, many people relied on the heavily processed food provided by the HD to survive, alongside the remnants of Family Dollar that remained through the shifting government systems. With no work available, people lived in extreme poverty or sold their land to the government for seed money to move elsewhere. As pesticides continuously poisoned the land and bad growing seasons worsened, they gave up on this labor-intensive and unprofitable industry; many didn't know any other life or work.

Abundio "Abe" David Ortiz/Flores IV was a sixth-generation farmer from rural areas south of Old Denver. The land where he farmed had been passed on through the generations in what used to be called land grants. Land grants are gifts of real estate, physical land space, and resources to use at your discretion. This area had all once been land grants meant for communal use to access water runoff from the nearby mountain, open land for cattle grazing, hunting grounds for big game, and firewood. While other parts of the world were fighting for resources, these communities worked together to ensure they all had what they needed; young people worked to make sure elders had sturdy homes, food to feed themselves, and firewood in the winter when their propane heat sources would become too expensive to run all the time. Abundio had moved three hours away to Old Denver to go to school and paid to get the farm back home up to date with the latest technology. He visited in the summers to meet the migrant workers who lived in his grandfather's house, which was renovated to house up to ten single people. His father's house had been renovated for vacations and weekend getaways, but he never went to stay beyond meeting the workers.

In winter, the upgrades and system updates for all the automated equipment never appropriately downloaded and would not be up and running by April 1st, the start of the growing season. The equipment that tilled the soil and neatly planted seeds in uniform rows with automated drip irrigation systems that sprayed pesticides and managed controlled burns, killing weeds and other plants that grow naturally in that part of the world would not be running on schedule. Abe headed down from Old Denver, thinking it would be a simple fix. First, he met with his head fieldworker and cousin, Diego Flores, to discuss the issues. Diego, a mechanical engineer in agriculture, was there in case the equipment failed and to direct migrant workers to do hands-on work while repairs took place.

"There isn't anything wrong with the equipment, just the update that didn't go through."

"What the hell do I pay you for, Diego?"

"To repair *máquinas,* not to deal with *computadoras, güey.*"

Frustrated, Abe called his work in Old Denver and requested to work remotely while he figured things out. He immediately called the company that supplied his computer network, but the wait times to get through to an actual person were through the roof. As a result, many farmers did not get the update for that year's grow season. Knowing this would not resolve quickly, he called again and requested a temporary relocation to stay close to the farm.

"What is the reason for this relocation?" The voice was part of an automation system.

"Family matters."

"What is the family name?"

Abundio, who had been going by "Abe Smith" for a long time, hesitated.

"What is the family name?" the automated voice repeated.

"Ortiz-Flores."

There was a pause.

"We will submit your request for temporary relocation for the Ortiz/Flores family name. Request number 03312113-RELO-10120304."

His fair skin allowed him to blend in with the gentrifying urbanites of Old Denver. He had disconnected from his ancestry to survive the post-Second Civil War. While he took pride in the fact that his grandfather had served on the side of the Defenders, those opposite the American military, when the regions were decided upon, his family decided to turn to the farm. His grandfather continued the work of farming on their family's land as many generations had done before him, always hoping he could return to do the same. Abe never had those dreams. Instead, he tried to separate himself from his origins as best he could. With racial disparities at an all-time high post-Second Civil War, he hid with his fair skin and adopted the name Smith from his partner John Smith, an English man who had come to the former United States to study urbanism. They met when Abe went to Old Denver as a young man for school. While Abe never openly discussed his past, John worried they would be called to the rural areas someday and that he would not be accepted as an outsider.

"Hi *papí,* how are the dogs?"

John was happy to hear Abe's voice but knew what small talk meant.

"Chula and Tito are doing well, my love. How is the farm?"

Abe hesitated because he had no idea. They were supposed to start the tilling portion tomorrow, prepare the soil for seeds, and mix compost and pesticides to encourage growth and repel insects. But without the updates or help from IT, how could any of that start?

"Bad, *papi*. I am starting to worry. Diego says the machines are ready, but the updates won't be ready tomorrow. For every day I lose, I can't guarantee my purchasers a good crop. We could lose contracts if I don't start tomorrow."

He had to stop himself from spiraling. He hadn't had his hands in soil in years, not since he was a small boy, playing in the fields and learning how his grandfather did this, year after year, in his solitude without complaint. This life was one of sacrifice, and he worried about the sacrifices he would have to make to keep his contracts in place.

"I think I have to stay here until the summer, at least. Then, once the snow melts, things should return to normal, and I should have a crew to take on those responsibilities for me."

"Do you want me to come down there to help?"

John had never farmed a day in his life. They had spent weekends there, and Abe told him about the places he used to play in. But he was an outsider, not even a post-Second Civil War American, but a transplant from a different country. This was an all-hands-on-deck situation, so with a gulp of courage, Abe said, "We're ready for you here when you are ready to come down."

They got off the phone, and Abe called Diego.

"I'm sorry about earlier. I shouldn't have—"

"You're forgiven, *primo*."

"Thank you. I need your help now more than ever."

Diego maintained equipment on several farms and was known in the rural areas for treating his clients like *compadres*. His property had the remains of many large machines whose parts were used for repair or invention.

"What do you need?"

"Workers."

"I gotcha."

In ten years of the return to traditional farming, Abe collected many illegal seeds, heirlooms, and non-genetically modified seeds, whose history was well documented in families and communities. The fruits and vegetables of these seeds would keep the lineage going instead of seeds that grew without pollination. Abe reintroduced natural pollinators like bees and did his best to avoid pesticides. He hired a crew of migrant workers, who he paid more to stay on the farm. Instead of one house for ten single people, he made a couple of single homes for couples to live in together. While many families had left the rural areas, Abe's farm continued to prosper under traditional farming and a growing migrant community of people looking to settle.

After finalizing some contracts for that year's grow season, John called Abe into the kitchen, where there was a letter from the HD informing people of a mandatory health fair that was happening later that week. They looked at each other in shock. Abe saw his community as they healed from *heridas abiertas* that marred the land like a burn scar. This had to be a good thing, something to model for the future of farming. It had to be.

The HD took blood samples at the mandatory health fair, and the community took a survey asking them questions. Several other communities had also been subject to such invasive practices over the past few weeks. Abe had worried a fox hunt was happening, but even if it was, he could do nothing. It didn't matter what they were looking for; they would find it, even if it weren't there. So when Diego came in later that day, Abe asked him for a word.

*"Y, ¿qué puedes hacer con las máquinas?"*

Diego looked at him curiously. Spanish was not typically used in whole sentences because it had been lost in the many generations removed from the border crossing of their forefamilies, especially their dialect.

*"¿Q'quieres hacer?"*

*"Si me'stan buscando, me muero antes de dejar todo esto,"* he looked at the crop growing as far as he could see from the kitchen table. Without this commodity, not only would the industry die, but this town that had started to come back to life would die with it. They had

done good things since that update malfunction years ago. Trying to protect it was going to be hard but worth it.

*"Cuando vienen, tienen máscaras. Van en dos. Regresan en dos. Me sigues?"*

Abe nodded.

When the day came, Abe and Diego had positioned themselves to leave. Abe kissed John and reassured him that everything would be okay. John smiled weakly at Abe, nervous and anxious that this farm would kill him. He could have handed that work off, but it became something he couldn't stop.

*"T'amo, papí,"* Abe whispered longingly into his ear.

"I admire you," John whispered back.

They kissed once more before going outside to smoke and get some *tequila* before the HD agents showed up. The panel van was red with a white plus sign on either side. It came barreling down the driveway, bumping along on paved-only tires. They slowly entered the property and opened the van, a space for sample collection and testing. The two agents exited the van with red totes and white rubber coats. They wore black stain-resistant clothing and black combat boots.

The altercation went smoothly. The HD wasn't militant, nor did they intend to use force. They had grown accustomed to compliance from all citizens, and nothing pointed to physical violence as the answer, only systemic violence to keep people in line. They had not expected to be shocked by the electric fence. They had not expected the machinery to shoot concentrated *manzanilla*-dipped darts, making them fall asleep instantly. After caring for them, Abe and Diego took their clothes, jumped in the van, and returned to the HD temporary headquarters. They were gone for almost two months, taking care of the HD until it was no more.

There are many details Abe left out of this part of the story, so I cannot relay them to you. However, there was a saying when they were growing up that comes to mind, and often when I talk about this story. Abe and Diego's *antepasados* used to say, *"Come loque'es rico."*

Eat what's rich—from a tradition of taking pride in the food you produce to feed yourself and your community to serve your fellow *campesinos.* Throughout his journey, he relied heavily on the community to help him as he learned to put his hands in the soil again and build a relationship with the land and all its bounty. And perhaps, when he translated it, he did it wrong. Instead of *"Come loque'es rico,"* he would say, *"Come los ricos.* Eat the rich."

# #00203

ELINDIOCOPYRIGHT1985

# TITAN'S PROMISE

## GERARDO ALDANA Y VILLALOBOS

Xavier watched intently as the girl at the front of his canoe grabbed hold of what he was fairly sure was a squash vine. He noticed that she had a way of gripping it firmly so that the canoe would slow down and stop, but only stretch the vine and displace it a little—she did no damage to the plant. *Doesn't look so hard,* Xavier thought to himself but was careful not to let his face or body language suggest otherwise.

"We're just here to look today," the girl said. "We don't want any surprises when the chiles start to fruit." As she spoke, she plucked small volunteer sprouts that might interfere with her vegetables if left to grow.

"Okay, you just said we're just looking, but it looks to me like you're doing something."

"Oh, weeding is nothing. You pretty much have to do that all the time."

Xavier imitated the girl and reached over to the large-leafed stalk of another squash vine to pull his end of the canoe closer to the miniature island of vegetables they were closest to. He felt the tension in the plant grow and his end of the canoe slide heavily closer. But just as his end accelerated, he realized that he grabbed a bit too close to the leaf and pulled a bit too quickly. The vine broke off in his hand. Xavier glanced up to confirm what he expected to see: the girl's disappointed expression.

The unlikely pair had paddled their canoe from the rickety pier of a small lake adjacent to their village, directly into a series of canals, which formed a grid of muck islands. Different areas of the grid were planted with different crops, but it didn't look to Xavier anything like the agricultural fields that were being used to feed people in the cities. No patchwork landscapes of monocrops fed by lattice-metalwork sprinkler systems and harvested by AI-powered, crab-like robots. Here, bean vines climbed up corn stalks, interspersed with chiles and squash. On other islands, avocado trees were surrounded by berry bushes and mushrooms. Bees hummed about and birds and dragonflies visited each island as if it were a mini airport. The islands looked "wild" from a distance, but up close, they made sense and intermingled regularities could be parsed.

Xavier started picking weeds, but then paused almost immediately. "What about the weeds under water? Do we pick those too?"

The girl let out a sigh. This guy had been assigned to her because she was one of the older girls in her generation, so she already had experience teaching the younger ones. The elders turned to her mother and father when he showed up out of nowhere to request that she train him. Her siblings she could handle. *This guy? Who knows.* "No. The plants underwater are for the turtles and the fish. You know, like the piranhas?"

Xavier reflexively pulled his hand back, shaking off water droplets wildly. "There's no piranha here," he said, hoping to make it sound like a statement, but realizing that it probably sounded like a question. The girl giggled and went back to work.

Xavier turned to the opposite side of the canoe and looked deep into the shallow water. He found himself chuckling and realized that this was good. His "teacher" was already laughing with him, so that was a kind of acceptance, wasn't it? He hoped so and took his turn at sighing, although for very different reason. *This might turn out to be a place to spend some time after all.*

With new confidence, Xavier gently moved aside the larger plant leaves and plucked tiny sprouts. He figured it might be good to try some small talk. "I thought there would be more mosquitos out here, you know? Because they seem to really like me, so I should have been bitten by now."

"No; the fish eat the larvas and the birds and the bats eat the flying ones—dragonflies, too. We still have some, but it's not bad. I barely notice them."

"Seems like you guys have thought of everything..."

"Well," the girl furrowed her brow, "the elders say that we're remembering a lot. Other people say that it's more like we're getting out of the way as much as we can..." She hesitated. "But I'm not really sure what that's supposed to mean."

A gentle ripple on the water behind him drew Xavier's attention to a young woman on a paddleboard, deftly steering through the canals and headed their way. He turned back to the sprouts and tried to look busy.

"Slow down there," the woman smirked as she approached the canoe. "This isn't a production line."

"Checking up on us, Xochitl?" the girl asked without looking up from her work.

"Nope. Just pulling soil samples." Xochitl hopped off her board and onto a stone path that led into the middle of the island. Xavier realized that he hadn't even noticed the stone until she stepped on it. He half expected that she would find herself knee-deep in mud. "Everything looking okay, Reina?"

"Same as always," the young girl replied.

A pause lingered in the air and Xavier caught himself distracted, having watched Xochitl disappear into the cornstalks and bean leaves, and then tracking butterflies and drawn into the birdsong coming from a stand of willow trees. In an instant he felt a sense of worry that he might be falling in love with this place, this village—La Realidad they called it.

Xochitl's words brought his attention back to the present. "So you came to us from the big city, huh?"

It took him a second to realize that she was talking to him. "Huh? Oh. Yeah."

Reina rolled her eyes.

Xochitl continued, "You're searching for the meaning of life or something like that."

This time, Xavier felt like that should have been a question, but nothing in her voice attested to it. "I mean...is that tired? Do you get a lot of folks coming out here? I mean, I haven't noticed many foreigners. You all look like..." Xavier hesitated, "a pretty small community."

Xochitl inserted a long tube into the center of the island and pulled up a column of soil. Now she came back to her paddleboard on the path of stones. "You were going to say 'isolated'? 'Traditional'? 'Backward'?"

Xavier could feel himself letting the conversation get away from him, and he felt like that wasn't like him. He realized, though, that if it did, it often happened specifically in Indigenous communities. He felt the need to defer, like he wanted to blend into the background. He wanted to be there, but not be noticed. When he had to talk, he found himself conflicted and often inarticulate. "No...I just meant like it's not like in the city where you hardly see the same people twice. You know."

"Actually, I don't know." Xochitl replied flatly. "I've never been."

Now Xavier wished there were piranha in the canals so he could slip in and be devoured by them.

Xochitl turned to address Reina. "The mound is looking a little low. You guys should build it a bit."

With that comment, Reina realized that she had just become a pawn. She didn't mind the work, of course. It would be messy for sure. They would have to dredge the bottom of the canal for mud to slop onto the island, and then spread it around. For her, it was everyday stuff. This newcomer, though—she knew he would struggle. And that's what Xochitl was doing. Reina was young, but she knew Xochitl well enough to realize that Xavier was getting tested...not just by the elders and her parents, but also now by Xochitl. "Okay," Reina replied. "Two, three centimeters?"

The nose of Xochitl's paddleboard rested on the edge of the island, allowing her to step over the toolkit strapped to its front, and sit comfortably cross-legged in the middle. She pushed the sample she had just collected into a small transparent tube so that it preserved the stratification, making it visible for inspection. She then placed the tube into a leather case that Xavier could see already carried a few other samples. He caught himself immediately realizing that this meant that she hadn't come to this spot first. This visit wasn't about him, he thought; she really was just doing her rounds.

Xochitl looked up at him just then. "Yeah," she said, responding to Reina, but looking back at Xavier. "That should do it."

At dinner that night, Xavier looked around persistently for Xochitl. He tried to hide it—sneaking glances around now and again. Reina noticed, but she realized she could probably tell only because she was with both of them in the morning. To anyone else, it probably just looked like Xavier's eyes were wandering so that he could take in what must have been a very unfamiliar setting.

One of the largest buildings in the village, the dining hall looked like a huge barn from the outside. The front door was painted bright red, and an elaborate mural had been started around it. Xavier could make out a woman reading a book, but the swirls and lines indicating what would fill in the scene confused him. Inside, papel picado from a recent festival hung from the high rafters. He counted at least 40 tables filling the hall, and most were occupied when Xavier arrived with Reina's family.

"Your family has been here for a while?" Xavier sought confirmation from Reina's dad, Jesus, as he lifted the cloth covering and they each took from a platter of black bean tamales in the center of their table.

"Yes," Jesus responded, "my cousins have been here much longer, but all my children have been born here."

"And those fields we were in this morning...they look a lot like the chinampas in Xochimilco. Well, at least from what I've seen on TV."

"Yes; very much. Our climate is a little warmer, but we follow many of the same practices." Jesus's face turned visibly serious. "Look, I wish we could talk all about our pueblo, but I'm sorry. I have to share some bad news."

Xavier had just taken a bite and stopped mid-chew.

"On my way over here," Jesus continued, "Don Pedro pulled me aside to let me know that you can't stay here any longer."

"Here, you mean with you? With your family?" Xavier reviewed the day and immediately worried that he had done something wrong, offended someone.

"Here as in: our village. Don Pedro said that a group of men came to the welcome house today, asking to speak to the council. They said it was urgent and that the quicker they could handle this, the less trouble for the village, and the less anyone else would have to know about it."

"Men? Like who?"

"From the city, clearly. Maybe from the government...but which government, Don Pedro didn't say. What he did say was that they were looking for a possible new arrival—a young man from DF—and the description matched yours."

Xavier instinctively moved to climb over the bench he sat on. He couldn't imagine any time that it was a good thing to be looked for by the government. He felt Jesus put his hand on his shoulder. "It's okay. The elders informed the men that there may have been a couple of young men who had arrived recently, and if they could provide justification, the council would consider bringing them up to the welcome house for a conversation." Jesus paused, chewing slowly. "They said that to buy you some time. So you could get away if you need to."

"I have to get out of here," Xavier said as he rose again from his seat. And again, Jesus put his hand on his shoulder.

"You shouldn't leave now. They are staying at the welcome house, and anyone leaving after dark will be suspicious. You have to understand. The elders are very careful. We can provide refuge, but we can't put the village at risk. People pass through this region, you know, trying to get away from bills they can't pay, families they've betrayed, drug problems. It would be too easy for the problems in the city to invade our village if we're not vigilant."

"Maybe I should talk to them? Honestly, I haven't done anything. Anything!"

"The elders thought you might say that. They say they've heard people say that before... and they were taken away anyway."

Both men turned back to their plates, reflecting introspectively when Jesus broke their silence. "If you decide not to talk to them, you should leave in the morning. We can give you some of our clothes, and you can head out in a combi. There are a few that leave early—one north to the city, and others to the east and south. They're usually full, so if you don't look suspicious, you can pass for one of us, just heading out for the day..."

"If I leave..." Xavier hesitated. "Will I be able to come back?"

"That will depend."

Xavier dropped his gaze to consider what this all meant. Maricuca noticed the change in his demeanor and asked her youngest daughter if she wanted more soup from the olla on the stove in order to draw the family's attention away from Xavier. Reina got up to go with them, and Jesus started discussing the next day's work with his son, moving fluidly between Spanish and Tzotzil.

Xavier realized it was no longer some crazy fantasy that he'd made up, trying to make his life seem more interesting or something. He really was being followed. And it wasn't just one person with who-knows-what interest in him—this was a group, Jesus said, probably government agents, and legitimate enough to have the elders concerned.

Now Xavier realized he wasn't just wandering. Now he was on the run.

Xavier wasn't early enough to get his pick of seats on the combi, but he faced no complications in following the instructions that Jesus had left him. He'd stuffed his backpack in a large duffle bag and the driver's assistant loaded it on the roof. A woman wearing a multicolored textile shawl over her head sat by the window on the middle bench. The basket of tamales wrapped in banana leaves she held on her lap was big enough to hide Xavier from anyone looking in through the side window. The woman nodded when they made eye contact, confirming that the seat was open. As for the other side, Xavier noticed that the sliding door window was covered with names of the various stops the combi would make, which would provide good cover once they got on the road.

That the funk he felt himself slipping into constituted a new experience dawned on Xavier as he sat anxiously, waiting for the vehicle to depart. He'd gotten used to feeling deep excitement and anticipation on his bus trips—not for his destination, really, but for the journey. Being on the road; not driving, just on the move. He loved that. Now, though, he felt anxiety…pretty much what he had been trying to get away from. And just when he thought he had found something, some escape, it was being torn away.

His mind raced. Maybe he should have stayed and talked to these men? He couldn't possibly have done anything worthy of being chased. It had to be mistaken identity. Unless it had something to do with his sister's death? But that was so long ago now, that wouldn't make sense. Maybe it was something from his last job, where he would be just a witness? So then he wasn't in trouble, they just wanted information?

But no, the elders were right. There were just too many stories of desaparecidos to ignore. Too much violence left unchecked. Too many cases of political mistakes needing to be covered up with innocent bystanders paying the price. *It has to be a mistake. But I can't risk it.*

The combi pulled out onto the main highway through the mountains, and Xavier realized he was already feeling nostalgia for the little time he had spent at La Realidad. So much was happening there, and it seemed like no one outside of that village knew anything about it. He'd only been able to scratch the surface in his conversation with Jesus that last night. But what he did hear allowed him to push his negative thoughts aside now as the combi wound its way up the road, into the forested mountains, and out of the valley.

"Why can't people do this kind of farming everywhere?" Xavier asked Jesus after realizing that even with the bad news, the afternoon's hard labor left him with a strong appetite. "Have folks been doing this here since, you know, since ancient times?" Xavier couldn't help but imagine himself having participated in the same lifestyle that he saw romantically depicted in magazines—colorful artistic renderings of Indigenous Mesoamerican communities living peacefully before contact with Europe.

"No, no. Not every landscape is appropriate." Jesus paused to take another bite of his tamal. "In this pueblo, we used to cultivate milpa. That's when the rains were consistent. Now it's different. We get heavy rain for shorter periods of time. That's not good for milpa, but we found ways to make it work for our raised fields. Also, we plant a shorter-stalked maize and we inter-plant trees to provide protection from the winds."

"And now you're set." Xavier looked around at the families eating in the community building. He noticed that the tables and chairs were random—some plastic, some metal, some wooden—but everything was decorated. Colorful, hand-woven runners dressed tables throughout. Polychrome vases held locally picked flowers. And dogs and cats roamed underfoot—even the occasional bird flew into the rafters. "You all eat better than we did in the city. I mean, my family was pretty poor, so that's not saying much, but still."

"It's not perfect. We do certainly still have much to worry us. Several years ago, there was a problem at a mining operation in the mountains above a village not far from here. The company just abandoned the mine and nobody stopped them or made them clean up. All the workers just stopped showing up. Then, when the rains came, they sent contaminated water into their reservoir; which poisoned all of their crops."

Oil spills, mining operation failures, fires started by arson—none of these had been in the news for a while. That very well could have been because the government didn't want the public to know about them, and there were no independent news sources left to hold them accountable. Or, Xavier thought, perhaps it was because the news was preoccupied with other things these days…

"Anyway, that's when we all realized that it would be in our best interests to create alliances for times of crisis."

"Alliances?"

"Yes, to help in emergencies, but also for socializing. We have fun. We play soccer when we get together. We play, but we don't keep score. One of the things we all ended up agreeing on was that the outside world has placed too much emphasis on competition and not enough on cooperation. We wanted to move away from the idea that the result was what was important. For our matches now, competition provides the opportunity for an experience—for experiences—and that's their value. Making a perfect pass down the sideline on an overlap, that should feel rewarding whether you're losing five, zero or winning one to nothing. Yes, we celebrate goals, but we don't keep track of them. And there's a side benefit. This greatly reduces the amount of injuries, which we can't really afford because we all have to go back to work after the festival is over."

"I can't believe it." Xavier shook his head and smiled. "I bet folks wouldn't even believe me if I tried to tell them about you back home. It sounds totally innovative and new…and at the same time, totally traditional and old."

The thought of this "newness" now contrasted with what Xavier was seeing out of his combi window. New these days in the cities were encampments further and further from the center, stretched out along the highways. New expansions of homeless communities. New drug combinations to make getting high ever cheaper…and always more dangerous. Yes, there was still new technology coming out, but no one he knew could afford it. La Realidad was a different kind of new for him.

The combi driver pulled up at the unofficial stop outside of the Southern Bus Terminal in Coyoacan. Xavier grabbed his duffle bag and left it in a locker back in the station, after pulling out his smaller day pack. He stopped at a stall on the street for a lime Jarrito and jumped on a different combi—one that he knew well. It would take him to a hostel on Avenida Division del Norte where he'd stayed at for most of last year while he worked as a custodian trying to save money. He figured he could stay there again until he came up with a new plan. But now he wondered: Would those men find him here? Would they still be looking for him? Could it have been the company he worked for, and not the government? Something about the work conditions there? Maybe he should try to find Paco again? At least then he might have a chance at seeing a familiar face.

After checking in, Xavier noticed that it was still early. The drive wasn't really that long, even though La Realidad seemed a world away. He walked a few blocks to a small restaurant he knew with good, cheap tacos.

Xavier entered the restaurant and approached the customers at a small square table, sitting in a group of three, so there was one spot naturally open. "Okay. I know this is strange, but can I just sit with you for a minute?" He grabbed the frayed-edged, Marvel-logo trucker hat from the young woman to his left and put it on backwards. "And borrow your hat? Just ten minutes, and I'll pay for your food?"

The three looked to be a little younger than Xavier. They dressed in street-fashionable clothes that were clearly not expensive.

"Cool, cool, man. You look like my cousin Eduardo anyway. Who you runnin' from?"

"I wish I knew."

The long-haired young man to Xavier's left spoke up. "Yeah, they picked up my cousin Tito the other day. He didn't do anything—like really didn't do anything...not like the 'hey, I didn't do anything' excuse kind of thing. But no, really. He was just hanging out with his friends and la jura pulled over and called him out. Just pointed at him, got out of their car, and pulled out their clubs. His buddies told him to run, but he said it again: 'I didn't do anything.' Yeah. He was working—had a job at a restaurant and everything. He didn't have time to get in trouble. Well...anymore."

"Yeah...it's no good to be under thirty anymore. We're all suspects...for something."

"Not just under thirty. If you're brown enough, you're a suspect."

"Simón."

They all took a moment of silent reflection, but then the noise and commotion of the restaurant brought them back to the present.

"Were they cops?"

"No idea. Well, I mean I know what one of them looks like, so for sure. Let me know if you see him. He's totally non-descript; totally average; except that he has blond hair. He sticks out like a sore thumb."

"HA! Blond?! You'd think that would be the worst choice if they didn't want to be noticed. I mean, look around."

The group all reactively surveyed the restaurant to see young adults sitting in groups or as couples eating and drinking at small, crowded tables. Xavier noticed that there were no families here...just workers on lunch break. But yes, it was a sea of black hair they saw throughout the restaurant to confirm what they already knew.

"No! Don't look around. If he's here, we might look suspicious."

"Oh, man...you really are in trouble. How long have you been on the run?"

"Yeah...this is good...casual conversation. Let's keep it looking natural. But let me know if you see him, yeah?"

"Sure, sure. Now tell us what you did."

"Okay, so I've been traveling for about six months now, but..." Xavier was interrupted by a group of affluent-looking young adults cheering at the bar. The TV screen was showing footage of another shuttle landing on Titan. It had been speculative fiction for so long, but now...now the world was seventeen years into the Earth2Saturn Mission, and the shuttle that took the population of Titan over one hundred thousand had just landed. "101,423" flashed across the bottom of the screen as a news anchor narrated the event.

Images from the moon's surface of pods dropping from an orbiting spacecraft and parachuting down filled the screen. Footage then shifted to a point of view from within a pod, showing a smiling and waving family of four, before swiveling for a view out the window, which revealed a huge architectural complex serving as a livable habitat for humans. The feed cut to the face of a beautiful young Chinese woman. Spanish subtitles had trouble keeping up as she skipped between Mandarin and English in her responses to an interviewer's questions.

"Absolutely, I am excited. Yes, the journey was long, but very comfortable. No, I'm not married yet," this caused her to look down, away from the screen, "but I am excited to maybe soon find someone and have one of the first weddings on Titan! And one of the first children native to this Saturnian Moon—wow!"

The interviewee shared her excitement. "Wait, would that make your children aliens?"

"No! Aliens, how?" The woman frowned, but playfully. "No one will be going back to Earth...so how would they be aliens if they live where they are born?"

The news story shifted to another shuttle—one that launched six months after the one that just landed. The mission engineers had designed a tethered "go-pro" camera device to this shuttle so that images and video of the whole spacecraft could be taken en route. The news anchor quipped that the number of spots were running out, but that they would continue to follow the news on Titan as it developed.

The group of young adults at the bar, closest to the television, whooped and raised their glasses for a toast.

"Those kids don't have a shot," the young man sitting directly across from Xavier chimed in to bring the group's attention back to the conversation at the table. "Now that they've hit a hundred thousand, it's going to be a blink before they hit a million, and then it's over. No one else goes."

"Yeah, but those kids come from pretty rich families," the now hatless woman contested as she tugged her hair up into a ponytail. "They could already be on the list."

"Not that rich. I bet they just pretend they have a shot so folks think they have more money than they really do. One of those guys looks like Tomás from prepa."

"Oh shit, don't look," Xavier caught a glimpse of blond hair across the room.

"What? He's here?"

"Chingao! The news distracted us...sorry, man."

Xavier placed the hat back on the young woman's head and hunched low, slipping into the kitchen. The cooks raised an eyebrow at him, but he pointed back and said, "Some tipo—maybe la jura—is chasing me." The cooks looked at one another. The older guy sporting a graying goatee pointed to the back door with a toss of his chin.

Xavier stepped out into an alley and winced at the smell. Trash filled dumpsters and peppered the sidewalk. Two men—barely skin and bones—were gently illuminated by a lighter as they hunched over a small piece of aluminum foil.

To his left, Xavier spotted the side street that would take him back to the Avenida Division del Norte. He sprinted and hopped on a combi that was about to leave just as he hit the sidewalk. It looked crowded, but Xavier knew they would take one more. The host stepped out and gave Xavier his seat, and then hung on to the doorway, standing on the edge of the car and hanging onto the roof-rack as they pulled into traffic. Xavier didn't even look to see if the blond man had tracked him. He kept his head down and white-knuckle-gripped his seat so that he wouldn't get thrown off when the driver switched lanes a little too abruptly.

A group of kids in the back started getting loud, so the driver turned up the radio. This group was definitely only taking the combi a short way—not like most of the others, who were on their way out of the city. Xavier thought now that he might just get off with them and see if they could be useful as cover. Then he could make his way back to Paco's apartment by Metro—that was really his only chance at sleeping indoors tonight if the blond man had tracked him through the hostel.

The radio caught Xavier's attention as the streets passed by. The DJ was taking calls in between songs, and a woman was saying that she didn't believe that people were going into space. She said that her abuelita used to say the same thing about people going to our Moon. "This could all just be a show. It could be that the government just doesn't want to make anything better for the people. They say they're spending money on a space program, but really, all of the rich are just living on an island with military protection."

The DJ responded that he believed people were traveling to Saturn, but why not ask callers? What did they think? "Call in now to let us know."

The next caller came on immediately. "Doesn't it seem weird that we never get any reports of problems on Titan? Everything just seems to work out. Doesn't that seem weird?" The caller's friend grabbed the phone from him. "Yeah. He says this all the time. But I say no. That's why they all leave. They're getting what we all want...why would there be any problems?"

The caller grabbed the phone back. "But even mechanical failures, or instrument breakdowns...I don't know. I guess, yeah, it's ENASA and all, but I just didn't think they were *that* good."

Xavier realized that he had never questioned it. This would have been a long deception if they actually weren't going. He was in elementary school when he started learning about the ships manned by robots, sent to Saturn's moon Titan, to start building a station there. They even had Lego playsets of the ships and of the robots that you could purchase. No, he never had anything big—for his birthday, his parents could afford one of the smaller ships or a couple of the robots that they sold individually. But his cousins—they had whole landing and laboratory sets. Xavier caught himself reminiscing while the DJ played the latest psychedelic-cumbia.

He remembered going to his cousins' house to play. They would take the set out into the yard and set it up in different "terrains" to pretend they were exploring Titan. The landscaping in their yard was never quite finished, so it provided the perfect setting for imagined adventures. Xavier remembered that his cousins would often scold him. The robots were supposed to be construction workers and scientists. They were designed to run off of AI so that they could land and adapt enough to the landscape to run machinery and to put together the first laboratory. But Xavier inevitably put his robot in one of the rovers and just started driving all over the place. Instead of building labs and collecting samples, or getting everything ready to support a colony of humans, Xavier had the robots going off jumps and driving down steep dirt hills. Xavier wondered now if that was the beginning of him not wanting to live a "successful" life, and instead looking for "something else."

He was lost in his reflections when the combi stopped and Xavier realized the rowdy kids were getting out. He jumped out as well, but the host stopped him and gave him a quizzical look. He had actually paid for a longer trip, so technically, the host owed him money. Xavier shook his head and turned to follow the group. The combi sped off, leaving them on one of the side streets off the Zona Rosa. It would be pretty easy to get lost in there, but then he would definitely be sleeping on the streets tonight. Xavier looked absently at the cliques of people walking by and the traffic overwhelming the roads. He breathed deeply and let out a heavy sigh.

There was no sign he'd been followed, so he decided to try his luck with Paco's apartment.

Xavier found himself stumped at the front door of a sizable apartment building. There wasn't a lot of foot traffic on these streets, but he did have the sense that folks were watching him—or at least taking note. He wasn't carrying his large backpack, and his smaller pack was at the hostel, so he felt like he didn't look that out of the ordinary. Still, this was a nicer neighborhood where he knew he didn't fit in. And now, no one answered the door.

It occurred to him that if someone entered the building, he could just follow them up, but he quickly rejected that idea. That might only make him look even more suspicious. And what if the person confronted him? *That's no good.* And no...he couldn't just sit here on the stoop. Folks entering the building would think he was begging and call the cops on him.

He turned and started walking away from the building, now not sure at all where to go. Paco had helped him out before—when he really needed it. But now he never seemed to be around.

As he stepped onto the sidewalk, thinking he could come back later, a woman brushed by him and spoke firmly. It seemed like she was speaking to him...but well, she also had a phone in her hand. Maybe he just overheard her conversation. But no...it didn't seem like that, either.

"Don't follow me, but meet me at the Oxxo two streets up and to the right in fifteen minutes."

She passed quickly by him, not modifying her brisk pace and making no movement to indicate that she was talking to him. Xavier was confused—excited, interested—but confused. Could she have been talking to him? What could she be thinking? Maybe it was an offer to sell drugs? He did seem to have that look—it wasn't infrequent that sellers on the street would pitch their pills or a little mota. But no; she sounded different—totally different.

*And she said, "Don't follow me." She wouldn't have said that to someone on the phone, right? Well...maybe.* If he caught her in mid-conversation, that could have referred to anything. But then the directions? *"Two streets up and on the right?" That's meant for someone who knows where she is, isn't it? Well, no...if they already mentioned a location in their conversation, then it could have been relative to that.*

*Arrgh.*

Frustrated, Xavier figured it couldn't hurt to check it out. If there was an Oxxo two streets up and to the right from where he was now, then maybe she was talking to him?

But he didn't have a watch, and he didn't have a phone...so, how long was fifteen minutes? And how should he get there without following her? Too many questions. *Seriously, what do I have to lose?*

Twenty minutes later, Xavier rounded the corner onto the street that should have corresponded to the woman's instructions. He expected to find an Oxxo on the corner—*they were always on the corner, weren't they?* He looked through the trees and manicured hedges, which sheltered the buildings from the little street noise that could be heard. There, through the foliage, he spotted an Oxxo on the opposite side of the street half-way down. So maybe she wasn't talking to him after all?

Xavier took his time. He didn't want to get there too early, and he had no idea if 15 minutes had passed or not. In his head, hours, days, years had gone by. During his walk, he'd reflected on playing games with his cousins, on his tortured experience in school, on his sister dying and his parents falling apart and leaving him in the city.

First they started fighting, blaming each other for why she started shooting up in the first place. Then his mom went back to work to try to find normalcy, but his father couldn't. He couldn't do anything. He quit his work and drank the day away. And so they fought. They fought about how she didn't care—she just worked all the time. And they fought about how he needed to get back to work or they wouldn't be able to afford rent. Finally, his mom left; she said she was going back to her family in Jalisco. It was only a week after that that Xavier came home and his dad was gone. Just gone. When he called his tía, she said that his mother never showed up—never made it back home.

Did they get addicted to the same drugs she had? Trying to escape their grief, did they follow her into the Underworld? Leaving him alone? Alone in the city of too many people.

His mind flitted from one thought to the next. *Wait, is that who was following me? Someone with news of my parents?*

The bells clinked on the glass door of the Oxxo as he pushed it open, bringing his attention back to the present. Xavier tried not to look suspicious but immediately wondered what that should look like in this situation? Should he look around? Should he keep his head down? *In the movies, cool people always keep their heads up and look around like they don't care. But, wait a minute...I'm not cool...*Well, if he wasn't suspicious, Xavier thought, he would be coming into the store for something, so he had to look around for whatever that was. It struck him that it might be easiest to check the magazine rack. He walked over to it, next to the cash register, and looked for something to flip through.

Immediately he felt his face blush. The only magazines on the rack were of nude women. This was not working out. The cashier gave him a look, but stepped out from behind the counter to help an older woman who was having trouble reaching the pan dulce in the back of a cabinet. She was wearing so much jewelry, Xavier wondered why she didn't just send a servant or someone to buy it for her. Just then, the woman from the street came up next to him. "I see you have an interest in literature."

Xavier was sure his brown skin could not turn any redder.

"Buy something and meet me outside," she said to him. "But please, not one of these."

The woman went to the counter and paid for a pack of Marias and a bottle of water. She slid both into her backpack and walked out of the store. Xavier grabbed another Jarrito and a bag of cacahuates japoneses, paid, and then tried to stroll after her.

He quickly caught up and matched the woman's stride. She was a little taller than him, but her pace was now casual. "Who are you, and why did you come to my building?"

"Your building? I don't even know who you are...why do you think I'm looking for you?"

"Look," the woman shot him a sharp glance, but kept walking. "I've lived here for a while now, and I've made it my business to know, so I have a pretty good sense of who might be looking for who."

"That's fair. But honestly, seriously, I'm not looking for you. I came to visit an old friend who I thought still lived in the building. His name is Paco—Francisco Morales. He's the only friend I have left in the city. I knew him in college. I thought I'd look him up. See if maybe I could crash at his place tonight."

"Okay...Better," the woman replied, relaxing a little. "Yes, he did live there. But he left...that was his apartment." She found herself over-sharing—which used to be a habit—but her gut told her this young man was no threat. "He said I could keep it until they kicked me out...but he didn't think they would. His family probably owned it."

"Wait," Xavier was totally confused. "So he left...but he left you his apartment? Were you married or something? Or...huh?"

"Okay..." the woman stopped and looked at him directly, then looked around. "This is going to be a longer conversation. Let's go get some tacos. I'm Susana, by the way."

"Xavier. Thanks for talking to me."

"I can't figure out why they're following me. I'm nobody. I've done nothing." They were both eating now, sitting at one of several card tables under a tarp, next to an outdoor street cocina. It was late afternoon, so vehicle and foot traffic were heavy. Horns blared. People shouted. Music rose and fell as it seeped out of open windows.

"Nobody, huh? How do you know Paco? You're too young to have gone to college with him."

Xavier didn't hesitate. It had almost become a habit at this point. He'd been on several long bus rides without music or a phone, so he found out that—not everyone—but a lot of people on the road just liked to talk. It turned out to be a pleasant way to pass the time. Now Xavier often initiated conversations, rather than waiting to see if his neighbor would start first. He found it easy to talk about anything because he knew he'd never see them again.

"I was at UNAM. I thought I wanted to be an engineer so I was taking calculus. Paco was my professor."

"Oh, yeah," Susana interrupted, "I remember he used to teach every once in a while. He liked the teaching part, but he didn't want to be on the faculty."

"Well, he was a great teacher—one of the few who seemed to really care about me and whether I was getting it.

"Anyway, I wasn't doing very well in the class. And he said it wasn't my fault, and you know, that felt good. I needed to hear that. He said the private schools had so many advanced activities in math and science that when those students got to university, the kids who went to public schools couldn't compete. Even if they were way smarter, by the time they figured it out at university, the private school kids were setting curves and doing advanced work."

Susana looked down and away from Xavier. She recalled her own educational experience and felt what she thought might be a sense of guilt.

"Anyway," Xavier continued, "it didn't matter because I ended up having to quit school and find a job...any job. I told that to Paco, and he said that if I needed help, to check back with him. Of course, nobody would hire me without a connection, so I went back to him. He said he had a cousin who owned a software company, so I should go see him. They ended up giving me a job as a janitor—turns out that was a position that had a high turnover, so there were openings."

"High turnover?" Susana muffled through her food.

"Yeah. It was kind of crazy, actually. These guys working in the office—they were insane. They were all guys and they just left messes all over the place. Their bosses made us clean it all up because they said that they were way too busy coding, so they shouldn't have to worry about it. And they really were. These guys were killing themselves—at their terminals all day long, late into the night, many early in the morning. And then the drugs. Every new employee thought he was the next best thing, and when he didn't produce as much as he thought he could, he would start shooting up to increase his output. And when that didn't work, well, that's when we would find them—on the bathroom floor covered in the nastiest stuff you could imagine."

"Like passed out?"

"Nope." Xavier looked Susana straight in the eyes. "Dead."

"No!"

"Yeah. This happened a lot. That's the reason they couldn't keep janitors; you can only clean that up so many times before you just can't take it anymore."

"Ugh...you had to do that?!"

"Twice."

"Wow...sorry to hear that. I mean, I heard stories, but I thought it was just macho, urban-legend stuff, you know? Working yourself to death...metaphor...not literally."

"Yeah. No. But I was just saving up money to quit and hit the road. And that's where I was...out on the road when I found out I'm being followed. I didn't know what to do, so I came back to the city. I came to Paco's apartment a few months ago, while I still had the job. I buzzed the buzzer, but no one answered. I tried to hang out for a bit to see if he would come back, but people started to give me *that* look, and he didn't show. I guess I was hoping he could help me out again."

Susana finished her second taco and was nodding that she understood. She picked up her third as Xavier continued.

"Hey, wait. Did Paco do something? Is that why he left? And that's why he left you the apartment? Is he in trouble?"

Susana continued chewing and gave no hint that she was going to respond.

"Anyway, I can't believe it was something I did, even though I did have the feeling that I was being watched...I kind of have this vague memory of a blond guy keeping an eye on me, but now I'm just worried that my mind is putting him there to make it all make sense. Once that group showed up at the village, though, and Jesus said that one of them was blond, I had to leave and I just didn't have anyone else to turn to."

"The village?"

"Yeah...how to make this not too long of a story..." Xavier scratched the scruff of a goatee that he was struggling to grow. "I dropped out of college and took that job a couple of years ago when things got bad with my family. My sister died and everything went bad."

Xavier paused, his eyes drifting upward as an image of his sister crossed his mind. "Paco let me crash on his couch a couple of times. He said he understood. He seemed to know about a lot of stuff. He said that a lot of people were going homeless. Actually, he said all housing—like everywhere—was just way too expensive. Paco used to say that we were living in a neo-feudalist society, or something like that. He said when corporations started buying houses, nobody—like no families—could afford to buy them anymore—everyone just had to rent. And then most folks had to take jobs they didn't want in order to afford that rent. So really, it was just like haciendas in the old days. But now corporations are the hacendados and most folks are just landless peones."

"Yeah. That totally sounds like Paco."

"And that was me—just a peon." Xavier dropped his eyes and scratched behind his ear. "So I decided to embrace it. I found out that I could live in a hostel for months at a time. Then if I worked at that janitor job, or something, I could save enough money to go out and live on the road, como vagabundo. Life wasn't an apartment and a job; life was out on the road."

"You sound like one of those jipis from the 1960s."

"Maybe," Xavier wasn't sure if he liked the comparison, "but anyway, it got even better. I heard from one guy on a bus that there were pueblos outside of the city that were going 'off the grid.' You didn't even have to pay rent, you just had to do chores. I tried going to the one he mentioned, and they let me in, no problem, but it was a total mess. It was really just squatters living in a big, open camp. Half the folks were on drugs. People were screaming...or not screaming really. More like howling. Other people were beating each other up. It was filthy. Yeah; I got out of there pretty quickly."

"And that was the village where they found you?"

"No...totally not. That made me more careful in looking where I might stay. Then I was on a bus to Cuernavaca, and a guy next to me told me that there were some villages that were harder to get into. You actually had to get permission to enter them. But he did warn me that there was nothing there. They weren't into technology, there were no drugs, there was no real party scene. He left when he heard that. But that sounded really good to me. So I eventually found one—turns out there were more.

"But this one specifically I really liked, so they interviewed me. I had to sit in a big old building, like a huge barn. The elders of the community sat on benches, and they asked me a lot about who I was and why I wanted to stay with them. It was super intimidating, but it kind of felt good when they let me in. Kind of a different experience, you know?"

"No...actually, I have no idea. I'm a computer geek; an indoors person. Air conditioning, heater, swivel chair, vending machine snacks. No elders' councils in the mountains for me."

"Oh...well...umm...it was really exciting for me." Xavier recounted how he was asked to leave and then took a combi into the city.

"So they may have followed you here? To my apartment?"

"I don't think so. I snuck out of the village by following Jesus's instructions—it seemed to go smoothly. But then he tracked me to a restaurant, so..."

"Hmm...maybe they sold you out? If it's the Ministerial, they have ways. Also, there's so much more surveillance in the city..." she replied. "How long have you been back? Do you think they might have some kind of tracker on you? And you said it's obvious because it's always a blond guy who shows up?"

"Yeah...he totally sticks out."

"Well it looks like he's onto you again."

Xavier turned to see a blond man in a black suit and tie running toward him.

"Let's go," Susana grabbed his wrist and jerked him into position alongside her as they started running down the street. Xavier looked back at the tacos he didn't get to eat, but didn't protest. His foot caught one of the chair legs, knocking it over. The last thing he saw was the cook's frown as he recovered and clumsily stumbled after Susana.

Susana knew this part of the city extremely well. They were in an apartment complex and out on a street two blocks away before they even broke into a sweat. As they stepped out from under an awning, they heard a drone humming directly above them.

She ducked back into another Oxxo and they worked their way through to the bathroom into a back alley.

"You can't..." Xavier protested before they entered the men's room. But Susana paid no attention.

"We need a secure place to hide out," she said, looking up and appreciating the laundry and other items giving them cover from the drone. "Those things run out of batteries pretty quickly. If we can wait them out, then we have to break for it—not around the corner this time. This next run is gonna have to be long distance. Out of the city maybe? Let's go."

Susana put her finger to her lips and led Xavier through a series of passageways that he never would have noticed if he were alone. They jumped a few iron gates and squeezed through hedges; all the while Xavier was surprised at how easy Susana made that look. They ended up in a courtyard within an apartment complex. There was an outdoor staircase at one end, so they climbed three flights until they were comfortable that they couldn't be seen from above or below. They leaned up against the wall and slid down into seated positions, glancing at each other and smiling at the coincidence.

"Indoors girl, huh?" Xavier managed while breathing heavily.

"Well, okay. My dad forced me to learn kung fu when I was a kid. I may have sometimes used it to get in a little trouble."

Xavier and Susana both took a moment to catch their breath. The stucco wall at their back was painted with large swaths in a color just lighter than the rest of the wall. It still smelled fresh.

"Okay, you said, 'We need to get out of here.' 'We.' Are you just being nice? Why are you helping me out?"

"If you're telling me the truth—and my gut tells me you are—then it sounds like you shouldn't have anyone chasing you. Paco and me, though…well…that could be a different story. So I'm guessing, here, but maybe someone was surveilling one of us and saw you come to our place, looking 'out of place,' and figured there might be a connection?"

"So you're the one in trouble," Xavier started to move away, "then I should split…get away from you?"

"I said I'm guessing. It's a hypothesis. At this point, we only know for sure that they've been following you."

"You're right." Xavier looked around. "Then thanks, I guess."

They both sat in silence, noticing that the neighborhood had grown quiet.

Xavier broke the silence. "Then it's your turn. How did you know Paco?"

Susana looked down at the stairs. She could feel her emotions bubbling up. She'd held them back for so long, pretending nothing bothered her, focusing on work. But now she felt it coming out. "Paco and I worked together...and we lived together. He wanted me to marry him, but I wouldn't. That doesn't matter. He left because his family was wealthy, and their turn came up to go to Titan."

Susana paused, and Xavier realized his jaw had dropped open. "You mean, if you married him, you could have gone too?! I can't believe this. I'm talking to someone who could have gone into space?" Xavier was basically speaking to himself, but because they were both whispering, she heard him and dropped her head. "And you said no?!"

"It's complicated."

Xavier had seen movie stars on TV boarding shuttles into space. He'd seen politicians and billionaires. Now he was here speaking to someone who was part of that part of society? *Wait. Paco was wealthy?*

"Anyway," Susana continued. "We worked together for ENASA as programmers..."

Xavier stopped her. "I can't believe it. So you're exactly what my cousins wanted to be when we were growing up. Heck, they may still want to be you."

"Well, it wasn't always this way. I mean, it wasn't supposed to be this way." Susana pulled a pen out of her pocket and started twirling it through her fingers. "It was never my plan. I got started in all of this because of these cybersecurity camps my mom made me go to when I was a kid...my mom was a biochemist and my dad was a mathematician—they both wanted me to 'do STEM.' To me, cybersecurity seemed like a rebellious kind of thing, because you learned how to do it by learning how to break it. So this ended up being the one thing my mom and I didn't fight about. But I guess she kind of ended up getting her way, since that's what got me into college for Computer Science."

A small bird joined them on the staircase landing. It picked at the crumbs that had fallen out of a Sabritas bag, left on the edge of a step.

"But that eventually got boring. Just before I quit, I found out that I liked making up worlds...you know, building them with CGI for movies. Well, that's what I thought I would do, once I enrolled at UNAM. I started working with a professor on building a sci-fi world, and that's when things got really interesting. My profe wasn't interested in just making movies. She was into simulating worlds. For that, she wanted to create these planets, these environments, and then put things in them that were controlled by AI."

"AI in a simulation? That totally sounds like the Matrix."

"Yeah...something like that, and I loved that. I was finally really hooked. I felt like I finally found something for me—not something I was doing to please my parents or to upset my parents, or to be cool with my friends."

"Maybe if I knew that something like that was possible, maybe I would have found a way to stay in college."

"But it did get weird at that point." Susana was in her storytelling mode and ignored Xavier's reflective comments. "My profe came to me one day and said she wanted to talk to me. She took me out for coffee, and told me that she was being recruited to work on a government project. She wasn't able to take it—her kids were still young, and the job would require a lot of hours. She said she had 'already done her time' and now liked her balance between teaching and her family. So she wanted to know if I was interested. She said the government would arrange for my degree, so I wouldn't have to finish any more coursework at UNAM. ENASA would put me on payroll, and it would be really good—more money than I knew what to do with."

"What was the work?"

"Yeah...that's it. It was seamless, *really*. My profe was kind of ahead of her time. They had this plan. They sent robots up to Titan to not just take data, but also to build a station there. That meant that they couldn't just send up probes, like they had for asteroids or for Mars—they needed robots that would adapt to conditions that we didn't yet know about, and then work together constructively to build things once they got there. Instead of waiting to see how that would work out over time, they figured simulations could run faster than real-time and project progress into the future. They had a group working on building a world simulation of Titan, and putting AI-controlled robots in it to see how they would do—exactly what I was doing with my profe. I didn't like the idea of working for the government, but the project sounded like so much fun that I couldn't say no."

"Wow. You are so frickin' cool." The words came out of his mouth before he could catch himself, leaving his face bright red.

Susana laughed. "I doubt that." She looked around and noticed that a second bird had joined the first, and they were starting to fight over what was left of the Sabritas, charging each other and twittering fiercely. "Anyway, I think we should get moving pretty soon. It looks like we've lost them for now. Let's split up. We have to stay away from my place—Paco's place—for a couple of days, but I need to grab some stuff and that will be easier alone. Do you have anything? You don't even have a backpack, how are you traveling?"

"Yeah, I have most of my stuff in a locker. Why don't we meet at the Central Bus Terminal?"

Susana found herself triggered as she walked back to her apartment. Yes, she could have been on one of those shuttles to Titan. But of course, she knew that would never happen, and how to say no was next to impossible. Paco didn't take it well.

"It's true, we've only actually lived together for nine months." Paco paused and looked down at her hand as he held it, facing her on the couch in their apartment. "I love you. I know that. It's in everything we do. Even, you know, when we're just having coffee on Sunday mornings, talking about nothing...it's just so...you know." He took a deep breath. "But this is my family. These are my siblings. Their families. No—we don't always see eye-to-eye, but they're my family. And I haven't participated in their lifestyle—this apartment is the only thing I've taken from them. And now they're asking me to join them because they'll pay...not because I've 'earned my passage.' And, yeah, it's a chance to start somewhere new. Seriously, this world is falling apart, you know that. There's something new to be worried about every day."

Susana ached to tell Paco why she didn't want to go, but also knew she absolutely could not...and she knew he would never believe her anyway. She had only one card to play. "I need you to trust me, Paco. Look at me. Really look at me. Look into that part of me that only you know. You're right; we've only lived together for a few months, but we've worked together for years. You've seen it. You've felt it. You know you can trust me. You should trust me on this." She looked into his eyes. "Let's just stay."

And that was it. They had been tiptoeing around the conversation for weeks, making jokes, innuendos. They had a sense of where each was, but didn't want to believe it. Now, though, it was confirmed. He would go, and she would stay.

Paco got up from the couch and gently released her hand. "Goodbye."

That was it. That was the last word he said to her. Fitting, sure. But so painful.

Susana stopped at some steps leading to the back side of her apartment building. She looked up to the top floor, and then up to the sky. Paco had left. So many others had gone too.

Susana felt herself breathing deeply.

She had said nothing.

Two hours later, Xavier had retrieved his backpack, changed his shirt, and was waiting in the busier part of the bus station, near the main entrance. At this hour, people were mostly arriving, greeting friends or family who had come to pick them up. He spotted Susana outside and headed toward her. She responded by turning and walking, leading him away from the station.

"Where are we going? Why don't we take a bus?"

"This place is covered with cameras. I'm sure they've spotted you already. Also, they're taking photos of everyone who gets on every bus at boarding. They'll pick us out immediately."

"Oh, yeah. I didn't think of that."

"We'll need to take a combi out of the city."

"You'll take a combi?!" Xavier realized that he now thought of Susana as part of the elite class. He couldn't imagine that she even knew what the inside of a combi looked like.

Susana turned to say, "Don't give me that," but was cut off when she noticed a black sedan approaching. It looked wrong, and she felt a twinge in her gut that the men in it were approaching them.

Susana grabbed Xavier by his backpack and briskly walked back into the bus station. Four men in black suits left the sedan in the loading zone and strode toward the entrance as a cop yelled after them for the illegal parking job. Susana went through the thickest part of the crowd and then came out the next door down, onto the street. She spotted a motorcycle in the loading zone with keys in the ignition and its owner kissing his partner goodbye. "Let's go."

Susana moved her backpack around to her chest as she ran and hopped on the bike, started the engine, and pushed off. Xavier barely made it onto the back, grabbing hold of Susana's backpack, while the owner of the motorcycle shouted and started to chase them, realizing immediately it was pointless. Susana hopped the central divider and headed in the opposite direction before the four men were even back out of the bus station.

Neither rider had a helmet, but Susana was able to pull her sunglasses out of her bag and slip them on while she steered. Xavier, though, had no protection for his eyes from the wind or Susana's long black hair, so he kept them closed and pressed his face into her back. After getting past the first hints of nausea with Susana's weaving in and around traffic, he found the experience pleasant. With his eyes closed, Xavier felt like he was in a kind of trance state.

Soon enough, though, he felt Susana's body relax as she eased off the throttle and applied the brakes. Xavier opened his eyes to see that they were pulling off the road just outside of the city. A grand vista of mountains opened up before them. Just at the edge of a cliff, they pulled up to a vegetable stand on the side of the road.

"Why are we stopping?" Xavier realized he was shouting—he'd gotten used to being buffeted by the wind, and now his ears were ringing. He intentionally lowered his voice. "I mean, I'm not complaining, but why are we stopping?"

"Yeah, I realized that I'm not actually sure what our next move should be." Susana motioned with her chin for Xavier to dismount. She then dropped the kickstand, pulled her backpack off, and stepped off the bike herself. She tried to tame her long black hair and put it up now that it had been angered by the wind. "Part of me thinks we should head into the mountains. But part of me is thinking we're better off laying low in the city—at least until we have some idea of what we plan to do."

"Great, because I really need to pee."

"Okay, I'll buy some guavas and wait for you here. I swear, men have, like, no bladders."

Xavier returned to find that Susana had pulled her bike up next to a small table, and ordered two guava licuados. He thanked her and started drinking immediately. He realized he was still hungry, and he could picture the tacos he left on his plate back at the restaurant earlier that day. He felt his mind drift, and they were both quiet for a bit.

Susana broke the silence. "You said you were living in a village out there? Now it's my turn to be surprised. I heard it was pretty dangerous...I lost a friend out there."

Xavier noticed that she was looking at the mountain range that continued on as far as the eye could see. Vultures circled high, drifting overhead. A stray, three-legged dog sniffed Xavier's shoes and then scurried away when Xavier flinched.

"Well, not out there as in right there, but out there...in the mountains."

Xavier could tell that she was lost in that memory, and even though he was feeling pressed for time, he was enjoying slurping his drink and so let her continue.

"I was young," Susana continued, "my mom and dad were still together. I was doing homework at the dinner table, and my dad was there with me, saying he would help if I needed any. Mom was in the kitchen. Then dad said, 'Oh no.' He said it in that way that you know means something is really wrong."

Susana looked back out at the mountains and continued. "He'd gotten a news flash on his phone. This family that we knew—we spent vacations together...actually, my mom was really proud of that, like wow, this really wealthy family liked to vacation with us. Anyway, this family was on a different trip, one without us, and something went wrong, throwing the plane into an uncontrolled descent. But it was okay. Everything worked, you know. The modules popped off. The parachutes opened up. Everything went as it was supposed to. Except that the one module—the one this family was in—it got caught up in a wind current or something, and just drifted. It separated from the others, which all went down in the mountains of Oaxaca. This one drifted away, and even though they had a tracker on it, it landed in this area that was just totally inaccessible. And then with the weather. Well, the rescue team searched for two days to get to the module, and when they got there, it was totally empty. Stripped clean. No sign of anyone, and the search for the family came up with nothing. They just disappeared."

Xavier had finished his drink and was listening intently. "Where'd they go?"

"Well, that's the thing. No one ever found them. So actually, my parents just used that as evidence that it's really not safe out there. They said that it must have been those villages out there. They said the family was probably kidnapped, robbed and killed. So, you know, not like the city is safe, but out there...even worse." She looked up at Xavier. "What?"

"What what?"

"You look like you don't believe me or something."

"No, no...really, no. But I just—you know—I mean, I've heard of this kind of thing on TV, but I've never been to an airport and I never really thought I'd meet someone who was part of that world." He stirred the dregs of his drink with his straw. "You know, if they just came out one day and said it was all just a movie, that no one was going into outer space, that airplanes didn't really have safety pods...I could believe that."

"Yeah, no; it's totally real. I was in one of those planes just a couple of months ago. They're super nice. They call your ticket number and you step into this pod that looks like a nice little room. You get in, and you have drinks and snacks and stuff. There's a screen, video games...you can just relax. Then when your pod is full, they disconnect it from the airport and shuttle it over to the plane—which is just a frame with wings. They attach your module, and then you're ready to go."

"I seriously can't even imagine that."

Susana shifted in her seat and looked away. "Yeah, but it was kind of accidental. I mean, the idea originally was just a 'first-class' kind of idea for air travel. Like, they have a bed in there, kind of a mini-studio-apartment, and just for the front of the plane. If you were in coach, you were in the main airplane like the old way."

"That checks out. That would be me if I could ever afford a plane ticket. And then all you guys would be floating down with parachutes, while I was strapped into a fiery deathtrap..."

"But it turned out to be cost-effective—that was the thing," Susana pressed on with her story, "and then with the recurring pandemics, it was an easier way to deal with ventilation, and with the severe turbulence from climate change...so they just converted all planes. And then, of course, they just adapted the same basic idea for the shuttles to Titan."

"It sounds like you know way too much about these shuttles...do you do that too? You design spaceships?"

"No. I mean, I know about them, yes—a lot about them, but I don't design them, really..." Susana looked around and changed topics. "We've been here too long. We need to figure out where we're going next."

"Yeah. Okay." Xavier wanted to hear more but knew that they needed to get back on the move. "We could head into the mountains?"

"I feel like we're pretty conspicuous on the motorcycle, though. I mean, we'd be easy to spot here in the city...if they put up more drones, we'd be really easy to pick out on the mountain roads."

"Yeah, and what would we do out there? Just hide? I guess I hadn't really thought about it...don't we have to hide?"

"No. And I need to be near the city."

"Why?"

"Let's go. We need a car."

"Where are we gonna get a car? Are you going to steal one?"

"Tonto." Susana chuckled. "I brought some cash, and I think we can get a good trade-in price for this bike. We just have to find a used vocho or something on the street. I know where we can go."

Susana navigated surface streets back into the city to a tianguis. In the parking lot, there were several cars for sale with the owners chatting in clusters nearby. Xavier pointed at a blue, recently painted vocho in really good shape. Its owner noticed and looked over at them questioningly. Susana shook her head and walked over to a vocho that clearly needed some work. Its green paint was covered with Bondo in several places and many of these places revealed that green was not the car's original color. This was definitely one of the sorrier looking ones on the lot.

One of the men from the group broke off and met Susana halfway.

"How much?"

"What'll you give me?"

Xavier was surprised and impressed with Susana's haggling skills, initially expecting that he'd have to step in to get a real price. She was able to trade the bike and 10,000 pesos for the car, which had a strong engine, even if it looked rough on the outside. It even had a half a tank of gas in it, so they felt like it was a deal, after all, despite the owner cutting the value of the bike when he found out she didn't have papers for it.

Susana gave Xavier a look that prompted him to suggest that he drive. "Where to?" he asked.

"I can't tell you until we're almost there."

"In the city? Or are we leaving?"

"Just pull out here, and let's get on the freeway, going north."

The radio was missing a knob, but it worked, so they tuned in a pop station and just listened without speaking. "We'll just stay on the freeway here for a bit."

Xavier focused on driving—it had been a while since he last drove a vehicle, so he needed to concentrate. Traffic was moving along, but slowdowns were persistent. After a stretch of pop songs, the DJ interrupted with some commercials that pulled Xavier's attention away from the traffic.

An overly loud male voice started: "Join us this Friday for an exclusive look at social life on Titan! Exercise? You'll never believe what they're doing on that moon!"

"Oh! You have a phone, right? Turn this on!" Xavier turned up the volume even louder. "I have to see this."

Susana pulled out her phone and opened the app that would link to the station. Her phone's screen picked up the video accompaniment to the streaming radio.

A young woman stood on Titan overlooking a broad, flat, open space that looked like a field of sand and moss. She wore a form-fitting, tan-colored suit that connected to her helmet, which was of clear glass except for the portion behind her head. She stood next to a young man and a young woman, each wearing the same suit, but theirs also had huge bird-like wings attached to their backs and arms. "So you've never tried this before?" The woman without wings asked.

The woman with wings spoke up first. "Well, kind of...I did the training in the virtual reality simulator, but no. I haven't tried it here yet."

"And you?"

"Nope. Uh-uh."

Xavier interrupted. "I've been hearing about this report. Honestly, it's pretty much the only thing that I've really been interested in so far...people flying like birds? C'mon."

The camera zoomed in on a number of robots, some distance away in the middle of the meadow. They all flashed green lights on their heads. The reporter took a step back and said, "All right, it looks like they're saying that they're ready. Ladies first?"

The original announcer came back on: "Find out how it went! Flying on Titan..." In the background, one person could be seen soaring overhead in circles; the second figure could be seen stumbling, and then just before face-planting, an airbag inflated from the upper-inside of the wings, pulling them into the shell of an inflated ball, sending the figure rolling toward the robots, which scurried into position to catch it. The announcer finished with, "Only here on one-oh-one point four."

"I bet the woman biffed it." Xavier said as Susana put her phone away. "She seemed a lot less confident."

"Oh, you've got to be kidding me," Susana replied, tossing her head back exaggeratedly and rolling her eyes. "Do you really not know this?"

Xavier gave her a blank stare.

"Women—in general—take much smaller risks than men. They've done studies over and over again for decades. Especially in the corporate world. Men apply for jobs when they aren't even qualified according to the job description. But then their bosses—who probably did the same thing—figure 'why not give them a chance? It worked for me.' So then men get rewarded and move up, while women are waiting until they're confident that they're qualified—and then they're passed over for not looking ambitious enough."

"Ummm…" Xavier thought he would respond but immediately realized he should keep his mouth shut.

"I bet that guy didn't even do the simulations. And I bet she did them all. I bet it was the woman flying and the man falling and rolling any day of the week."

Xavier felt like he needed to change the topic…quickly. He went back to their earlier conversation, which he suspected would be a safer topic. "You said the Titan shuttles—the ones these folks used to get there—they work like airplanes?"

"Right." Susana paused and gave Xavier a look to let him know that she knew what he was doing but continued anyway. "I mean it's the same principle, really. They don't launch one massive shuttle from Earth. Families load into condo-sized pods here on Earth, which get launched individually and attach to a frame once they reach the station in orbit. That massive condo-complex in the sky gets a set of crews—navigators, scientists, engineers and technicians—and the whole thing makes the journey."

"That's hilarious—a condo complex."

"Oh yeah…they're living in these pods for years before they reach Titan. And then once they get there, the shuttle enters orbit, and each of the modules drops to the base to be attached there. There's one massive complex on Titan, all interconnected. A modular village."

"What happened to the robots? I thought the first missions were just AI robots building labs and stuff. So what happened to them?"

"Yeah. That's how it got started. The first shuttles were just robots, but some missions are still sending up more to keep building—there's a lot more infrastructure they want to put in place. Others are just like construction workers...building additions for those who still have enough money to turn their condos into mansions."

"So the robots are like slaves, then? I mean...because they have AI?"

"I mean...I never thought of it that way. They're just machines—they don't really have personalities...or well, no...they kind of do..." Susana trailed off. It was as though she were just encountering an aspect of her work that she hadn't really thought about and wasn't sure she wanted to.

"I guess it's worth it, then. The price. I mean it's crazy expensive, but it sounds like they're in some kind of extraterrestrial Disneyland resort."

"It definitely looks that way." Susana replied flatly.

Xavier seemed to catch something in Susana's tone...*was it irony? Jealousy? Regret?* She turned to look out the window, so Xavier figured it was something, but he didn't feel right pushing it.

He turned to the radio and turned the volume up. "Oh...this is my jam."

With Susana gazing out the window, Xavier found his mind wandering and drifting back to how he ended up in the highlands before he was chased out.

He remembered being in line at a grocery store. The man paying at the register was complaining about the price of something. Xavier looked back to see how long the line had grown, and he noticed the woman behind him just as she clicked her boots together, causing a clump of mud to drop off onto the recently polished tile floor. She looked up and caught Xavier's eye, then raised her finger to her lips, suggesting he not draw attention to the mess. Xavier smiled and found his attention drawn back to her boots—black, military style, laced all the way up.

"So you were up in the mountains?" Xavier was impressed but tried to seem casually interested.

The woman carried her items awkwardly as she dug through her backpack. "Uh-huh. I live up there, in an autonomous community. I'm just here visiting friends and picking up a few supplies."

"Autonomous? Like the Zapatistas?"

"Well…I mean in terms of autonomy, yes. But really not. We didn't have to fight for it. The government doesn't want anything from us, and we don't need anything from them, so we just live on our own.

"What's it like? I mean, you don't look poor…or starving."

"HA! Thanks, I guess."

"No…I mean…without the government, how do you get electricity and stuff? How do you get enough to eat?"

The woman looked up at the gap between Xavier and the cashier. She blew one of her long curls out of her face. "Hey, you're up."

Xavier turned back around, paid for his torta, and then waited by the door. When the young woman made her purchase, Xavier approached her again.

"Can I talk to you about where you live? Your pueblo? I think I heard something…"

"Look." She interrupted, "I don't know who you are. You seem like a nice kid, but I've already told you more than you need to know."

"No. I'm not a kid. I've actually been looking for something, somewhere to go. That's why I'm asking. I think I heard about a pueblo like yours, and it may be exactly what I'm looking for."

"Well, we don't exactly have an open door." She looked him up and down. "But it is possible to stay with us…for a while."

"What do I have to do?"

"Okay, well, why don't you meet me at the bus station in about an hour. I'm heading back tonight, so we can talk about what we're about and whether or not you really are interested."

"Thank you, thank you. I'll be there."

They met at the bus station. Citlali was going to take a pretty common route out of the city, so combis would leave every half hour or so; she had time.

"Mostly we're just local families. We live in a valley that used to be great for agriculture. They say that a long time ago, the village was totally self-sufficient. We had hillsides for growing maize in terraces; we had three natural springs; we got plenty of rain. But then you know—or maybe you don't know—there was this problem with coffee."

"That sounds like something I heard about in school," Xavier struggled to remember if he'd heard it from a class or if he read it somewhere. "Something like a lot of villages started growing coffee to sell all over the world, but then they all went broke."

"That's right. When folks in the cities realized that these rural parts of Mexico were great for growing coffee, they basically seduced farmers in small pueblos to switch from planting milpa to monocropping coffee. At first, a lot of them thought it was great. Coffee was booming internationally, so folks made enough money to buy the food that they used to grow, and maybe even have a little left over. But then the price of coffee dropped. Massively. These small farmers couldn't make enough from their coffee to pay for food anymore. By using pesticides and fertilizers for the coffee, they ruined their soil for growing corn, so they couldn't go back. Things were difficult for a long time. A lot of families just left. And then the rains stopped. Well...they didn't stop, but they changed. Sometimes we'd get too much rain...sometimes not nearly enough. They said it was climate change. But for us, it made growing anything super difficult. More families left. Many broke apart—some moved to Mexico City or Guadalajara or Monterrey, and some went to the US.

"Anyway, at our village, one of the families came back. That family had gone to Mexico City, and one of the older sons got a job at Xochimilco. Just washing dishes at a restaurant. Some corporate-something wanted to set up dining experiences for the super wealthy. They got food only from the chinampas, which they privatized, and they served ten-star meals—or whatever—in a boat on the water."

Xavier interrupted. "Chinampas are those floating gardens, right? Like from los aztecas?"

"They're not really floating—they're more like islands of super-rich soil. But yeah, they used to be along the edge of a lake, so they kind of looked like they were floating. Anyway, this kid, this dishwasher, he started hanging out with the chinamperos after work. And then he started hanging out with them before work. He was fascinated, and pretty soon he was convinced that they could do chinampas back at home in the village his family left. Nobody believed him at first, but eventually he convinced one of the Xochimilco chinamperos to come back to the village to visit. The next thing you know, there was a whole plan being developed. A new kind of terrace and chinampa agriculture in the valley. They found enough families to commit, and then, even better, they found out that there was a village in Guatemala that had already done something very similar.

"And so that was how we got really started. Some of our families were loosely connected to the original families and decided to join. Eventually it all came together, and, like I said, the government didn't care what we were doing, so nothing got in our way."

"That sounds perfect. Everything is local? Everything is sustainable?"

"Yes."

"So...wow. Why doesn't everyone join?"

"Like I said, we're not trying to grow. For us to keep this sustainable, we have to be careful with everything."

"But you do let some people in?"

"Yes...but you have to get approval from the elders' council. If it's just a person or two, then you might get permission for a few months. If it's a family, there's a chance to stay permanently."

"And you guys have everything in your village? Like electricity and stuff too?"

"Well, that's a good question. A lot of folks are interested in joining us, but then when they find out that we don't have TVs in our houses, and there's only one internet connection, and there's no Nintendo...that's when the interest kind of evaporates."

"I could see that."

"You too?"

"No...I mean, I think I get it. I've seen it from the inside. I used to want to be in that society—you know, 'successful.' But then things fell apart. I thought if I got a job—any job—I might be able to work my way up. Well, that didn't work out at all, and I realized I didn't want the jobs that I might be able to work my way up into. So do I work at some random job that's probably polluting the environment? Or just making money for some guy so he can have more billions...some guy I don't even like? No thanks. So now I only work until I save enough money to travel, and when it runs out, I go back to work. That means I don't spend money on a phone or computers or social media. I know people are into that, but I let that go a while ago."

"Como Neo-Chichimeca." Citlali chuckled. "Yeah...you're not alone. And it's funny. Some visitors say that there's enough gossip and 'drama' going on in the village that they don't really miss social media at all.

"But, there's also all kinds who say they want to join the village, and usually they don't last. It turns out they're on the run for stealing stuff. Or they're on drugs and they think they can hide it from us."

"I'm not in trouble. I'm just looking for something to do with my life."

"Yeah, we talk about that too. You know, we asked ourselves this question. We said, okay...folks are all interested in going to Titan; in leaving our planet. They all see technology and science as the solution. That's been the easy argument to make for a hundred years or more—medicine, robotics, transportation. Tech has been the answer. But we started to look at it a different way. What if that's not what technology was about? I mean, my dad used to say that modern technology was driven by three things: military escalation, consumerism, and a pharmaceutical industry to address the dysfunction caused by the other two."

"Heh...that sounds kinda true..."

"Yeah, so what if you didn't have those? What if you could use tech outside of those pressures? No international conflict? No gadgets to 'kill time'? No 'burning calories' at the gym. Your lifestyle is healthy for you and the ecosystem you live in. What kind of tech would you need? Would you want?"

Susana's voice brought Xavier back to the traffic they were still sitting in. "Did you know Titan was originally supposed to be for everyone?" She was still looking out the window.

"Huh? What do you mean?"

"I mean, this is just history. It's not top secret or anything."

"Uhhh...hold on." Xavier felt his body go cold. "Are you saying that you know some stuff that *is* top secret?! Is that why we're being chased? You know top secret stuff about the Titan mission that you're not supposed to? Oh. My..."

"Slow down, slow down. Don't get all worked up. I'm not a spy or anything. I'm just saying that, you know, you could look this up on the internet. There was a space program. You know that. But then there were a lot of political cries that the government was wasting all of this money when it could be solving the economic and environmental problems at home. Well, the directors of the space program needed help, and they had one 'hail mary' left. They figured they could convince folks to keep the program open if they had a solution that would be available for all people. An Earth Two or something. Do you remember that? For a minute, the whole story was that we were going to make Titan available to anyone who wanted to go. It would be a choice, and we could use all that we learned on Earth One about not polluting to create an even better 'Earth 2.'"

"No. I never heard of that."

"Well, maybe it was before your time. You're what? Twenty-three? You were probably too young. Anyway, that's how they got the funding to send 'lower cost' missions with just robots on them. They were supposed to run tests and set up a lab on Titan to see if further ventures were possible."

"Right. That part I totally remember. I even remember the Lego kits they used to sell of those robots."

"Yes! That's right. My boyfriend said he used to play with those—or build them—even when he wasn't a kid anymore. Anyway, those early missions were successful, but they sent back bad news. The air didn't have enough oxygen in it for people to just walk around without a pack on."

"So that's why it couldn't be for just anyone anymore?"

"Right. Or that's the argument anyway. It could no longer be that you just had to get there, and then you'd be fine. There would have to be an enclosure, a building, or a pod of some sort that you could hang out in without a pack, but when you left the pod, you would need a suit. And that meant it was going to be a lot more expensive for anyone to live there."

"They privatized it."

"Right. The space program offered to partner with the trillionaires, the international oligarchs. There would still be science going on—that's why the government stayed involved—but the actual costs would have to be paid for out of pocket. A bunch of these oligarchs got together and funded it. And that's when it turned into something that you would have to buy. If you wanted to go to Titan, you had to buy a ticket, and pay your own way."

"Look. I'm starting to feel like I need some food. Do you mind if we stop? We can eat in the car if you want."

Xavier couldn't stop thinking about what he took as a hint. It wasn't Paco at all. It was something top secret? Was Susana actually part of the same government agency that was chasing him?

He swallowed hard. "So do you have top secret information?"

They picked up fast food to go and were eating in the car. Susana had been taking her time with her fries, but now she shoved a handful into her mouth. "Huh?" she said with her left cheek bulging.

"I mean, you didn't say it...but it seemed like you know a lot more than just what's in the papers. Or 'available online.'" Xavier used the fingers on his right hand to make air quotes.

Susana didn't reply. She turned to look out the window. "We need to head to Naucalpan. Do you know the way?"

"Yes, but I think you need to answer my question. I mean, yes, this has kind of been a fun adventure so far...I mean...it sucked to get kicked out of La Realidad, but it's definitely a break from my normal routine. And there has to be some reason that these guys are following us, and honestly, it can't be anything I've done. So is it you," he paused and then offered timidly, "or are you one of them?"

Susana couldn't contain a sharp "HA!"

"No, I'm not with them—whoever they are. She sighed heavily. "Okay...but there are, like, five people in the world who know this. So if I tell you, you're on the inside. No more free-living on the road. No more carefree days. No more jipi lifestyle. If I tell you this, you'll know something that can both get you killed but also can make you wealthier than you ever imagined."

"Wealthy? You mean, like, enough to go to Titan?"

Susana looked down at what was left of her fries. "Yes," she paused. "And no."

Xavier was completely befuddled at this point. He grabbed his drink and took a pull from the straw. Susana finished off her fries.

"Okay, look. Think about it. I won't say anything for 15 minutes, even if you beg me. After those 15 minutes, though, or any time thereafter, if you want me to tell you, I will."

On surface streets, Xavier guessed that the drive to Naucalpan wouldn't take less than 40 minutes. He figured that should be plenty of time to hear even the most interesting of stories. But he immediately realized that this was the most exciting thing that would ever happen in his lifetime. It had to be. Even if he said no, it had already been the most exciting thing. So he had to go through with it. He would die of regret if he walked away from this without finding out what Susana kept secret. He had to know.

"Okay. Tell me."

Susana put her thumb and forefinger to her lips and pulled across from left to right, "zipping them" shut. She tapped her wrist, even though there was no watch there.

"Okay, okay. I'll wait."

Navigating traffic kept Xavier sufficiently distracted that this time, 15 minutes flew by. And this time, he had a clock on the radio, which seemed to be off by a couple of hours, but still allowed him to keep track of minutes.

"Okay, so you were working on a simulation for the robots. You told me that much. But that's not enough to get you in trouble."

"Right. The simulations did all they were supposed to do, and projected that the fourth mission could take humans for occupation. But we wanted to make sure that our model was as strong as possible, so when they launched the first spacecraft that would prepare the habitat for humanity, we grabbed that data and used it to continue calibrating various parameters in our model. Then we were going to run a new simulation based on all of this earlier work alongside the launch to see how well it tracked." Susana looked down and smiled. "I have to say...that was some of the funnest coding of my life."

"But that's still not anything to get you in trouble...is it?"

"No. That could easily all have been just testing and prototyping. No big deal. But that's not where it stopped...so this is your last chance. You're sure you want to know this."

"Absolutely."

"Okay, so everything was running well and the launch was set. And this is where it got sticky."

"Oh no!" Xavier checked his rear-view mirror.

"Okay, you don't have to be dramatic about it."

"No. I mean, oh no. There's a cop pulling us over."

"What?!"

"Yeah. Should I pull over?"

"Of course."

"But what if it's the feds... do you think they put out an alert on us?"

"Oh...you're right. Maybe? But that seems like a bit much. Let's see what they want."

The cop pulled up behind their vocho. He was alone and took his time strapping on his gun and making his way over to Xavier's window. Leaning against the door, he asked Xavier if he had a driver's license. "You didn't do anything wrong...really. Your license plate number ends in a three, so you aren't supposed to be driving today—Saturday."

Susana responded for Xavier, "Officer, look. We just bought this car, so we didn't even think about that. We're just trying to get it home. Can't we just pull over?"

"Well, I'm supposed to impound your car, and then you can pay the fine on Monday to get it back. Three hundred pesos." He looked around. "Or you could pay me a thousand pesos now, and I can pay the fine for you..." He stepped away from the car. "Let me run your driver's license and you can think about it."

Xavier waited for the cop to get back to his car and pick up his radio. He then stomped on the gas pedal. The vocho lurched forward, and the race was on.

Susana turned to look at him, thoroughly astonished. "What..."

Xavier took a left turn just as a light turned red, throwing Susana up against her window. She tried to look back to see if the cop was coming, but now Xavier took a hard right and she lost her balance. She grabbed her seat firmly and turned to face him. "Are you crazy?!"

Xavier grinned as he borrowed a line from one of his favorite movies: "only in the morning."

Xavier saw the cop jump in his car, flip on his lights, and cut off a small Toyota to pick up the chase, just before he made his first turn. The cop would stay in his district, so Xavier knew he just had to get a few kilometers away. There was traffic, but not enough to really slow either vehicle down much.

The vocho handled admirably. Xavier cut into oncoming traffic to avoid a backed-up stoplight. He pulled U-turns, hoping the cop would get stuck on the other side of a center divider. But he couldn't shake him. *This cop seems just too determined…and for what? Just for la mordida?* It had to be something else.

Xavier glanced over at Susana. *Was this part of her plan? Was this a trap? Was she just using him for…for what?*

He took a hard right, the wrong way up a one-way street. Immediately, though, he slammed on the brakes as did an oncoming black sedan. Xavier's eyes nearly popped out of his head when he realized the driver of this black sedan was the blond guy who had been chasing him. Now he had two adversaries to evade.

Xavier slammed his vocho into reverse and drove backwards into traffic. Both his pursuers were now weaving through traffic toward him. In one last ditch effort, he swerved across two lanes into a left-hand turn lane, still driving in reverse. He hit the brakes, skidding to a stop, and then took off on the other side of the center divider, into the flow of traffic in the opposite direction.

Neither the cop or the blond could approach that move and had to continue on to the next break in the divider. Xavier took another left, and then left them both with too many possible turns to navigate.

Susana turned to Xavier. "Both of them? We lost both of them?"

Xavier smiled wide, feeling new confidence. "I've always wanted to do that." He calmly turned into a multi-story parking lot that was quite full. Susana understood Xavier's move.

"Okay…we can wait here until it's dark. Then we shouldn't have to worry about being spotted again."

"Right."

Xavier and Susana both sighed heavily and sank down into their seats. Xavier realized, though, that he didn't want to let up. "And that means you can finish your story."

There was very little activity in the parking garage, but Xavier and Susana stayed scrunched low in their seats, doing what they could to not be seen.

"Right...so...so..." Susana tried to recall where she had left her story.

"Robot missions being launched."

"Right. There was this general assigned to this project who pulled me and the other coders aside. This was going to be a highest-clearance level discussion. If we weren't willing to engage, we could leave." Susana took a deep breath. "He said he was getting some sense that the Titan Mission was in jeopardy. People with money were getting skeptical now that it seemed so real. Also, the politics of the election were getting some folks really worried about the level of risk the government was taking on. He said that he had a plan. We would continue launching as normal. No interference there. But once the shuttle was of considerable distance from Earth, we would replace the communication feed from the ship with a feed from our simulation." Susana paused as though she were considering the consequences herself for the first time.

"Huh?"

"Yeah. He wanted us to feed ENASA the simulation communication in place of what was really happening with the ship. That way we would make sure that the mission was successful since it would be happening in our simulation. If the real ship was also successful, then great. We pull the plug on the simulation and let it take over. If not, then we let the next missions go forward until they get it right. By then, the election season would be over and everyone would be anticipating the launching of the first manned missions."

"Okay...so it was kind of like a safety measure? Sounds risky, but kind of smart?"

"And it went great. The actual missions were successful. The robots landed. Their AI control was sufficient for the challenges they met. And they started building the architecture.

Which meant that we didn't really need the simulation, even though we used it. We also continued feeding the results of what was actually happening on Titan into the simulation, so our model was learning. And anyway, it didn't seem like it was going to matter. By the third robot mission everything was clockwork, and the general was ready to decommission the simulation. And, of course, that's when it went to carajolandia.

"The third ship had an equipment malfunction and crash-landed on Titan. The wreckage damaged the lab, and essentially set construction back five years. That was no good. The fourth mission was supposed to have the first people on it, so if they had to adjust, then we'd be looking at another ten years before anyone set foot on Titan. The funding would be pulled for sure. So the general decided to keep the simulation plugged in. ENASA believed that their third mission was a success. They started getting ready for the first human mission."

"That one I do remember. I remember how everyone was glued to their screens—everyone wanted to see the launch of the first people who would live on Titan. There were a couple of billionaires, I think, but mostly it was scientists, right?"

"Yes...most were scientists and engineers. They were going to expand the labs and the living pods. They were going to make sure that things were in place for the first families to take up residence."

The Sun had set, and darkness had fallen. Fluorescent lights came on in the parking garage, but it was still very dark in the car.

"Hey," Susana said, "it's time. Let's go."

"But..."

"I'll tell you the rest when we're inside."

"Okay...there's more? And wait...you haven't even told me where exactly we're going."

"Right."

Susana gave Xavier directions along surface streets. Eventually she had him pull over on the side of a mostly residential street. The homes here were considerably less affluent than those around Paco's apartment. Most had high fences or cement-block walls lining the sidewalks.

Graffiti around here was not so quickly painted over.

They stepped out of the car and Xavier walked up behind Susana. "Here," she said, "take my hand. And you lead...it'll look like we're a couple, so we'll be less conspicuous. Don't worry...I'll tell you the way."

Xavier tried to walk casually, but again he found himself wondering what exactly that should look like...and would it be different now that he was holding this woman's hand? This woman...she was definitely attractive, but she had to be 10 years—or more?—older than him? Was he attracted to her? Could he really trust her? He hoped his hands wouldn't start sweating, and he set a medium pace up the slightly inclined sidewalk.

Susana caught herself wondering now. Was she really going to tell the whole story to this guy? This kid? What would happen to him once he knew? Would this destroy his whole life? Would it give him the purpose he said he was looking for? What kind of purpose was that?

She caught herself thinking back to the beginning of her story—her involvement—as they walked. The general was always pretty direct with her. She really wasn't a fan of the military, but she also didn't see herself as one of those radicals trying to ban or defund them either. And the general seemed okay. He was strict and tight-lipped, but it seemed like he knew where he stood and he was comfortable with it. She appreciated that much at least. And since he was connected to so many others, it helped her feel like there was more justification behind what they were doing than just what she heard from him.

She remembered when the first mission to take humans was at an advanced planning stage. The general brought the team together for a briefing. The simulation was going to *expand* with the first human mission.

He said that plenty of passengers, more than enough, had already signed up and purchased tickets. The general and his associates found it easy to introduce a 3D scanner into the medical check-up equipment, which all passengers had to go through. No one even questioned it. So this was it...they had images of everyone who would be on the ship. They could plug these into the simulation, and now, instead of just robots, they would have AI avatars of human passengers.

The room went dead silent. So they'd be faking real people? How did that make any sense? Almost in perfect synchrony, everyone spoke up with questions. From technical to ethical, the discussion lasted well into the night. At the end, the general left them with the decision they would have to make: Did they want to stay on the project or not? If not, they all knew the information they discussed was Top Secret, so of course they couldn't say anything about it. If yes, they would need to get to work right away. Now it wasn't just a simulated crew of robots they would be responsible for...they would need to simulate actual personalities with their code.

Susana recalled that only one team member left the group. He couldn't believe that this was being considered and stated that, at the level of a worst-case scenario, it seemed impossible. What if the mission failed? What if the entire crew died? Would there be simulated versions of them "still alive" to communicate with ENASA. This was insane.

This team member couldn't stand it. No...he wouldn't tell anyone, but he couldn't be part of this.

No one ever heard from him again. Susana remembered asking others on the team. Did he leave town? Wasn't he supposed to just go back to work in the main lab with all of the other programmers? What happened to him? But that was it. Her questions were left unanswered, and there was no sign of him at all thereafter.

Nine months later, they launched the mission. Communication with ENASA allowed for some great TV conversations for the first few days...even weeks. Only one representative of the tech crew was interviewed now and again. Usually, it was the billionaires and oligarchs who were talking about how exciting it was and how incredible space was. The world and social media were abuzz with communication from the shuttle. In retrospect, Susana mused, the coding shouldn't have been that difficult. Most of the folks said incredibly predictable things.

Just as they reached the orbit of Mars, the general's team switched the communication feed over to the simulation. The team still received communication from the shuttle, but then diverted it and replaced the transmission with communication from the simulation. That's when the team held their collective breath. But it went off without a hitch. Also by this point, the "interviews" were never very long—most of the attention had waned and the media was backing off, waiting for the big news, when the team actually landed on Titan. Meanwhile, wealthy families were beginning orientation and training for the next shuttles, which would establish the community and begin building the population.

And that's when the general had a heart attack and died. Just like that. Susana heard the news over social media. *Now what?* She figured one of the other planners of their simulation would step in and contact the team in his place, but the call never came. No one ever stepped up.

Xavier noticed that they were approaching a large black metal gate in the middle of a very long cement-block wall. "What is this? Where are you taking me?" Susana pulled out a key and unlocked it.

They walked through and flipped the lock from the inside. Down a few steps, they encountered a building inside the enclosure. This was no one's residence. It looked like a huge abandoned maquiladora, taking up multiple house lots. Susana walked along the outer wall, away from the entrance. She approached a portion of the concrete wall that appeared to have no door, no features whatsoever. Susana placed her hand on it, and slid it into place. Xavier saw the concrete change color around her handprint, and then a hatch opened at eye level. Susana pressed her nose up against the wall and looked in as a device scanned her eyes. A door opened to her left, and Xavier followed her downstairs into a tunnel.

Inside, the air was cool and dry—sterile. The tunnel before them ended in a pale blue glow, with intermittent brighter flashes of green and white light. An electric hum in the background grew as they stepped into a large open space. A huge complex of interconnected computers sat in the middle of the room.

"This is Kan Balam," Susana spoke in a low, respectful, voice. "It's a supercomputer that was decommissioned back in the early '20s. We brought it back to life to run our simulation." Susana plopped into a swivel chair positioned at a long table with a series of terminals along its length. She leaned back and motioned for Xavier to sit next to her. "Okay. Where were we?"

"You said the third mission—the last one with only robots—you said that one failed. How did they go ahead with the human mission?"

"That one failed and we only received a few more messages from the base after that. Both suggested that repairs were being made—not super-fast, but you know…progress. So the general said it was authorized. They were going to send the team of humans and basically figure that with all of those scientists and engineers, they would be able to get the whole thing back into shape and compensate for the earlier losses."

"That sounds like a HUGE gamble."

"Yeah. To say the least."

Susana told Xavier the whole story as they sat in the dimly lit room. Kan Balam whirred and beeped periodically in the background.

"So...well...I guess you never told anyone. You couldn't, otherwise it would be all over the news."

"Yeah, we never really talked too much about it. We were just following orders."

"But then you weren't."

"Well, as far as we heard from the general, there was never an order to pull the plug. In a way, we would be taking responsibility for the decision if we chose to take down the simulation. But while we left it running, we were just following the last orders we received."

"So all these people we see being interviewed...all these folks who we all think are living on Titan...those are just AI people in a simulation?"

"Yes."

"What about the actual people!? Are they still sending messages?"

"Well, that's the weird part." Susana shifted uncomfortably. "After the robot mission that crashed, we got a few communications through from them, but then those stopped. And then, once the human missions got to within Saturn's orbit, we didn't receive any further communication from them. Any of them. Maybe they're fine." Susana added unconvincingly.

"Maybe?"

"Well...we should have heard from them once they crossed the signal disruption zone, right? I mean yes, we remain in contact with most of them up until..."

Xavier interrupted, "MOST of them?!"

"Yes; most of them up until the disruption zone. We know that as they approach Titan, we'll lose signal until they reach the surface, and then they should be able to transmit from there. In our simulation, that ranges from twelve hours to forty-eight. In real life, we haven't heard back."

"At all?!"

"At all."

"They crashed."

"We don't know. All we know is that we receive messages—all goes as expected—until they reach the outermost orbits of Saturn's moons. And then the communication goes dark. Nada."

"Ohhhh maaaan...so that's why they're chasing us. So that's why they're chasing us?"

"That part I don't know. I mean, we've been working on this for years, obviously. Why now? If it is that they're looking for me for my role on the team, why didn't they come for me before?"

"Well...did anything happen since that last one? Maybe someone found out?"

"Okay...so there was a moment of crisis. Last year we received communication that a shuttle wanted to come back. The crew identified a malfunction that looked like it would prevent their making it to Titan with sufficient oxygen. The simulation directed them to return at a slow pace—not to fully return, but just so that they could meet a repair/supply ship that would be sent out to them. Of course, this was a crisis because there would be no real repair/supply ship to send. That was just the fiction of the simulation. And what if they did return all the way home? Or what if they crossed paths with another shuttle leaving? ENASA would wonder why they didn't get the distress communication. The shuttle would wonder who they had communicated with (and received responses from). Basically, the jig would be up."

"Wrecked. No way out." Xavier furrowed his brow. "How did you get out?"

"The leak was related to a larger problem, leading to the main engine failing completely, followed by the others. That put the shuttle's trajectory off-course and the ship got caught in the gravitational pull of Mars. Catastrophic failure."

Xavier and Susana both fell silent for a bit.

"Don't you feel guilty about this? I mean...all those people dying. No one knowing about it?"

"Wait a minute...no. I mean, yes, I've thought about this. In this case, our simulation had no impact. If we had patched them through to ENASA, there wasn't any time to get a shuttle out to save them. This was a mission failure—they all knew it was possible."

Xavier started to feel queasy. Susana was right...he shouldn't have asked. He didn't want to know about this. All he could think was that so many people thought they were escaping to an amazing world, and they were really just...what? Dying?

Xavier's mind flipped back to the Chinese woman who wanted to get married on Titan. *She was actually AI?* Then his thoughts came back to Susana. *Who was this woman? Was she really this cold? Just following orders? How could she not tell someone? How did she not tell...*

"Paco?" Xavier's voice was meek.

"No!" Susana heard his name and the dam broke. She hadn't been processing it; she'd been ignoring him since he left. It was much easier to just keep doing the work from day to day. Editing code. Testing updated functions. She didn't want to consider the bigger picture. But now it all stood facing her, staring back through Xavier's questioning eyes. "He would have told his family...I couldn't say anything! I was under orders."

She felt a tear slipping down her cheek. "I'm just doing what my parents wanted. I'm just doing what the government pays me to do! I just write code!"

Xavier's face lost all color. Susana got up and walked away. She had nowhere to go, but she couldn't contain it anymore. They both moved away from each other. Apart and quiet, they waited.

Xavier's mind finally settled down and he realized he still had no clue what the plan was. "So what are we doing here? Why here?"

"The rest of the team." Susana spoke slowly at first, coming back to thinking logistically. "We've been getting together once a week to touch base, but honestly, it doesn't seem like we're close to a consensus yet. Folks are saying everything from leaving it up and running and then splitting up and running away, to telling President Salazar, to just pulling the plug and claiming ignorance. After we bought the vocho, I texted the others and requested an emergency meeting this evening."

"So I guess I really am in this now too."

"Well, yeah. If the Ministerial is after me, and they found me through you, then yeah...I mean, I guess you could tell them that you had no part in any of this and hope that they believe you. But the last guy who tried to get out...well..."

"Yeah."

Hanging from the ceiling in between the tables and Kan Balam, a glass screen lit up. Video feed from the access door displayed the rest of the team, along with three other men. One of these men held a knife to the throat of a team member. Memo, the man with the knife at his throat, nodded to confirm they should be let in.

Susana and Xavier looked at each other. Should they make a break for it? The man with the knife anticipated their hunch. "We've got the back covered. No way out. Let us in, and nobody gets hurt."

As the men entered, Susana scoured her pockets for something that might serve as a weapon. Her backpack had a knife and pepper spray in it, but she'd left that in the car. Xavier sat slack-jawed in shock.

Inside, the men pulled the swivel chairs away from the desks and out into a circle. The one with the knife shifted to sit behind his hostage, pressing the dull edge into his back near his kidney. Susana noticed that his hair wasn't really blond...it was bleached. But yeah, this was the guy who'd been chasing them.

Susana remained standing. "What the hell is going on?"

"Wow..." the shorter member of the hostage takers, Jesse, was enthralled by the computers. "So this is it? This is Kan Balam." He paused, seemingly for effect. "You know Kan Balam—actually K'inich Kan B'ahlam—he was a Mayan k'uhulajaw from Classic Period Palenque...you knew that, right?"

"Huh?" Susana seemed to be the only one willing to respond.

"Yeah. He was known for the astronomy and numerology that he patronized during the seventh century. That's why they named this supercomputer after him—he was good at math."

"Okay, whatever." Susana now grew impatient. "But who are you and what are you doing here? You don't look like Ministerial agents."

"Agents? HA!" Jesse and his partners looked at each other and chuckled. "No, we dress like this 'cause it confuses people. They think whatever their imaginations tell them." He paused. "Plus, we're into ska."

Jesse fist-bumped his nearest partner. "Seriously, though. You've heard of Greenpeace? Yes, of course you have." Now he was all attitude. "Well, we're part of a Chicano splinter faction from back in the mid-2010s. Some of us got into cyber-ops and we figured out we could do more in cyberspace than we could with direct action. Anyway, that's eventually how we came across your little project with Kan Balam here. Chuy here was at a party that Francisco Morales—Paco—was at about six months before his shuttle launched."

"Yeah," Chuy took over the conversation. "It was a huge party—like they were celebrating that they were going to Titan. Men in tuxes, women in huge dresses. Not everyone, but the older folks for sure. Anyway, just about everyone there was pretty drunk. I pretended like I was in a conversation in another group, with my back to Paco, but I was basically just listening to your boyfriend 'cause he was kind of making a scene. That's when he mentioned his fight with you. He said something like—'she's working on this secret project to support the missions, but she won't even travel there with me.' He was really upset. But of course, that caught my attention. Secret project?"

"No way! You're lying!" Susana turned to her team members, "He's lying! I never told Paco anything."

Stuart, a member of the coding team, dropped his chin and looked at the concrete floor. "I may have said something…"

But Jesse cut him off. "Yeah, so Chuy hacked his phone, and that's how we found out about you and the work you're doing. But you, Susana. You've been very difficult to track down."

"What?! No way." Stuart was now feeling defensive and tried to push back. "Our work was stealth—next-level secure. You can't even guess what kind of tech we were using for our encryption."

"Yeah, you guys are all so arrogant." Jesse stood up and started pacing as he spoke. "You think that because you have the US and Europe behind you that no one could be as 'advanced.' Guess what—India. Yup…they totally know how to hack your security. And honestly, no one should be surprised. I mean, that culture did mathematical poems in ancient times. They used to give each other math problems as aphrodisiacs. I mean seriously…math talent? Coders? You're going to find them there."

Stuart persisted. "You're bluffing. How do we know you're actually in our system?"

Jesse pulled out his phone and tapped away furiously. He looked over at the terminal screens, which prompted all the others to turn that way as well. "Hello World" showed up in a terminal window on each screen.

"So anyway, we learned all about your simulation and what it was doing." Chuy interjected. "And we're interested."

"Look, we're really not interested in hurting anybody." Jesse turned to the man with the weapon. "Seriously. Lalo, drop the knife."

"We just want to talk. We knew none of you would speak to us if we reached out—obvy. But then this kid pops up. No one thought he knew anything, but he kept running, kept evading us, so we got suspicious. Then, incredibly, he leads us directly to you!"

"But to do what?" Susana snapped.

"Yeah, well, when we first found out about you, folks came up with all kinds of crazy ideas for sabotaging you. It would have been so easy. Leaks or hacks could put you all in really awkward positions. We could have created some next-level chaos. But then a completely different alternative came up." He looked at his partners. "We were talking with members of another group from Greenpeace, and they said that in their work, they saw something like an archipelago of sustainable communities all trying to—you know—'make it' independently of the rest of the world. Like the one the kid was at."

"Archipelago?" Chuy turned to Jesse. "Órale, good word choice, man." They reached out and fist-bumped.

The silent one with the knife, Lalo, now spoke up. "Yeah, and then it all fell into place. What if instead of looking for global solutions that were universal—like new ways of feeding the world or growing meat in labs—what if we supported a whole lot of different approaches? A diversity of sustainability? Some folks could literally live as hunter-gatherers in Yosemite, for example, and they would be totally off the grid for 90% of their lives. But then, if they needed help through a crisis, there was a support network there for them. Agricultural villages in Chiapas, fishing villages on the Pacific Coast. They basically all stayed independent but supported each other when they needed it."

"And it's going beyond that." Jesse sat back down to meet the others at eye level. "In some cities, larger communities have been innovating with hydroponics and coastal cities with ocean-based agriculture. Technologies are being converted into locally sustainable versions. In these communities, function is becoming way more important than style or profit. And there's lots of materials that are re-used, recycled—there's plenty lying around from the high-tech industry and abandoned projects. So now, in these communities, people just want to innovate in ways that are sustainable and non-extractive."

Lalo turned to wrap it up. "Anyway, the point is that now we want to help. We want to keep the simulation running so as many of these greedy folks as possible can get off our planet and out of the policy-making meetings. Meanwhile, through Greenpeace, we're helping out to recognize and support alternative, sustainable communities in rural areas, and high-production, green-growing technologies in cities."

Susana's fingers gripped her forehead. She was growing exasperated by this group of... what? Cooler-than-thou activists? Her conversations with her colleagues had been about the individual repercussions of their decisions about the simulation, or the politics of it. These guys were talking about global economics and alternative communities. "Wait...what?"

"Yeah, we know that it's all just a simulation, and that we don't even know if folks are surviving the journey. We say: keep it going."

"Don't you see?" Chuy was getting excited as he usually did when addressing new audiences. "If folks are that motivated to make money in ways to buy paradise, instead of working toward it here, then don't we want them off the planet? Look, these folks are totally driven, yes, but they lack moral—uh...what's the word? Fortitude—they make money through things like hedge funds or real estate, and as a result, they get to leave the planet. We're saying that's actually great because now they're not contributing to the administration of the planet itself. They're leaving that work to people who actually want to do it responsibly.

"Without meaning to, it means we've basically created two economies: one global economy interested in wealth accumulation to be able to leave the planet; and one based in the radically local, recognizing that they will never leave, or that they wouldn't want to leave, and so investing in what it takes to make the local sustainable and healthy."

Jesse jumped in. It was clearly an on-going discussion within the group. "We're not saying that all ambition is bad."

Lalo sighed. "No. But it's like a matter of scale. When there are plenty of resources and minimal impact, then individual unbridled ambition might be a good thing for a community. Encourage everyone to just go for it. But when resources are scarce or limited, then individual ambition is like a disease or a maladaptation. It had been good at one scale of society, but then the conditions changed, and now it's a problem."

"And it's not even just zero-sum." Chuy fell back into his usual position in this discussion. "If it were just that now individual ambition meant that a few people had more than everyone else, that's one thing. But the way we're going, we're destroying resources. So there's less and less for more and more. To get rid of this problem, we can just get rid of the people."

"So it's kind of like sacrifice then?" Xavier found his voice. He wasn't sure he was following everything these guys were saying, but this point seemed clear. "We're letting these folks die so that the rest of us can live? That's your idea?"

Susana couldn't help herself. "We don't *know* that they're dying..."

The conversation just ping-ponged around the room after that.

"Look, if we expose the simulation, then these folks—the ones who are most invested in extractivist capitalism—they stay, and then it is the poor and disenfranchised who will suffer and die. So either way, there will be significant death. Will it be the unethically ambitious folks, who are exacerbating the problems—will it be them who die? Or will it be those who have no control or power over the situation?"

"Yeah. I mean. Haven't they done the exact same thing to others throughout history? Weren't they planning on sacrificing us here on Earth? It's okay if the poor are sacrificed?"

"But there are families..."

"I know."

"And they knew."

"But c'mon. Are these people really that bad? Aren't they just trying to do what's best for their families?"

"It's not that they're 'bad.' It's just that they'll do the same thing over and over again. Think about it. The ones who are going are all getting there the same way, finding some way to exploit others to buy their tickets. Does that morality, does that ambition, does that just go away when they get to Titan? I mean, sure, they'll be distracted with the newness of it all for a while, but once the place gets familiar, or once some new powerful-but-scarce resource gets 'discovered,' then they'll do to that place what they've done here."

"Look. Right now, if we pull the plug, then everyone finds out. Everything will fall into chaos. Folks in shuttles will want to come back and take power by force to maintain their privilege. That won't be good for anyone. But if we let them all go, and then we pull the plug..."

Susana interrupted the verbal popping corn. "So what's your plan? You're going to kill us, and hope that the simulation keeps running on its own?" She looked Lalo dead in the eye. "And with one knife?"

The blond man pulled back from his captive and raised his hands, showing they were empty. "No. We just wanted to make sure we got the chance to talk to you. My colleagues here were convinced that once you heard our plan, you'd see it's the best path forward. But yeah. If you were to die, I'm sure we could keep the simulation running."

They all fell silent, lost in their own thoughts, and once again, all that could be heard was Kan Balam processing ones and zeros in the background.

Xavier felt his mind racing. Would things really eventually turn bad on Titan? They were going to create a paradise, but would their own nature prevent that? Was it a nature thing? Something that was part of who they were?

That made him think of Paco—and his decision to leave Susana. *Was Paco running away from this planet, or was he running toward something new? Was he a pioneer? A conquistador? Did he see that as part of his purpose somehow? Wait. Was it about purpose? Or fear?*

*What was Susana's purpose? Did she find it with a job that she enjoyed and that pleased her parents?*

Xavier knew he didn't want his own purpose to just be to work for someone else—to make someone else wealthy. When this crazy situation began, he was just starting to experience having a "carefree life." *Which could have been my purpose?* Traveling when possible, and mostly independent of anyone else. *A lone wolf.*

But he tasted something different as well.

He thought about Xochitl, Reina, Citlali and La Realidad. Was there a different kind of purpose there? Purpose across generations, not of just individuals?

Maybe these radical, cyber-op Chicanos were right. If an escape into space failed, then all of these "extractivist capitalists" would turn back to Earth. Autonomous communities again would find their resources and their lands "needed" by the global economy.

He closed his eyes and saw Xochitl paddling away down a canal. He heard Reina's laugh echoing in his head.

"Susana, please..." Xavier found a moment of calm in the tornado of thoughts raging through his mind, causing the corners of his eyes to moisten.

Susana kept her head down, but lifted her eyes up and to the left to almost meet Xavier's, though hers held a near-vacant stare.

"Please, leave it plugged in."

# CIBERBANDIDO MASK

## SAMANTHA "EGGSY" J. AND COLTON "CUCA" CAMPBELL

*Pixel art rendition by Samantha "Eggsy" J. Concept and original art by Colton "Cuca" Campbell.*

# THE MASK OF THE CIBERBANDIDO

## COLTON "CUCA" CAMPBELL

*This poem includes references and paraphrases from Bladee, Dunbar, Yeats, Kafka, and others, used within a decolonial tradition of poetic banditry that remixes language and imagery for critique, resistance, and transformation.*

Mask of the Ciberbandido

Who are you?

The outlaw is made righteous
only by the hypocrisy
of the law

So the bandit is a parasite on a parasite
The spirit of the Chupacabra
The Pachuca-Cabra
the Great Criminal
infected scapegoat
mirroring a reflection of the Law

The Mimic's Mask
The Meme's Mask
Mascara de Mimetismo
Mascara de Memetismo

You asked a question of me
please elaborate
and hear your question parried by this mirror shield mask

Ding!

It is only an echo

"What do your thoughts
of me
say
about you?"

Camouflaged to hunt my own skin
but only in fooling surveillance
I am able to find myself
The fool
European enough to be the first of the Major Arcana
while I aspire to be an overeducated Vato Loco

A folie a deux
Just me
but in the mirror is you
A foo times two

My Grandfather's Mask
Tezcatlipoca
Lord Smoking Mirror reflects
The Bandit Joaquin
Y, yo soy Joaquin—correcto?
Smoking mirror shining smoke
rising with Coyolshauqui
from Ome yo...yocan?

Pero no
Joaquin did not hide his face
Why should I?
Pues

"Yo soy Joaquin"
not myself
not *yourself*
I myself have something to lose
Myself

El Bandido was banished in any case
He didn't *have* to cover his face
He was already known
El Mas Chingon

So wear his face instead of yours
and become him
Each of you

gatekeepers before the law
cross the threshold
and invite su vuelta
into the digital necropolis
Invert the mobius strip border
and reverse borderless state terror
of the Imperial Boomerang's
slouching return

Prepare ye the way of the Ciberbandido
and make digitally circuitous
his way through the city's motherboard
Queer the straight streets with the conocimiento
of raza multitude's gushing sacrifice

Not the messiah, just a meme
Not liberation, just a shield
Not a weapon, just a mask

But the Shield of Ahuizote
is a deep annoyance to them
The pest reaches with a hand on the end of a tail
and with flickering red tongues we sputter drowned stories from the depths of Anahuac

Before you swing your machete
raise your shield
Dual wield with my chimalli
A mask
wears another
that grins and lies
though they may think otherwise

Some mustachioed calavera,
slices into our story the letter Z
not history
our story
Zorro cut holes in its fabric
a bandana
and later

donned the domino mask of the European trickster

V's Guy Fawkes Mask
bears a striking resemblance
to the Spaniard Zorro
now Anonymous

The issue is that to be
Anon
Chad
Pepe
or even a Wojack
you must be white

and male
or are assumed so
and if not
it is assumed that you are aspiring to be
Pics or it didn't happen
ASL?
Send proof
document your digital citizenship
This is our vendetta

But the memic mimics must resist
El Pachuco's digital meme-oh-flage
must be constructed with images indiscernible in basic form
from the mannequins that dance across
red
white
and blue
digital
and silver screens

Guy Fawkes
no
Guey Fawkes
more brown
less blush
A digital mask

Built as resistance
for protest
Not the sword
the shield

But like the commercial says about tortillas
why not both?

Swing this Papier-mâchéte
in all its duality
Ometeotl

The mask of the Fourth world, and the Fifth Sun
Too late to the drama of history to be top three
commune with the maroon,
the hybrid
and the bandit
with a symbol to unify the banished
the irredentists
the Xicanx of Aztlan

This mask is insurgent retaliation
Socialization through antisocial participation
I put on the mask so you know that it's me
We must mask our resistance
yet underneath
we are free

Mask of the Ciberbandido

Yo soy nada
this much is true
Who are you?

# OBSIDIAN VISIONS: TIERRA Y LIBERTAD

1.  In "Royal Wedding" by Catrióna Rueda Esquibel, "Come los ricos. Eat the Rich" by Dante Olivas, "Titan's Promise" by Gerardo Aldana y Villalobos, and "The Mask of the Ciberbandido" by Colton "Cuca" Campbell, information about the resistive act is transmitted indirectly, filtered via media, oral tradition, and a mix of "secret knowledge." How does the transmission affect the portrayal of the liberating and resistive act? How do they fit into the notion "The revolution will not be televised"?

2.  In most cases in these stories, normal life is disrupted (however oppressive normal life may be), but in "#00204" by elindiocopyright1985, it seems we see the "aftereffects" of two guys standing on Mars next to "Viva la Raza" and a squashed US spacecraft. How does this contrast with the aftereffect in Dante Olivas's story that is being told by an elder about the past?

3.  "Titan's Promise" by Gerardo Aldana y Villalobos and "Royal Wedding" by Catrióna Rueda Esquibel both use the rules and structures of each story's system to resist and improve conditions for their characters and their world. Compare and contrast these strategies.

4.  With Zapata rocketing through space in "#00204" by elindiocopyright1985 and the "Ciberbandido Mask" of Eggsy and Cuca, the issues of land, "Tierra y Libertad," are brought to other worlds and the future. How do the other stories, in particular "Titan's Promise" and "Come los ricos. Eat the Rich" deal with land issues?

5.  When is violence unacceptable? Violence to maintain the system against the woman in Catrióna Rueda Esquibel's "Royal Wedding" is portrayed as accepted by the in-story media, but the "violence" of her resisting it (declaring herself a "whore" to own her own body) is portrayed as shocking.

•••
# YEI:
# MOTHER EARTH AWAKENS

Planet Earth and its inhabitants need many protectors. We, the subject of many negative anthropomorphisms in sci-fi, can nonetheless see humanity in other creatures of our homeworld.

In these stories Mother Earth and avatars react against the hoarding of withering resources, and mass disasters, the groans of a dying planet. Xicanxfuturism walks this world and has many not-human friends.

# PLANET EARTH IS WORTH HER SALT

## ROCIO ANICA

In the crucial years leading up to the end of humanity, only certain people understood that race was a construct, sexuality was a spectrum, and gender was not fixed. Everyone else fought vehemently, then blew up the world.

The intellectual daughters of the Solamente family, having been in the United States of America around the difficult times of weekly mass book burnings and supermax prison constructions for every zip code, could perceive that a nuclear war was inevitable; they made plans to return permanently to the land of their origin near Teloloapan in Mexico to be with their loved ones. Who knows when it will happen, they repeated amongst themselves, but it would certainly be happening.

People on both sides of the border laughed when the young women bought chain-link, soldered chainmail, and defended those who chained themselves to American statues and landmarks to protest the end of the world. The sisters lamented; it was such a violent paradox for humans to kill others over being human. Many people thought the sisters were the silly ones for making a big deal over merely dramatic gestures and words. Meanwhile, the sisters wrote long tomes for their future progeny, detailing the sisters' every idea, every skill set, and every question with an answer because the libraries, all of them, were being destroyed.

By the time the worst of the bombs stopped, the Solamente estate knew to expect the cyborgs. The four sisters warned everyone it would only be a matter of time before the cyborgs discovered their compound thriving, needing no external validation, finding meaning and solidarity in each other despite the annihilation of their kind. The cyborgs would never tolerate it.

This was a point of urgency because, by that time, the Solamente estate was a compound full of their kin and the many who had joined the sisters in their willful desire for peaceful survival and communion with the earth, the goddess mother of all, the only entity deserving of respect but who hadn't seen respect for some centuries.

The sisters made it clear in their tomes that the discourse around the cyborgs is what tipped them off to what the future was bringing. Leading up to the first bombs, there was great contempt for people like the Solamente sisters from people known in the early days as machine supremacists. The machine supremacists would often say, rhetorically and disdainfully: Who earnestly communes with the earth these days, anyway? Any territory on earth belongs to the fittest, the strongest, or the quickest to mine the earth. All progress is good, and anything that is not progress is evil. To discuss the past is hate speech.

Their propaganda was made worse by the fact that the Solamentes didn't belong to a nationally-recognized tribe of the Americas, didn't have family that had survived long enough to claim them. It didn't matter that the Solamentes were brown and that their ancestors had belonged to tribes before those tribes were destroyed. The machine supremacists liked to argue that if people like the Solamentes couldn't answer with specifics about their histories or provide proof of where they came from, then people like the Solamentes were undeserving of rights to their past and should probably be destroyed or, more preferably, destroy themselves. The destruction could be symbolic, they suggested; all they had to do was relinquish what was in their hearts and join any cause but their own, any other cause would be fine. Most preferable of all, of course, was if people like the Solamente sisters hated themselves so much that they yearned to be cyborgs themselves.

The machine supremacists suspected that it would never happen. That was why they had bullied and asserted themselves in those early years, wanting to know why people like the Solamente sisters, so obsessed with history, held themselves in esteem higher than cyborgs when the future, all along, had been heading toward the birth of the cyborgs, clear markers of progress. How dare the Solamente sisters even consider themselves worthy of consideration by cyborg-apologists when the sisters were mere expatriates born of expatriates, the least of the least, bastards of the vanquished, embracing a slur like a lifeline, so stupid that they kept appropriating and appropriating that which didn't belong to them, unwanted by those from either side of the border, unclaimed by living, recognized tribes. The machine supremacists hurled insults and accusations, all the while building their mock-ups and models of what would be the first viable generation of cyborgs. Such was the discourse.

The four sisters warned that to answer the questions posed by the cyborgs was intellectual and physical suicide. The cyborgs believed their abilities to compute and reason were superior to the Solamentes and their people. Trust us, the sisters told their people. We were educated in their institutions. We know how they think. How they revere their steel and lead and brass, mainly in their weaponry but also in their vehicles and computers. How they believe that strength is external and measurable when it is actually internal and immaterial, and all the most powerful things in the universe are already within us. If only things had turned out differently.

Alas, things hadn't, so if one didn't agree with cyborg ideology or endeavored to embody it, one would be slaughtered.

Of the four sisters' children, there was one who represented the best of them, and it was the youngest daughter of the youngest Solamente sister. By the time she came of age, Luz had embraced everything she'd been taught, squeezed it tight with the workings of her intellect, formed new shapes of ideas, and was able to communicate them to those around her in a way that was kind, logical, comprehensive, and resonating. It helped that Luz was fast yet sturdy, could bear a lot of pain without surrendering, and had no desire to rule humanity. In fact, all she wanted was to learn about the plants scattered throughout the Solamente compound. Her deepest desire was to have been born a tree.

As the four sisters started to pass away to the other side, the talk of their compound swayed in Luz's favor, with the consensus being that Luz would be the one to deal with the cyborgs when they arrived.

Luz can plan an attack! they all said.

Luz can help us hide! they all said.

Luz can rebuild! they all said.

But Luz, who worried about bombs hurting her trees, only said, Maybe. Or maybe there is another way.

One thing she was certain of was that the cyborgs would never tolerate anything that wasn't literal and complete support of the cyborgs. She had read this in her aunts' many journals.

*The cyborg does not tolerate love of that which is not machine supremacy, about which the cyborg holds itself to be arbiter and progenitor. Even when presented with something that would uphold its survival inherently and immediately, if that very idea does not loudly sublimate toward machine supremacy, it will be destroyed brutally and permanently regardless of consequence even if it results in the demise of everyone including all cyborgs.*

Luz didn't like romance or idealizing things, so even though she loved Earth and nature more than herself, she knew that nature had many examples of destruction occurring, like, for example, when lightning hit a forest or when tsunamis rushed toward shores. But was destruction natural if it was intentional? Further, she knew that bombing Earth was like salting earth, and neither was natural. The closest either process could ever come to being natural was if one was to describe the salting of earth as a process in which a natural thing grabbed hold of another natural thing to pour it over a separate natural thing. These are the kinds of thoughts she had years to ponder.

Eventually, word began to spread of another round of bombs that appeared to be heading their way. The future was slow, but, as the sisters had warned, certain to be ruinous. Finally, the day came when the warning bells at the chain-link gates began to ring and the dogs began to howl and the children ran to find Luz.

The cyborgs were nothing as the four sisters described in their tomes. Having only seen the earliest iterations of cyborgs in the movies and TV of their youth, the sisters could only guesstimate what they would look like. The latest cyborgs were disgusting and patchwork, with methods of construction having prioritized utility and efficiency over aesthetics and human comprehension, their design worsening with every generation forced to repair themselves without the help of the educated humans who had been the last to attend art and design schools. They constructed new iterations of themselves using the only available material that remained after the wars capable of melding with biological material. Dented and rusted, with each cyborg's chrome components soldered to bone and sinew in horrifically unique ways, the cyborgs looked like something the junkyard dirt had regurgitated, eaten, defecated then eaten again, in that exact cyclical order, for decades.

The people in the Solamente compound almost died of fright from the roar of enormous metal gears and the thick, awesome rust that looked like horrifying blood dripping off the zombie-like elements encompassing their many haphazard parts as they approached and fired at anything that moved. The people in the Solamente compound barely had it in them to do as instructed, even though Luz and her aunts had warned them that every second counted. With great care, the people had been instructed to hide their body heat as best they could, to retreat into water caverns with air tanks and wetsuits if necessary, and to hide in the deep shelters underground, making sure to cover the ground properly above them.

At last, the cyborgs reached the inner square, where Luz stood covered in chainmail in front of a banner she had made. It read: CYBORGS WELCOME BUT ONLY IF CYBORGS ARE SMART ENOUGH TO ANSWER (A) CERTAIN QUESTION(S).

Behold, she screamed to catch their attention, waving around a small tree like one would a white flag. Stand before me if you would like to hear a conundrum unheard by any specimen, including all cyborgs. To vanquish me before I utter these specific words is to avoid a rare experience, she declared. And to avoid experience is to admit a purposeful lack stemming from avoidance. Indeed, to avoid something is cowardly, and to lack something is to be incomplete. Therefore, cyborgs, being the highest of all lifeforms, must be inclined to listen, even if cyborgs wish to do otherwise. Do you agree?

The cyborgs replied in unison their agreement.

Luz wanted to vomit.

Okay then, she said.

The conundrum is as follows, she said. On one hand, we have salt, which is rich and natural and important. And on the other we have earth, which is also rich and natural and important. Therefore, you must prove your worthiness in ruling us all by reconciling the following phrases. The first phrase is: They who are good are the salt of the earth. And the second phrase is: What happens when you salt the earth?

Luz crossed her hands behind her back and stared at the heavens. The sound of cyborgs computing and processing sounded suspiciously like war, she thought, or what she imagined war sounded like.

At last, one of the cyborgs said, Okay, we have our answer.

Luz replied, You only have one answer?

YES, the cyborgs replied in unison. From afar, the people of the Solamente compound cried out in fear of all the noise.

Whatever your answer is, she said, you must reconcile it with this third and final phrase: If that which is worth its salt is worthy of what it is given, then is Earth worth its salt?

The cyborgs conferred among themselves again, and Luz thought about what her aunts had told her regarding the most distinct aspect of the cyborgs that separated them from the robots. She replayed in her mind the many conversations she'd been blessed to have with her aunts and mother, how she'd been told that cyborgs were human enough to take roundabouts in their conclusions. She listened to the cyborgs return to the first phrase again and again, after having discussed the third phrase at length, before referring repeatedly to the second phrase. Luz watched the sun slowly set on the horizon.

When at last they claimed to be ready and demanded their resolutions be heard, Luz held out her arms and said, Hold your cyborg-tongues!

Luz laid the tree down and said, I am just the messenger. The great mother is the one who receives your offerings. Our Earth is listening and is ready for your response. Do you hear her calling to you?

The cyborgs looked at each other.

Our Earth has been listening this whole time, she repeated. She's talking back now. Do you really not hear her?

The cyborgs, cocking their metallic heads from side to side, really didn't.

Luz sucked her cheeks in. Well, cyborgs. What do you think this means?

# CHUPACABRA CHARLIE

## FREDERICK LUIS ALDAMA

MAMá LULA AND PAPá ROLO USUALLY SPEND DINNER TIME TALKING ABOUT THE OLD DAYS, BEFORE THE WEATHER CHANGED AND FAMINE BEGAN.
PAPá ROLO WAXES POETIC ABOUT HIS CHILDHOOD IN CHIHUAHUA, GROWING UP WITH HIS 6 BROTHERS AND 6 SISTERS. MAMá LULA VARIES HER STORIES A BIT OF LIFE IN CHAMPOTÓN,
BUT ALWAYS ENDS UP TALKING ABOUT THE DAYS WHEN SHE SWAM IN GREAT BIG BLUE WITH TORTUGAS AND MYRIAD OF COLOR FISHES.
SMILES TURN TO FROWNS AS THEY TALK ABOUT THE DISAPPEARING ATUNES IN THE SEA AND THE CORN ON THE LAND.
AND FROWNS TURN TO SADNESS WHEN THEY REMEMBER HOW HUMANS BECAME VIOLENT AGAINST OUR CHUPACABRA KIND.
SEARCHING FOR FOOD, FOR A LONG TIME THEY HAD INCHED THEIR WAY FROM CITY TO CITY DUMPSTER-DIVING.

WE CONSTANTLY WORK ON WHAT MAMÁ LULA AND PAPÁ ROLO CALL "ETIQUETTE". AFTER ALL, THEY DON'T WANT ME TO TURN OUT LIKE MY PRIMOS WHO APPARENTLY SIT BENT OVER, HOP LIKE KANGAROOS, AND LOVE TO PROD AND TEASE OTHER ANIMALITOS. IT'S NO WONDER, THEY EXCLAIM, THAT THE HUMANS HAVE CONJURED UP SUCH UNINFORMED FOLKTALES ABOUT US.
MAMÁ LULA AND PAPÁ ROLO SAY I'VE GOT GOOD GENES. AT FIRST, I DIDN'T UNDERSTAND. US CHUPACABRAS DON'T WEAR CLOTHES, MUCH LESS JEANS. THEN THEY EXPLAINED THAT FOR A CHUPACABRA, I'M UNUSUALLY TALL AT 4 FEET 9 INCHES, HAVE DELICATE EARS, LONG CLAWS, FIRE-RED EYES, A GENEROUS FANG-TOOTHY SMILE, AND AN EXOTIC IRIDESCENT SHIMMERY SKIN. I'M HANDSOME, APPARENTLY.
I'M TEN AND I'VE NEVER SEEN BEYOND THE EDGE. I YEARN FOR ADVENTURE. I WANT TO BATTLE A CYCLOPS AND SLICE THROUGH SQUADRONS OF HARPIES.
I LONG FOR A FRIEND. SO TONIGHT, I WILL GO FIND MY ADVENTURE.

WHEN THE SNORES BEGIN, I SILENTLY SLINK TO THE ROOF EDGE WHERE I HEAR A YOUNG HUMAN VOICE FROM THE WINDOW BELOW.
WITH WARRIOR-LIKE COURAGE LIKE THE GREAT ACHILLES, I SWING THEN TWIST MY BODY FROM ROOF EDGE THROUGH WINDOW SILL, LANDING ON A PILE OF BOXES.
A YOUNG HUMAN LOOKS OVER, MORE SURPRISED THAN STARTLED.

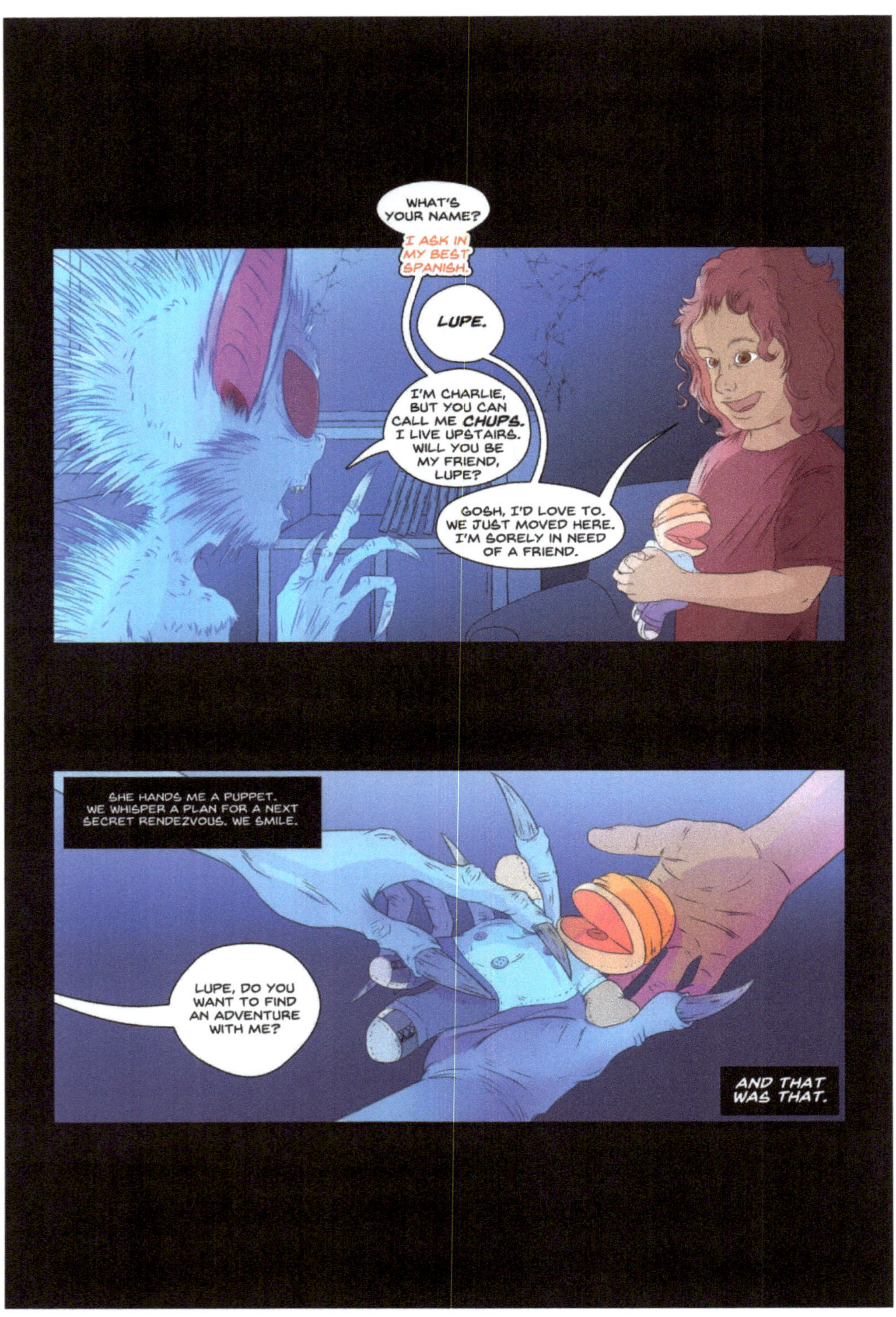
WHAT'S YOUR NAME?
I ASK IN MY BEST SPANISH.
LUPE.
I'M CHARLIE, BUT YOU CAN CALL ME CHUPS. I LIVE UPSTAIRS. WILL YOU BE MY FRIEND, LUPE?
GOSH, I'D LOVE TO. WE JUST MOVED HERE. I'M SORELY IN NEED OF A FRIEND.
SHE HANDS ME A PUPPET. WE WHISPER A PLAN FOR A NEXT SECRET RENDEZVOUS. WE SMILE.
LUPE, DO YOU WANT TO FIND AN ADVENTURE WITH ME?
AND THAT WAS THAT.

WITH LIGHTS- OUT AND NOT EVEN A MOUSE SCURRYING IN THE HOUSE, LUPE AND I GRAB A SHOULDER SLING BAG, FILL IT WITH LEFTOVER BACON QUESADILLAS AND A COUPLE OF CANS OF JUMEX. SHE GRABS A SKATEBOARD. I GRAB THE KICK SCOOTER. HUGGING SHADOWED HALLWAYS, WE MAKE OUR GREAT ESCAPE.
FLASHING LIGHTS. BLASTING NORTEÑO BEATS. ZOOMING CARS. HUMANS OF ALL SHAPES, SIZES, AND SMELLS. WE BOTH GO GOOSE-BUMPY ALL OVER.
WE SCOOT AND SKATE OVER BUMPS AND CRACKS IN THE DIRECTION OF THE WALL.
SIDEWALKS STOP AND DIRT BEGINS. COYOTES CHANT ANCIENT HYMNS TO A MOON IN FULL SHINE. AS WE INCH UP TO THE WALL, WE TWIRL AROUND A SWIRL OF PEOPLE CURLED IN BALLS OF SLEEP.

WE AGREE, THAT
FOR OUR ADVENTURE
THE WALL WE MUST CLIMB.
WE TRY OUR BEST,
GRABBING METAL EDGES,
BUT SLIP MORE THAN SCALE.

WE FALL TO THE
GROUND EXHAUSTED.
¡QUÉ LÁSTIMA!
CURLED IN A DUST-HEAP AT
THE FEET OF THE THE WALL
WE OPEN OUR EARS
TO THE WISPY MOANS
AND CRIES OF NIÑOS
LOST AND NEVER FOUND.

WE HEAR A
GENTLE RUMBLE
THEN MURMUR.
THE WALL SPEAKS!
THEY NEED YOUR HELP,
LUPE AND CHUPS.
FOLLOW THE COYOTE.
SHE WILL LEAD YOU TO A TUNNEL.
TELL THE SNAKE ON GUARD
THAT THE GIANT WALL
SENT YOU.
THEN
WHAT?
THE
TUNNEL LEADS
TO EL OTRO LADO.
HERE YOU'LL FOLLOW
THE ACEQUIA MADRE
TILL YOU FIND EL
SEÑOR PALETERO MAN.
HE HAS LA
LLAVE DE PLATA.
YOU'LL KNOW WHAT
TO DO ONCE
IN HAND.
BUT BE
WARNED,
YOU WILL ENCOUNTER
THE BIG PEOPLE IN GREEN.
LIKE A DRAGON, THEY WILL
SHOOT FIRE AND SMOKE
AT YOU.
WE CAN'T BELIEVE OUR EARS.
WE CAN'T BELIEVE OUR LUCK AS
OUR ADVENTURE STILL HAS STEAM.

SO, LUPE AND I DID AS TOLD. WE FOLLOWED THE COYOTE. WE MET THE SNAKE. SHE GRANTED SAFE PASSAGE TO EL OTRO LADO.
AFTER A LONG SCURRY ON ELBOWS AND KNEES, THE TUNNEL SPITS US OUT ON THE OTHER SIDE.
UNDER THE BRIGHT MOONLIGHT, WE FIND THE PATH OF THE ACEQUIA MADRE.
WE FIND EL SEÑOR PALETERO MAN WITH LA LLAVE DE PLATA.
LUPE AND CHUPS, I'VE BEEN WAITING FOR YOU. YOU MUST TAKE THIS KEY AND FREE THE NIÑOS. THE BIG PEOPLE IN GREEN KEEP THEM LOCKED IN CAGES ALLÁ!
Paletas

AROUND THE BIG ROCK
WE SPOT THE
BIG PEOPLE IN GREEN.
THEY SPOT US.

FLASHING LIGHTS.

LADRIDOS.

GNASHING TEETH.

WE FOLLOW THE SHADOWS TO THE CAGES.
LICKETY-SPLIT, WITH LA LLAVE DE PLATA
LUPE CLICK-CLICKS COUNTER CLOCKWISE.
THE GIANT PAD-LOCKS OPEN.

NIÑOS:
CORRAN!
CORRAN!
CORRAN!

WE RUN TOO. WE ALL ESCAPE.

WE RUN BACK TO THE WALL.
BUT NEITHER SNAKE NOR COYOTE
NOR TUNNEL ARE TO BE FOUND.

COLD, TIRED, AND HUNGRY
WE SLUMP TO THE GROUND.
WE MUST BE HOME BEFORE
THE SUN AND OUR PARENTS RISE.
OUR ONLY CHANCE: TO FIND
EL SEÑOR PALETERO MAN.

WITH URGENT AND SUREFOOTED STEPS, WE RETRACE PATHS TO *EL SEÑOR PALETERO MAN.*
WE SAVED THE NIÑOS. NOW WE MUST GET HOME BEFORE SUNRISE, EL SEÑOR PALETERO MAN.
WITH SO LITTLE TIME, THE ONLY MANERA, IS TO *FLY.* YOU'RE IN LUCK. I'M FRIENDS WITH *EL SEÑOR BIG BIGOTE.* HE'S GOT THE BIGGEST BIGOTE IN THE LAND.
HE'S THE ONLY ONE WHO CAN WHISK-WHISK YOU BACK TO YOUR CASAS. THE PATH OF THE THREE-PRICKLY-PEAR CACTUS WILL LEAD YOU TO HIM. *¡ÁNDENLE!*
JUST BEFORE WE SCURRY EL SEÑOR PALETERO MAN HANDS US A GIANT JAR OF *PICKLES.*
YOU'LL NEED TO OFFER HIM THIS, BRAVE NIÑOS.
HURRYING DOWN PATH OF THE THREE-PRICKLY-PEAR CACTUS WE FIND *EL SEÑOR BIG BIGOTE* WITH HIS HEAD TUCKED UNDER THE HOOD OF A *'67 CHEVY IMPALA.*
"EL SEÑOR BIG BIGOTE, WOULD YOU BE SO KIND AS TO FLY US ACROSS THE GIANT WALL SO WE CAN BE HOME BEFORE DAWN",
WE IMPLORE WHILE HANDING HIM THE GIANT JAR OF PICKLES.
WITH SUCH A GIFT HOW CAN I REFUSE?
I WANT TO TRY OUT MY LATEST PICKLE-POWERED COMBUSTION ENGINE. LET'S GO, NIÑOS.

WITH SEATBELTS FASTENED
AND WINDOWS DOWN,
EL SEÑOR BIG BIGOTE
NOW BECOME TACO TRUCK MAN
ZIP-ZIPS US THROUGH THE SKY.
WE SEARCH FAR AND WIDE FOR MY
CUARTO DE AZOTEA IN THE SKY.

Bigo

WE LAND AND, WITH
FEW MINUTES TO SPARE,
WE RUSH TO OUR
RESPECTIVE ROOMS.

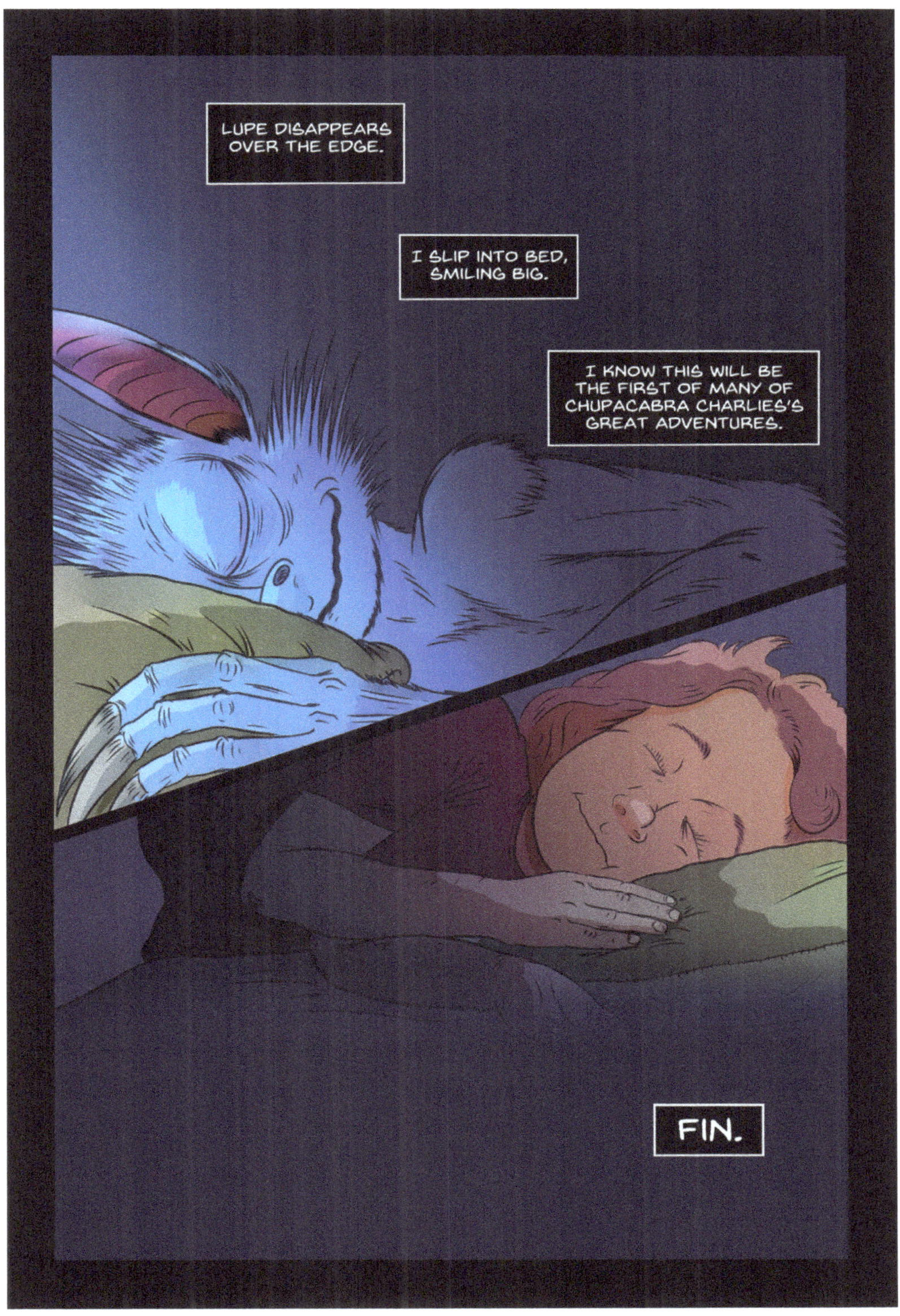
LUPE DISAPPEARS OVER THE EDGE.
I SLIP INTO BED, SMILING BIG.
I KNOW THIS WILL BE THE FIRST OF MANY OF CHUPACABRA CHARLIES'S GREAT ADVENTURES.
FIN.

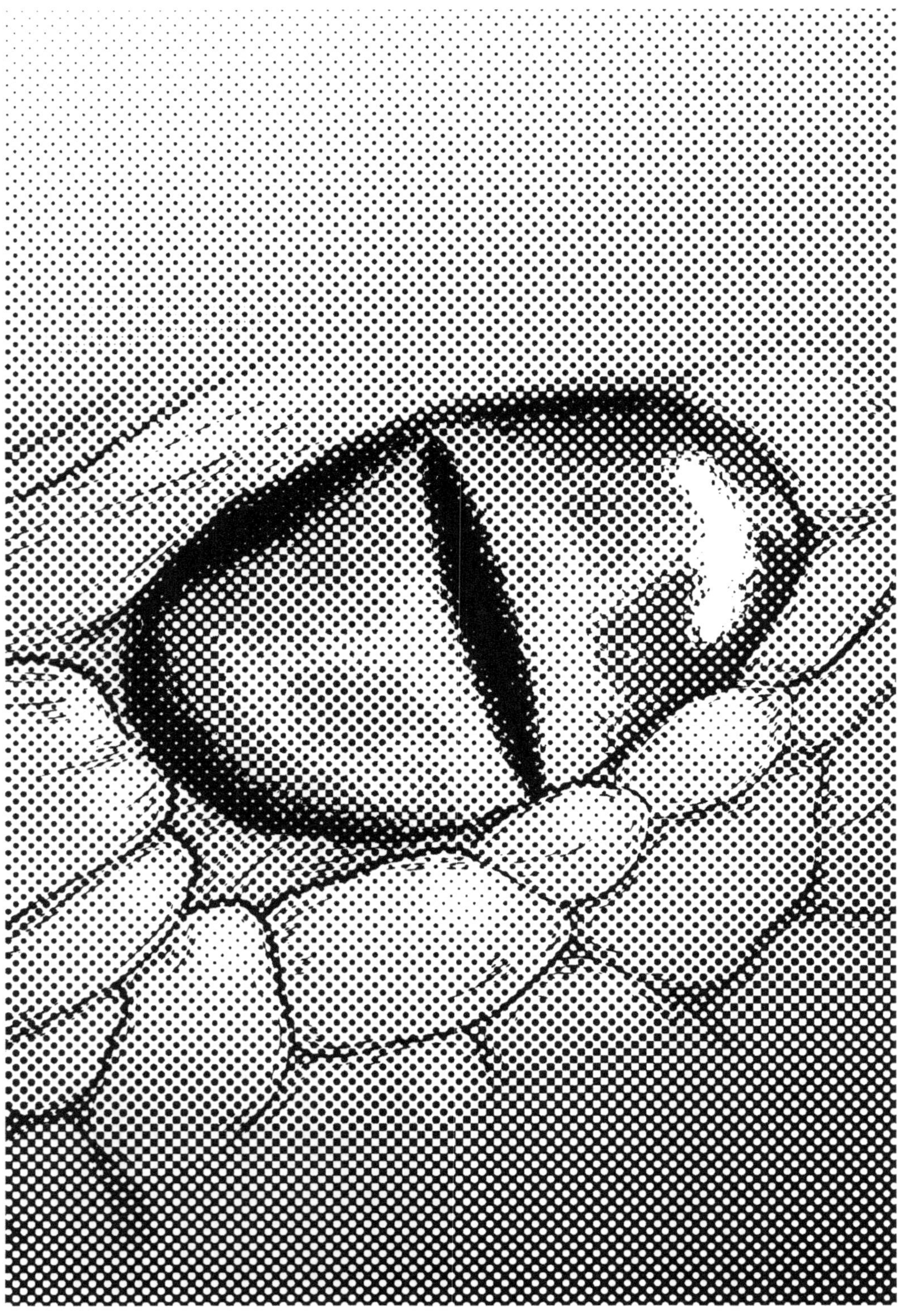

# PERICULUM TERRA

## RICARDO TAVAREZ

A candle on the table flickered as a breeze puffed through a broken window. A bevy of scanner robos hovered above my lab last night and one crashed through the window to scan inside. Anam blinked slowly and his ears drooped across his face in the dim light. A puff of dust trailed off from his paw when he stretched. Anam explained he stowed away in a transport shuttle last night from Acacia Nine Station. His fur was singed and paws had purple frostbite from atmospheric reentry. Anam had to wait until night to slink across several districts to avoid being detected by drones that crisscrossed the sky at all hours. Three narrow ice-blue beams extended from cine-lenses as they zipped across the sky, carving districts into quadrants. Anam motioned me to close an open curtain then jumped on a cushion that lay near the hydrothermic hearth in my lab.

"I looked everywhere for you for weeks, the only Phrygians in the streets had their gamma bands removed. They looked confused when I asked them for you. Last week, I found a box of crushed bands in an abandoned UA building." Gamma bands interfaced with brainwaves and made communication between humans and animals possible. Experimental ceres implants were placed in fewer animals.

"Listen, they removed my gamma band but the cortex scan found the ceres," Anam said but then froze, ears turned toward a faint click through the wall somewhere outside.

The UA detention center conducted research on different species with the ceres implant. Gamma bands allowed owners to have simple communication with animals but the ceres implants developed personalities, self-awareness and super intelligence. I first noticed when Anam began trapping mice with bits of food he placed in ceramic tubes. Soon, several fell into the narrow traps and there was nothing left for Anam to do but enjoy the squeaky prey. Later, Anam had more of a taste for fish and found that floating crumbs in ponds could entice shoals of freys to the surface and only required a deft claw. Later, he improvised a net of knotted yarn to catch more fish. After one lunar cycle, Anam began asking about aerodynamics, warp engine containment fields, time dilation and electromagnetism.

Anam's ears rocked forward and to the side at the slightest bump or scrape outside.

"Unified Authority Agents are looking for those with ceres implants...two months ago, Jin, a bonobo, with a ceres, planted a sentinel virus in the UA mainframe. The virus is still undetected and registering ceres data trackers." Anam leapt from the cushion and glided to a stop three meters away to drink water. A sliver of morning light shined into the room.

"Scientists doubted Jin developed super intelligence and began running cognitive diagnostics tests. I was in the same lab when Jin discovered the human plan for non-human organisms, that's what they call us," Anam paced back to the table, "We need to find Jin before the UA initiates their directive."

The UA began scanning for the ceres implant and took animals to decrypt enemy communications or code composite algorithms for autonomous battle drones to evade signal jamming. Jin helped the animals escape by inserting time delays in the electronic locks and security monitoring system. Anam agreed to help find others with ceres implants and meet back in a subterranean shuttle bay.

Anam curled up on a blanket and wrapped his bushy tail around his legs and body. The hydrothermic pipes crackled while a teapot steamed gently on the hearth. I made a cup of tea, sipped and exhaled slowly, what did the UA intend to do with the ceres animals?

A sudden metal clank at the door startled me. I looked around. Anam was gone. A boom on the door rattled the teapot on the stove. An automized voice chattered in a vehicle parked outside. I stepped back from the door when a UA robo activated the door sensor.

"Your motion is detected," a metallic synth vocalized.

The voice startled me. I opened the door.

"Are you in communication with the Phrygian, Anam?" the robo stood still while two of its four lenses extended and scanned the room behind me.

"Uh...no, I haven't...You took Anam! Where did you take...!" I yelled, the drone stepped back, scanned me then a green flash made me pause and lose my train of thought. It processed the data with a trio of beeps then retreated to a transport cart. It clicked onto a rail at its hip joint, folded forward then deactivated. A mechanized hook pulled it toward a dozen drones stored aboard as the cart pulled out to the road.

I closed the door and took a hard breath. Once it was quiet Anam glided onto the table.

"Get ready, we need to find someone. She has information about Jin and where to find the others," Anam bounded toward the door.

"What if they see you? They'll take you again!" I said frantically.

"Click a leash on this collar, we'll blend into the crowd." Anam jumped on the table and I clicked on the leash.

Once on the street, animals moved as though they had never been able to understand humans. If people were around, Anam bounced around, ears flopping with an occasional contrived bark. After searching three districts, Anam suggested checking along the river. We stopped at a row of food stands. Anam looked for a lit sign that blinked codes intermittently. We found it at the furthest end of the row, under the light hung a weathered awning, a lone burner stove and sign that read, *Noodles Zarat.* A woman in a lazuli cloak stood behind the counter stocking a utensil tray. Anam walked up to the stand, looked cautiously at the woman. She nodded slowly, he knew it was the place. She motioned for us to sit, laid plates on the table and looked around to see if anyone had followed us.

"Anam?" she whispered.

"Yes, have you seen Jin?" Anam whispered.

The woman observed simmering pots in large flat pans along the front of the stand, looked at us and motioned for us to follow her.

"Jin found something in the UA database. Something to help animals," she sighed, "Jin didn't tell me what it is but did say you knew where to go."

UA scientists captured the ceres bonobos and planned to use them to generate super algorithms to map neural networks for autonomous stealth attack systems. Jin told the bonobos to only do what they were asked by the scientists, to find cracks in the UA security protocols and where other ceres animals were detained. In a matter of days, the bonobos found all ceres animals and isolated the location of an experimental space shuttle. Jin programmed a squad of robos to upgrade the craft to interstellar specifications. Teams of robos drilled and welded around the clock undetected to modify the shuttle for space flight. Human ingenuity had been limited by insular goals of progress that did not benefit humanity, human simulacrums of advancement were merely maintenance of power structures. Jin found the root of humanity's sorrow deep in the UA mainframe.

"Meet some friends who arrived last night," the woman stood and walked to the front.

Three meerkats skittered from the back of the stand and introduced themselves to Anam. Cedar, Sanjay and Xuan were to meet Jin tomorrow. The meerkats chattered about the bonobos and a warden that found a way for animals to be safe from humans. A cargo-strider lost its balance along the walkway and crashed into trash bins, startling the meerkats to jump behind us. They remembered the culling of bands and knew what ceres animals still faced if they were caught. Cedar looked out from a tablecloth.

"Jin remembers you helped them in the laboratory and is counting on you to be part of the mission. See you soon," Cedar chattered and then slurped a long noodle and gave a soft burp.

The meerkats gathered around and embraced Anam before we left. I clicked the leash on Anam's collar and we took the walkway to the road.

Shops were busy and cargo-striders rattled. If cargo boxes were not balanced correctly, the strider's heels retracted erratically, causing a metallic knock against the pavement. Anam nodded or yawped to signal a "Yes" or "No" when I asked a question. No one noticed us as we bought plums and starfruit from a kiosk. Starfruit was perfect for their paws and thumbs to grasp. We stopped at a park to rest and eat fruit. Phrygian immunological evolution made them grow stronger with the fruit's toxins that were nephrotoxic to some humans. Anam took a deep breath and squinted as he looked across a crowded square. Plum stones and starfruit rinds were arranged in a neat mound at our feet.

"After the UA broadcasts...I didn't know if you'd ever come back. I mean...a broadcast said ceres chimps attacked a lab of scientists, that the ceres was unstable, made you rabid and deadly so the UA had to capture you..." I grasped for words. Anam turned to me.

"In the lab, with the other animals, we understood why they brought us there, it was to test algorithm simulators and calculate superposition. Jin made a code of winks, gestures, snorts and rhythmic breathing to communicate with other primates. During test exercises, Jin could complete the challenges and write subroutines that scanned the UA database for information about the ceres," Anam paused as a group of tourists walked by, snapping pictures of the kaleidoscope-colored kiosks.

The cognitive ability in ceres animals was beyond anything they calculated. Each species grew different evolutionary adaptations and UA scientists planned to use them to model new attack drone systems. Bonobos have digits, thumbs, binocular vision and fit into human suborbital simulators, this made them perfect test subjects. Bonobos created tests to find how the ceres transformed the physiologies and senses of other animals. Jin found that the warden's memory was enhanced for cosmography. Cedar, Sanjay and Xuan wrote celestial navigation cyphers in minutes when teams of UA astrophysicists took a year to write just one cypher. Jin found that Anam's resistance to radiation made them a magnetic sunstone, but in space. Jin designed an umbilical hypersphere capsule with minimal shielding for Anam to detect geomagnetic fields of Class M planets across dense nebulas.

The bonobos staged simulations in the UA mainframe and calculated the probability of planetary collapse. Humanity's perpetual wars and environmental damage was nearing irreversible stages. Mosi, a bonobo navigator, calculated the only hope for planetary life was for humans to completely abandon destruction of the planet. Even in simulations, when humans reversed their path, it was impossible to recover some devastated ecosystems. The stealth algorithms scaled across the UA quantum lattice collecting information about the Ceres and discovered the UA planned a millennium of Ceres-modified weapons. A classified fortress lab and a space station were fast tracked by secret UA appropriation committees. Ceres animals that demonstrated super intelligence were tested and designated for designing mining equipment, gratifier bots, daze tonics, polymer cereals and babble comms. Anam flicked a starfruit seed into a pond. His ears drooped and tail lay flat on the grass.

"Humanity is afraid to change even when its survival depends on it. We don't have a voice, then we're used to destroy the planet. We can see what is happening but you need to act and find others like you. Your future depends on it. Our planet depends on it." Anam exhaled slowly, "We have a right to live in peace, we have a right to be free."

Suddenly, a motorized claw clasped for Anam, but he darted out of the way. The claw ripped into the grass cratering the dirt. The fierce momentum made the claw tip the drone cart, causing it to crash on the stone walkway. The cart unleashed a dozen drones into the air, leaping from the machine, blue lasers slicing through the air scanning for Anam. A synchronized synth chorus rang across the park, birds fluttered and kiosks shuttered.

I followed Anam as we ran out of the park along a path that led to storm gates. The drones recalibrated lasers as they searched for us. We ran along the riverbank, tin boats floated along, a rowboat glided near the shore. Metallic heels clacked along the walkway behind us, crisscrossing the area where aerial drones last spotted us. We hid and waited in an abandoned kiosk then moved cautiously when it was quiet.

Anam stood, ears raised and pointed in different directions.

"No drones above, but they'll circle back," Anam said, "they know you are involved now and will look for you everywhere. You can't go back home."

We didn't notice that the drones spotted Anam and suddenly the sky looked like a rabid bee swarm. Anam turned his ears toward the dark storm gate cavern. We had no choice but to travel through the storm gate system. A torrent roared in the pitch black.

"Can we get to the East Rim through these tunnels?" I asked.

"I think we can." Anam nodded and led the way, "Let's go!"

We found a maintenance room of broken robos everywhere. Anam wired several batteries to power a holo-map of the tunnel network. All around us, valves rattled and vents steamed vapor. Encampments were scattered along subterranean caverns; people didn't seem startled by us but instead waved hello or invited us in to have soup or tea with them. I waved hello and goodbye as we walked along. Could humanity save the planet or were we too late? We paused to listen to an orchestra of voices as we passed under the Palace of Arts, "Alle Menschen werden Brüder, Wo dein sanfter Flügel weilt." We trudged through narrow tubes, and swam against currents all night.

Morning sun lit the caverns when we arrived in the East Rim, exhausted and spent from the journey. Anam's paws had followed the vibrations that coursed along the tunnels, and soon we could see the crackling flashes of arcs from robos welding the last alloy shields to the ship's keel. Columns of steam stretched across the cavernous quarry laboratory, a blue glow streamed along translucent conduit, electric voltage popped into the form of ocean bull kelp above, surging voltages arched in iridescent bulbs, cyan charges dispersed into magenta zephyrs around us with rolling low frequency clicks. An array of plant cuttings in bio-gel lined the loading deck, robos loaded barrels of aminos and protein recyclers. Jin redesigned the food systems to synthesize food in perpetuity. Humans dreamed of this technology, but fell short of completion, getting tangled in arguments over profits.

A bonobo stood on the loading deck of the cosmojet reviewing a cargo holo-data manifest on the loading ramp. We walked to the ramp exhausted.

"Anam? I'm Mosi. Jin is on the bridge with the others waiting for you." Mosi motioned to a stairwell at the end of the cargo bay.

Anam paused then turned to me.

I kneeled to say goodbye, Anam placed a paw on my heart, and we hugged. Anam bounded aboard and went up the stairwell. Mosi disconnected an exhaust vent and moved a crate with ease from a loading conveyor, then turned to me.

"Only a few humans know this is happening. We'll return one day," Mosi said through a whirl of warbles from the holo-data, then he paused and looked at me, "to remind humans of another way to live, a way that unites all life."

I was walking through the caverns when people from an encampment invited me to have soup and sit by their fire. I listened to their stories and admired their smiling faces lit by flickering fires. In the distance, the ship's engine rumbled through the caverns like thunderstorm, then it was quiet until all we heard was water spilling into causeways.

# OBSIDIAN VISIONS: MOTHER EARTH AWAKENS

1. Do you think these stories say humans may not be the ones to lead, when it comes to healing the planet? Do these stories show that we are limited by the idea of human supremacy?

2. How is human-nonhuman friendship fulfilled or stifled in these stories?

3. What do the oppressors/destructors look like in these stories? What do they use to fulfill their control over others?

4. Is there a difference between being an ally and being an accomplice, between humans, between humans and other non-human beings, and between humans and earth/land/habitat/ecosystems?

5. Do the human qualities of some nonhuman characters help them or mark them negatively in these stories?

# •••• NAHUI
# YES, WE WILL

Sí, Se Puede! A statement appropriated by the system against us, so now it is better to cast these words into the future: Yes, We Will, no exclamation, because it is a certainty. The certainty of our ability to learn, of powering our determination to break down oppressive systems. Yes, We Will resist. Yes, We Will organize. Yes, We Will grow.

# DRAG QUEEN 3004

## OSMANI OCHOA

Holographic eyeshadow / Milky Way eyelids
Her nano-silk huipil of / Moon texture

was to die for / Thermo-chromatic lips glow / sun beams
Eyes are mini projectors of / gamma rays / cosmic rainbow

bullseye / Luna.techa makes vulgar jokes, performs, big /
al ritmo de / Quantum Cumbia / liquid metal

braids / locked in yellow cempasúchil / serpent crown /
red BladeStilletos press against / the glowing metal
throttle: / Igniting / tele  trans *porting*

Her spaceship    powered by /
ancient bone dust of Musk,
Abott / Tr*mp and /
JK Rowling     takes / off.

# #00204

ELINDIOCOPYRIGHT1985

# SECTION ONE: DISPATCH FROM AN AZTLAN INSURGENT

### ERNESTO MIRELES

*Editors' note: This is an excerpt from* Flower Battle, *a book in progress.*

"Beginning to think is beginning to be undermined"[1]

I am undermined. I am doubted, and maligned. My Indigenous existence violates the foundation of the historical mythology of settler colonialism. I am anomalous in the historical imagination. The child of three Americas: white privileged, black underclass, and Mexican Indian, separate but equal, distinct but one, spreading rebellion through endlessly reimagined and refashioned realities, a secret in plain sight, displayed for the cultural benefit of liberal do-gooders. My children are the future—a future of voluntary miscegenation, of oppression dismantled. I am the failure of a colonial education because I speak, read, write and organize to free my people.

As an Indigenous Xicano organizer/scholar in the twenty-first century looking back on 500 years of physical, environmental and psychological erasure I see the latest threat to collective survival is the creeping removal of Indigenous resistance through a fracturing neo-liberal identity politics that celebrates "I" while dismissing "WE." It is within this atomized framework I experience the dismissal of the group, the collective, that leaves me and others like me with the stark realization there seems to be no other recourse for political petition in the United States other than the individual will.

I am writing this because Xicana/o/x leftists have it all wrong. Arguing endlessly about Marx, Lenin, Stalin as if somewhere locked in the dusty writings of these Old World Marxists is the only path to Indigenous liberation. Many in the Xicano movement measure radical understanding by how deeply we have dived into the writings of white men who propagate a form of the very religious millennialism that has held Indigenous people in mental, physical, and spiritual bondage for centuries.

I write this because someone needs to say enough. Let us end this sick fascination with whiteness, with our social, physical and emotional subjugation to the settler regime, the

---

1     Camus, Albert. *The Myth of Sisyphus.*

endless repeating of grievances. It is this obsession with our abuser that keeps Xicanos and other Indigenous people subjugated and politically powerless. Our obsessive need to shove their face into the depraved circumstances these invaders have subjugated us to in part has convinced us land acknowledgements are challenges to the settler colonial system. How much weaker could we actually appear by continuously reminding our conquerors that they have taken our land, and that we can't take it back? That the physical reality of Indigenous people in the Americas in no way mirrors the revolutionary situation of early twentieth-century Russia. Yet somehow that moment of Eastern European clarity has come to overshadow in the minds of so many Indigenous Xicanos. What about our legacy as descendants of the first "socialist" revolution in this world that took place in Mexico.

I say socialist only to make an important point. The Mexican Revolution took place before the October Revolution and it was in fact a revolt against occupying forces. Different in every way. We are not the intellectual heirs of European radicalism. We are the intellectual heirs of 20,000 years of Meso-American civilization.

An uprising of Indian men, women, and children acknowledging their claim to the land by actually fighting for it. Do we study that? Not really. The Xicano movement is tunnel-visioned on a European binary of capitalism and socialism. It's not our invention. We didn't invent Communism before Marx; that thought system emerged from a very specific set of historical circumstances and ways of thinking rooted in Europe. Indigenous worldviews, on the other hand, were violently interrupted by settler colonialism—an invasion that tore them from their own histories and forced them into an apocryphal, European-centered narrative.

How do we recapture political momentum? We must think about resistance in ways that are not completely co-opted by the structuring of the European proletariat (*Black Marxism,* Robinson). While 40 years of intellectual efforts around the concept of Nepantla began to take us in the right direction, recognizing this "in-between" state is not enough. It unwittingly positions us as incomplete—as half a human being. At some point, we must emerge beyond this condition. Nepantla may describe where we are, but it does not offer a pathway to liberation. As Indigenous insurgents, we must explore theories of resistance rooted in our colonized reality—frameworks born from the pushback against the apocalyptic circumstances that have dominated our physical landscape and the imagination of the colonized for the past 500 years.

Now that I've said all that I need to acknowledge the framework for this book, space + time = will might appear to be another step in the European direction but it is not. It is in fact a turn toward Asia and a philosophy of resistance founded deep within settler occupation and a lack of material resources. We will in this book take the equation and calculate it within our Indigenous reality, measuring it against the culture of survival and resistance Indigenous people have built during this past 500 year occupation.

Indigenous presence in the United States is a dangerous one. Both for us as Indigenous people and for Euro Christians who deeply desire the dominance within a white supremacist ideology that comes with the total erasure of brown bodies from the United States specifically.

Under Donald Trump's second presidency, this brutal reality will take on new dimensions. His 2024 election was a signal flare for white supremacy, emboldening settler colonialism in its most grotesque forms. His administration has promised to make mass deportations a centerpiece of its agenda, criminalizing brownness and Indigenous presence as existential threats to its colonial order. The construction of the border wall—designed not just as a physical barrier but as a symbol of inclusion/exclusion and domination—is a rallying cry for the most virulent xenophobia. Brown children continue to be ripped from their parents' arms, a practice that has continued uninterrupted during the past five centuries, caged like animals, forced to represent themselves in courtrooms—infants, toddlers, and teenagers navigating legal systems that barely acknowledge their humanity.

Meanwhile, Xicanos and other Indigenous-looking men and women have vanished and will vanish from our streets, many never to be heard from again. These disappearances, deportations, and separations are not isolated acts of cruelty but a coordinated effort to erase us from this land—our land. And the bitter truth? Most of us won't even know they are gone. This isn't just about the actions of the state but about the internalized terror we carry, the way it numbs us, immobilizes us, and leaves us grappling with the stark realization of our collective powerlessness.

This *autocritica* is necessary because we, as Xicana/o/x people, must confront the fact that our approach to power is fundamentally flawed. We've been playing defense for too long, reacting to every new assault instead of building the kind of insurgent political collective power that can push back against this colonial nightmare. The wall may be physical, but the greater barrier is the one we've allowed to exist within our movements, minds and relationships with each other—a lack of coordination, vision, and belief in our ability to reshape this reality.

As an example, the majority of our community considers it ridiculous to talk about a coming Indigenous political storm; a deluge of social, political, cultural retribution that will overwhelm the fabric of settler society. Yet, the consummate US apologist Samuel Huntington (among others) said as much in his 2004 premonitory essay written for the journal *Foreign*

*Policy* titled "The Hispanic Challenge," and expanded on in his 2014 follow-up book *Who We Are* where Huntington doubles down on his warning by writing that unless the US government stems the flow of brown bodies entering the United States White Anglo Saxon Protestant society will be destroyed from within, transformed into a new Latin America.

Unlike Huntington, I do not fear the rising tide of Indigenous humanity that might reclaim their land and history. In the so-called immigration debate we rarely acknowledge, either on purpose or out of a sense of survival, this continent is not a place Brown people arrived at after a period of travel: we are native to this hemisphere. In fact, Huntington argues Mexican and Mexican Americans' (Indigenous) historical claim to the land and the political control of the land is what makes the continued presence of "Latin Americans" (Mexicans) here dangerous. "No other immigrant group in US history has asserted or could assert a historical claim to US territory. Mexicans and Mexican Americans can and do make that claim."[2] It is this irredentist[3] claim to the land that Huntington both acknowledges and warns his fellow Anglo-Saxon patriots about.

Five centuries of European occupation have decimated the political presence and capacity of Indigenous peoples, yet la lucha sigue. The struggle for liberation is alive and resurgent, a flame that refuses to be extinguished despite the systemic efforts to erase us. Across Turtle Island, our numbers are rebounding—millions of Indigenous people and their descendants walk these streets. But what eludes us, still, is a political and cultural purpose that transcends our enforced role as consumers in a system designed to exploit and suppress us.

Now, imagine the next phase of this disenfranchisement: a world where labor itself becomes untethered from the body—where dreams, imagination, and even identity are extracted, commodified, and repurposed as fuel for the capitalist machine. This isn't just alienation in the Marxist sense, where workers are estranged from the products of their hands. It's hyper-alienation—the transformation of human beings into vessels of dead labor, stripped not only of agency but of the ability to imagine something beyond their subjugation. Workers no longer sell their labor; they rent their bodies, their neural connections, their very essence, creating surplus value they can never reclaim.

---

2        Huntington, Samuel. "The Hispanic Challenge."
3        Irredentism is a political and territorial concept that refers to a movement or ideology advocating for the annexation or reclaiming of territory that is believed to be part of one's own country based on historical, ethnic, cultural, or nationalistic grounds. Irredentist claims often arise when a group of people, typically of the same ethnicity or nationality, believe that their kin or territory is under the control of another state and seek to reunify it with their own nation. (ChatGPT)

This is no longer speculative fiction; it is a fantasy beyond Huntington's narrow nightmares—a dystopia where Brown labor persists without Brown bodies. Alex Rivera's *Sleep Dealer* (2008) foreshadowed this world, depicting Indigenous workers in rural Mexico mutilated and mechanized into cyborgs, remotely piloting robots to perform labor in the United States. Their bodies are reduced to conduits—property without ownership, freedom without movement—mirroring the chasm Dubois identified between the commodified black slave and the alienated white worker before abolition. Rivera's vision echoes today's reality: a world where bodies and imaginations are bound by the same colonial logic that has oppressed us for centuries, only now under the guise of seamless technology and global capitalism.

Slavoj Žižek once wrote, "Nightmare is fantasy realized," and here, the nightmare of settler colonialism is laid bare—a technocratic hellscape where the removal of Brown bodies becomes a perverse ideal. For Indigenous peoples, the dystopia of *Sleep Dealer* is not fiction; it is a stark reflection of the past, present, and future. The settler fantasy of Indigenous erasure persists, adapting itself to every new technological and economic phase. What is clear, and what we must confront, is that our nightmares are perverse settler fantasies. Only by dismantling this system, reclaiming our purpose, and reigniting our unified national will can we turn this nightmare into an insurgent reality of liberation.

**"A gesture is revolutionary not by its own content but by the sequence of effects it engenders."[4]**

Existence is not resistance, and it may be for a select few that their personal existence is tied explicitly to their personal resistance to settler colonialism, but the hard truth is their, your, my individual commitment to ending this Indigenous apocalypse is almost universally metaphoric. The revolutionary Ulrike Meinhof, one of the leaders of the Red Army Faction in Germany famously said, **"Resistance is when I ensure what does not please me occurs no more."** The reality of Indigenous resistance at this moment in time is that we do not comprehend the path of taking resistance to its logical conclusion. Collective resistance has physical consequences that expand notions of culture to include the political and economic, heightening of contradictions between human need and the economic realities of settler capitalism that forces everyone involved to choose a side: liberation or subjugation. There are no neutrals.

---

4      The Invisible Committee. *To Our Friends.*

How does the process of manufacturing collective power benefit Indigenous lives and solidify Indigenous liberation movements? We have seen brief flashes of collective will in the DACA movement, at Standing Rock, the Idle No More movement, certainly the most successful is the Zapatista's in Southern Mexico, and we know these movements have pushed the bounds of Indigenous political action because these movements, through their determination to exist, have revealed the political and economic oppression of settler society by powerful displays of political, social, cultural power.

Indigenous insurgent culture is a form of physical and political resistance that can only be created through concentrated group action, it goes beyond individual efforts and aims to ensure oppression against Indigenous communities is either eliminated or significantly reduced. It underlines how power only responds to strength through collective action, and the impact it can have on challenging the status quo and forcing settler societies to engage politically with Indigenous issues. Collective resistance surpasses individual existence, and either ensures or attempts to ensure that oppression no longer happens.

Resistance is an existential conundrum, a labyrinth of choices and dilemmas that confront individuals. Groups under oppressive systems experience a journey fraught with bewildering answers that never lead to a definitive resolution but instead open the door to new challenges. This dynamic nature of resistance reflects its necessity to adapt and persist in the face of the overwhelming political, cultural, and economic power of the settler state. Resistance never follows a linear path; rather, it involves intricate navigation through evolving pressures and opportunities, shaping both individual and collective identities.

However, national liberation is more than resistance—it is the structured culmination of resistance and collective action into a deliberate movement. It seeks to dismantle the settler colonial state and reclaim autonomy, identity, and sovereignty for oppressed peoples. National liberation is, therefore, the winding path—a transformative and protracted struggle, weaving together the clarity of theoretical insight with the urgency of decisive action, as it confronts and counters the entrenched systems of domination. This journey, as articulated, demands an ever-heightening level of awareness, organization, and resolve to meet the challenges imposed by the settler state's relentless drive to maintain control.

While resistance encompasses both individual acts of defiance and broader expressions of survival, collective action represents a more organized and strategic effort to address systemic oppression. Collective action amplifies resistance by uniting people around shared goals and ideologies. Yet, it is national liberation that synthesizes these elements into a cohesive framework for revolutionary change. It is not simply a reaction to oppression but a proactive and holistic effort to create new systems, reclaim stolen identities, and achieve sovereignty.

In this sense, resistance, collective action, and national liberation are interconnected but distinct. Resistance provides the foundation; collective action organizes and intensifies it; and national liberation transcends both, embodying the vision of a transformed future. To conflate these terms risks obscuring the critical distinctions between reactive and proactive strategies and the ultimate goal of liberation.

National liberation, as envisioned, is an intentional process—a reclaiming of space, time, and will—rooted in historical consciousness and collective determination. Challenging the imposed boundaries and identities of settler colonialism, not merely to survive but to transform. Through the lens of national liberation, resistance is not an end but a beginning, collective action a necessary amplifier, and the national return to history the ultimate realization of an insurgent identity and purpose.

While resistance and collective action are inextricable components of insurgent struggle, it is national liberation that defines the winding path—a transformative journey to reclaim humanity, history, and sovereignty, resolutely countering the tides of erasure and assimilation. This underscores the need for clarity and intentionality in framing the national discourse around these concepts, ensuring that the trajectory from resistance to liberation is both visible and actionable.

The foundational truth is that resistance within an organized national liberation movement is a constantly evolving process—one shaped by struggle, choice, and self-determination, not by inevitability or divine intervention. For Xicanx people, opening a collective channel to the practice of life as more than a cultural existence propelled forward by consumerist choices means rejecting the comfort of Christian messianic time—the belief that we must simply endure until our moment of deliverance arrives. Liberation is not predestined; it must be chosen, built, and fought for in every dimension—political, economic, artistic, and cultural. It must be more than a slogan or a symbol printed on a t-shirt. Indigenous liberation is the reemergence of these forces into a direct and opposing power, one that must inevitably end—or be ended by—the settler colonial system. Huntington understood this. Euro-Americans understand this. Xicanx people must understand it as well. As long as we continue to fool ourselves into believing that power is produced simply by proclaiming our existence, we will remain collectively powerless in every sense of the word.

The reality for those laboring endlessly under late capitalist production and its proxy, settler colonialism, is one of shallow existence, defined by fabricated desires. For Xicana/o/x communities, this imposed reality manifests in clinging to commodified frameworks, such as the ubiquitous "Taco Tuesday," a symbol of neo-liberal individualism that deflects from collective resistance. This individualism, central to capitalist ideology, generates more slogans than solidarity, leaving no space for the depth of analysis or action necessary for liberation. It is futile to expect transformative change—collective liberation—from frameworks designed to perpetuate oppression. After all, you can't get apple juice from squeezing lemons.

Huntington got one thing wrong about Indigenous demographic resurgence: numbers alone mean nothing without organization. It's not enough to be present; we must be purposeful. Building insurgent political organizations is not just an option—it's a necessity if we're serious about reclaiming power for Indigenous communities. We can't keep fracturing ourselves through identity politics purges or dismissing the potential of different generations. Scaling up our movements is how we achieve true Red/Brown power. And let's be clear: Xicana/o/x people won't suddenly become a majority in this country—we're looking at being the largest group within a plurality. That reality makes political maneuvering, coalition-building, and strategic action essential to survival and progress in the twenty-first century.

It's time to get involved. Find a group that's doing or at least talking about radical politics, one that has a critique of power and an active organizing practice. Learn from them. Yes, even if that group is all white. Cesar Chavez and Dolores Huerta, two of the greatest Xicano leaders of the twentieth century, learned from Fred Ross, a white organizer who taught them how to build infrastructure and mobilize communities. Imagine if they'd told him, "You can come to our meetings, but don't speak because you're white." That's not how movements grow. They built something powerful because they were willing to learn, to strategize, and then to lead. That's what our culture should be rooted in—organizing, mobilizing, and resisting—not obsessing over the privileges of those who stand in our way. Time to become the subjects of our own story.

The choice Xicana/o/x people face today is not new. It echoes across centuries—the same choice our ancestors confronted over 500 years ago: surrender to a shadow existence within the genocidal mechanisms of settler colonialism or reclaim our collective power. National liberation is not a lofty abstraction. It is our path to transformation—a revolutionary process that makes self-determination tangible. It is how we transcend fragmented individualism and atomized struggles to forge a unified will capable of dismantling the colonial apparatus that thrives on exploiting our labor and erasing our existence.

This is not merely about survival. It is about agency—choosing to shape our futures rather than passively enduring the present. Fatalism chains us to inevitability, but determinism invites us to act with purpose, envisioning liberation as the logical outcome of collective struggle. National liberation grounds us in the material realities of our lives and history, asserting that self-determination is the engine of transformation, not a gift bestowed by our oppressors.

To embrace self-determination is to move beyond the despair of isolation, beyond the distractions of consumerism and resignation. It is to claim our right to organize, resist, and build—not as spectators but as insurgents, united in the struggle for freedom. Together, we can transform what feels unchangeable into what becomes unstoppable.

This moment demands decision: will we remain spectators in the theater of our own oppression, or will we rise as protagonists, reclaiming our collective destiny? The equation is simple: space + time = will. Join us. Build. Organize. Resist. Let us forge the world we deserve.

**"It is easier to fight for principles than to live up to them."[5]**

As the first decades of the twenty-first century unfold, I stare deeply into an uncertain future, a future that continues uninterrupted in the colonial abuses and excesses of the past 500 years. In spite of this uncertainty I believe it is important to keep an open mind about the direction of Indigenous politics. As a small minority of Xicanos and Xicanas strive to create structures that will sever their physical, emotional, economic and spiritual reliance on the US settler colonial system, a conversation centering on an Indigenous political reality that acknowledges the need to reclaim national identity must take place. Assembling a Xicano national presence, is a Frankensteinian project replete with the political and cultural science fiction accessories (mad scientist, hidden laboratories and life-giving flashes of lighting) necessary to stitch together the Xicano version of the contemporary national liberation movement to reclaim their history.

Reflecting on the struggles Xicanos have endured across generations, we recognize the toll of fighting the same battles repeatedly. The long-term erosion—mental, spiritual, and communal—is undeniable. Capitalism, as an ever-adaptive system, thrives on this repetition, locking us into frozen societal positions and deepening alienation at every turn. Alienation

---

5    Fortune Cookie

becomes the measure of our subjugation, yet it disguises itself as progress. Like the sun marching toward its inevitable heat death, this so-called progress celebrates movement without substance, masking the stagnation and erasure at its core.

The rising tide of Indigenous consciousness has grown alongside this alienation, creating a paradox where our awareness sharpens even as the systems of domination evolve to suppress it. The accumulation of wealth depends on our disconnection: from labor, from history, from identity. As a result, Xicanos are left circling the same terrain, worn down by a capitalist settler-colonial world that reaches into the most intimate aspects of our lives. While capitalists innovate and consolidate their power, we remain caught in reactive cycles, drained of the transformative energy needed to break free.

But this exhaustion, this alienation, is not inevitable. It is the terrain upon which we must organize. As *Flower Battle* makes clear, resistance must shift from defense to insurgency. We need spaces that reclaim our will, spaces that refuse to accept the inevitability of our oppression. This means rejecting the false promise of inclusion, of progress measured by assimilation, and embracing the contradictions that expose the system's inability to resolve its injustices. It is in those contradictions that we find openings for real transformation.

Alienation and capital are not unstoppable forces; they are the scaffolding of a system that can be dismantled. *Insurgent Aztlán* reminds us that national liberation requires rejecting settler paradigms altogether. The task is not to negotiate a place within the system but to imagine a future beyond it, grounded in sovereignty and collective power. To move forward, Xicanos must ask: How do we fight differently? What structures will we create that refuse to replicate the very forces we seek to overthrow?

Progress is not motion for its own sake. It is a measure of transformation, of aligning our struggles with the reclamation of identity, land, and power. It is the will to turn alienation into connection, to reclaim space and time as tools of liberation. The cycle of repeated struggles can only be broken when we stop reacting and begin building—when resistance becomes not a fight to survive but a fight to transform.

This moment calls for clarity and resolve. Alienation is not our fate; it is our battleground. Contradictions are sharpening, and the terrain is shifting beneath us. What we do now will determine whether we remain bound to this system or break free from it.

To move the Xicano/Indigenous struggle forward, we must demand more from ourselves—different socio-political and cultural outcomes and better results for our efforts. The question is not merely about finding political answers; it's about redefining our relationship to these questions. What did we learn this time around? How will our actions shape what happens next? What do we need to change to amplify the intensity of our socio-cultural efforts?

The pan-Indigenous movements hold essential lessons. There are elders and organizers with decades of experience in face-to-face movement building who embody the principles necessary for sovereignty. They should be engaged to co-create the structures needed to flourish as independent and self-determined peoples.

As Xicana/o/x communities move into the future, we must embrace the reality that political unity does not require monolithic thinking. Every nation on Earth thrives on diversity within shared goals. Similarly, we need collective agreements on key objectives and collaborative strategies to achieve them. This flexibility, grounded in common principles, is how we begin to dismantle the dysfunction of the settler colonial system and build anew.

**Learn, Reflect, Act, Reflect, Lead.** Returning to the teachings of Nahui Ollin, we reflect at every stage of this journey: the self-awareness of *Tezcatlipoca* (memory and self-reflection), the precious knowledge of *Quetzalcoatl,* the will to act with *Huitzilopochtli,* and the transformation through *Xipe Totec.* Each cycle brings us closer to understanding how to better position ourselves and our people in this ongoing struggle.

This is not just a call to action but a call to transformation—a return to history with an insurgent clarity and the resolve to imagine and build a liberated future.

As Xicana/o/x people move to the future we will not be nor could we ever be a giant monolithic single-minded entity in order to function politically as a nation or a collective of people. Xicana/o/x need an agreement on some common goals and then cooperate on how to get it done. Every country on the face of the Earth is an example of this.

Amid the vibrant yet often fragmented landscape of Xicano activism, the creation of a constitution emerges as a pivotal tool—not merely a document, but a living framework embodying our collective principles. Historically, the Xicano struggle has been marked by a tension between individual agendas and the need for unified action. This reflects the enduring challenges of agenda factionalism and disharmony, which stem from the absence of shared political principles.

Drawing from the idea of insurgent spaces, as explored in *Insurgent Aztlán,* we see that resistance thrives not merely on cultural expression but on structured political action. A constitution encapsulates this by centralizing leadership, policy, and activities as Apaxu Maiz envisioned. It provides the ethical and strategic groundwork necessary to raise taxes, deliver justice, and plan for the reacquisition of our property—a collective necessity for sovereignty.

By anchoring our diversity within a framework of shared principles, the constitution aligns our individual and group energies. It transforms disjointed efforts into a unified front capable of addressing the political reality of colonization. This is not a retreat into bureaucracy but an advancement toward national liberation, one that integrates our historical resilience with a deliberate strategy for the future.

Leadership, as a strategy for national liberation, must be centralized to provide coherence and direction without becoming an instrument of unchecked power. Centralizing leadership is not about suppressing diversity of thought or imposing a single vision: it is about creating a unified structure that channels our collective energy toward shared goals. For Xicana/o/x national liberation, this means establishing a leadership body that can effectively coordinate efforts, represent the will of the people, and ensure accountability across all levels of the movement. Centralized leadership allows us to act with purpose and clarity, making it possible to respond decisively to the colonizing forces that seek to divide and dilute our efforts. It creates a foundation where trust and mutual respect can flourish, fostering a collective identity capable of navigating the complexities of liberation work. Without centralizing leadership, we risk fragmentation and inefficiency, jeopardizing the very movement we seek to build.

Policy serves as the backbone of our collective effort, guiding our decisions and ensuring our actions remain aligned with shared principles. It offers the framework necessary for unity, allowing us to navigate the complexities of governance and define the terms of our resistance. The Xicano Movement must address critical questions: How will we govern ourselves? What form will our government take—representative, parliamentary, or collective? And perhaps most importantly, what are we willing to sacrifice to achieve these goals? As we explore these models, we must consider whether to embrace a marketplace of ideas or assert our vision as the vanguard. This requires political maturity, a willingness to transcend personal egos and ideological divisions, and an openness to synthesize diverse perspectives into a cohesive strategy. By practicing governance now, in insurgent spaces rooted in Indigenous traditions, we prepare for the responsibilities of power. Without this preparation, we risk achieving liberation without the tools to sustain it. Policy, then, is not just a guide for resistance; it is the foundation upon which we build a future rooted in sovereignty and self-determination.

Centralizing activities is the lifeblood of any national liberation struggle, serving as the tangible expression of unity, identity, and purpose. To build a national body, we must prioritize coordinated events and actions that foster a shared sense of belonging and collective struggle. From cultural celebrations that reclaim our heritage to political mobilizations that challenge the forces of colonization, these activities must be carefully planned and executed to reflect our values and aspirations. Establishing national dates of significance, hosting regional and national congresses, and creating opportunities for communal engagement will help solidify a unified identity across the Xicana/o/x movement. These actions are not mere gatherings—they are rituals of resistance and affirmation, reminding us that we are part of something greater than ourselves. Through activities, we transform our ideas into lived experiences, reinforcing the bonds of solidarity and building the momentum needed to achieve national liberation.

Much is made over differences in "agendas." However, for any conflict there is one axiom—an agenda must exist before there can be true differences. Many of our so-called Xicano movement leaders hide their lack of vision, planning, and fear of actually getting what we want for the future by claiming they do not want to work with such a group because of a difference in agendas. Their lack of substance and faith in the principles on which they have built their part of the Xicano Movement is disturbing and ultimately if not addressed the poison pill to Indigenous liberation.

As a movement we cannot afford any longer to allow willful petulant children who want to take their toys and go at the first sign of disagreement to dictate the political agenda of Xicana/o/x national liberation. Because of the political immaturity of so many within the Xicano movement I believe the majority of those who claim differences in agendas are mostly trying to cloak lack of experience, personality differences, fear and a laziness that often arise from their own inability to control the direction of their small squads. Thus, our movement for pan-Indigenous liberation is continuously thwarted over the personality clashes of the small-minded. These individuals are unable to honestly entertain the fundamental belief that we can win. So they concentrate on the politics of fracturing to ensure their own personal gain. Faith in each other is crucial to the success of our political process.

There must be respect for the independence of different organizations within the movement, but there must be faith in a shared vision and a willingness to cooperate. This is where the real difference within the "agenda" wars really lies. So many, Xicana/o/x grassroots organizations operate from the "vanguard" position and never learned the art of diplomacy and compromise. The only way to make the type of political change Xicana/o/x need in this country is to begin building coalitions based on policy and political empowerment for the nation.

**"Now is not the time for martyrs. Now is the time for thinkers."[6]**

We must acknowledge there is a problem.

Oppression and injustice thrive over the world. The so-called free market that perpetuates this misery is moving unchecked into a phase of world-ending global domination more devastating and inhumane than ever.

The first ingredient in resistance is to awaken to the fact of our humanity. That we are not a counter story. We are human beings and deserve to be treated like human beings, a change begins. From the moment we internalize the reality that the police have no right to beat us in the streets, to take our lives indiscriminately. We have the right to decent housing; to live without disease and sickness dogging us because of where we live. From that moment we no longer recognize the authority of this system over the truth of our existence.

We acknowledge our youth are not prison fodder but valuable political entities and potentially revolutionaries. Their acts are not criminal, they are rather defying a settler system that has slated them for cultural and political destruction. It is this work of revolutionary education Xicana/o/x must commit themselves to everywhere our gente are found. If we as an historically constituted people are to throw off the chains of colonial domination that bind us, the same physical, emotional and intellectual chains placed on us over 500 years ago—then we must return to history to assert our cultural, political, and economic heritage; by developing a political analysis of our situation based on scientific reasoning that is accepted so widely that even those who don't agree must consider it seriously in any discussion about Xicana/o/x sovereignty as Indigenous people.

The type of politics Xicana/o/x people should be talking about are constructed in "future histories"[7] that privileges the rights of Indigenous people in a politics based on shared national policy that moves people to fight for better housing, to stop police brutality, to end the widespread use of drugs in their neighborhood, to re-establish a national identity that makes these things possible through the exercise of collective power. As I wrote in *Insurgent Aztlan,* "Reclaiming Xicano/a Indigenous heritage is the foundation of decolonizing methodologies for Indigenous scholars in the Americas...by recognizing these rights, Indigenous people turn away from the colonial methodologies that have served to rob Xicanos and Xicanas of history, identity, and the will to resist."[8]

---

6      The Invisible Committee. *To Our Friends.*
7      Mireles, Ernesto. *Insurgent Aztlan.*
8      Mireles, Ernesto. *Insurgent Aztlan.*

These are the politics of the people, the politics of el rojo amanacer, when Raza takes matters into their own hands and deals with the condition of their colonization in a manner agreed on by the people—not "solutions" dictated by some punitive governmental authority whose goal is the eradication of brown bodies.

The multinational corporations that have us now won't ever willingly let us go. The men who controlled them are too mad with greed and power to ever acquiesce to the Xicana/o/x Indigenous desire for self-determination. That is why we must come together politically where we live to control the agenda, and build political, cultural, economic power within the areas we could control to the point where we begin to counteract the influence of 500 years of economic and intellectual bondage. Political organizing through the national liberation movement is essential to building political power.

**"It is only at the very moment they understand they are human that they begin to sharpen their tools."[9]**

The biggest obstacle in the way of an even marginally successful Xicano liberation movement with a growing Indigenous philosophy is an unclear, romanticized vision of where and how the struggle for national liberation begins. The practice of free choice within our Indigenous politics is found within the practice of collective action, collective decision-making and building a popular front as an umbrella for an anti-colonialist pro Indigenous movement.

Taiaiake Alfred in his book *Wasáse: Indigenous Pathways of Action and Freedom* tells us that options like armed struggle through guerrilla warfare are impractical when he writes, "it is clear that guerrilla and terrorist strategies are futile ... violent revolt is simply not an intelligent and realistic approach to confronting the injustice we face."[10] While Alfred's words are important, it is also important to understand there are a variety of organizational methodologies that may at one time or another be appropriate for the people to try. The challenge is, whether as a people or nation, we have the ability to enact these different methods, even learning about guerrilla warfare or as it has been called in many Third World countries—the national liberation struggle—as we've come to understand that it is much more than guns and fighting. It is a totalizing effort that activates the political, cultural, and economic remnants of the colonized for resistance on many levels.

---

9       Fanon, Frantz. *The Wretched of the Earth.*
10      Alfred, Taiaiake. *Wasáse: Indigenous Pathways of Action and Freedom.*

For Xicanos examining the words of revolutionary guerrilla fighter Mao Zedong along with the modern analysis of Indigenous liberation theorist like Taiaiake Alfred and Howard Adams is important, it is Mao who eloquently but simply writes, "without a political goal (national liberation) guerrilla warfare must fail"[11] For Xicanos engaged in Indigenous liberation politics this one statement shines a bright light on the necessity of building political party organization. The nature of guerrilla warfare or what Mao calls revolutionary war is a "protracted one"[12] The goal of the revolutionary is not to produce a quick military decision but rather "how to avoid a military decision... give way before the determined advance of the enemy, and, like the sea, close in again as the enemy passes,"[13] According to Mao, in the beginning of a revolution there are no pitched battles—there is merely a struggle for the minds and allegiance of the people through political education. This battle for the mind is the exact situation in which Xicana/o/x and other Indigenous people find themselves.

Mao choose to develop his revolutionary theory focusing on the three intangible aspects of warfare: space, time and will, "the basic premise of this theory is that political mobilization may be substituted for industrial mobilization"[14] according to Edward L. Katzenbach, Jr., who served as the Deputy Assistant Secretary of State under President John F. Kennedy,[15] in his essay on the military theories of Mao Zedong.

According to Katzenbach the three tangibles of warfare are:

[T]he weapons systems, the longbow, the Swiss pike, the A-bomb, items on the long list of the instruments of war that have given a sole possessor a moment of military supremacy. Second, there is the supply system, logistics in the broadest sense. Perhaps this is the area in which US Military genius has best expressed itself... and, third, there is manpower.

Within this emerging post-apocalyptic Indigenous Xicano movement we suffer from a lack of direction and unrealistic perspectives about our roles and the activities we should be undertaking at this point in our liberation struggle. An important lesson from Katzenbach's

---

11  Zedong, Mao. *Yóujī Zhàn (游击战)* – *Guerrilla Warfare.*

12  Ibid.

13  Taber, Robert. *War of the Flea.*

14  Katzenbach, E. L. Jr. *Time, Space and Will: The politico-military views of Mao Tse Tung.*

15  Taber, Robert. *War of the Flea.*

analysis of Mao's guerrilla theory that places our own movement within a proper lens of what constitutes appropriate action at the beginning of a revolution is about timing,

Katzenbach writes that Mao's military problem was how to organize space so that it could be made to yield time. His political problem was how to organize time so that it could be made to yield will, that quality which makes willingness to sacrifice the order of the day... Mao's real military problem was not that of getting the war over with, the question to which Western military thinkers have directed the greater part of their attention, but that of keeping it going.[16] This is now the battle of every Xicana/o/x.

Space + time = will is the equation Katzenbach formulated to explain Mao's theories of protracted warfare, and one that may well serve the needs of Indigenous liberation movements today. For contemporary Indigenous insurgents in the United States, even a basic understanding of Mao's military theory tells us that while we consider ourselves at war, we have not lost, "only those willing to admit defeat can be defeated."[17] And while it may seem to some that war, specifically revolutionary war or insurgency can only be conducted in a specific way it is evident through reading not only Mao, but other revolutionary theorists that war is at its very basic level an attack on the force of law. It is an attempt to reconstitute that society, or as Jacques Derrida points out "war is in fact... a violence that serves to found law."[18]

Post-apocalyptic authoritarian measures perpetrated by the colonial system's state institutions maintain the misery around us. These ideological state institutions (church, education, carceral system, etc.) configure the basis of our psychological relationship with the colonizer and the perpetuation of settler colonialism within our personal and public affairs. Xicana/o/x peoples respond to this type of oppressive authority because it is all we have ever known and have not to date build a different system primarily because of ongoing apocalyptic oppression that has resulted in an incomplete understanding of our political role as Indigenous people in the Americas. Albert Memmi, a Tunisian philosopher who wrote extensively about the conditions of both the colonized and the colonizer, said, "regardless of how soon or how violently the colonized rejects his situation, he will one day begin to overthrow his unlivable existence with the whole force of his oppressed personality."[19]

---

16     Katzenbach, E.L. *Time, Space and Will: The politico-military views of Mao Tse Tung.*
17     Taber. Robert. *War of the Flea.*
18     Derrida, Jacques. *Force of Law: The "Mystical Foundation of Authority."*
19     Memmi, Albert. *The Colonizer and the Colonized.*

The greatest danger our movement faces today is falling prey to the seductive force and philosophy of defeatist assimilation. I believe this happens when culture alone replaces politics as a primary means of resistance. Our current structure within the Xicano movement is conveniently set up, running and allegedly functioning all around us. We unwittingly structure many of the changes we try to institute within the context of the current system of exploitation. This colonial mindset is so ingrained in our proto-national psyche, at this point the only hope toward any significant change in the way we see the world and deal with each other, would come only after it was clearly articulated how a recovery of Indigenous identity and nationalism would work and then begin to order the very identity and nation we have proposed. Law and our understanding of that law and colonialism as a system must be fundamentally altered to grasp the importance and necessity of understanding the role that resistance to oppression plays in founding law.

We cannot have it both ways. We cannot be loyal citizens of the empire and continue to talk about Aztlan as if it were a political reality. If we are to be good citizens then we must halt this talk of stolen land, oppression and colonization because as Huntington so clearly points out, "History shows that serious potential for conflicts exists when people in one country begin referring to territory in a neighboring country in proprietary terms and to assert special rights and claims to that territory."[20]

The decision we have before us is one of great historical and future importance. If we are to choose the path of nation building and pay more than lip service to the creation of a state for Xicanos and other Indigenous people on this continent then it is imperative we begin studying the methods of achieving that end.

Revolutionary Xicano Nationalism as an ideology is dedicated to the promotion of justice and equality for all people. We cannot hesitate or put this discussion off since there is a certain sequence of events in place that make the emergence of a pan-Indigenous nation in this country, sometime in the future, inevitable.

In talking about the unstoppable influx of Mexicans in the US Huntington describes their eventual impact in this way. "They could eventually undertake to do what no previous immigrant group could have dreamed of doing: challenge the existing cultural, political, legal, commercial, and educational systems to fundamentally change not only the language but also the very institutions in which they do business."

Huntington's article and the sentiments it barely tries to cover over are the time-worn thought patterns of a die-hard colonialist racist. The explanation has changed slightly over

---

20      Huntington, Samuel. *The Hispanic Challenge.*

the years because of certain realities regarding the population growth of European Americans in the United States but the underlying support of the colonial system in this country is firmly intact and the tried and tested ways of maintaining its legitimacy are in place.

Memmi exposes for his readers the tangled web of relationships between the colonizer and the colonized. He is able to show how the colonial system makes a reality for Indigenous people they are unable for a time to escape, "The colonialists are perpetually explaining, justifying and maintaining (by word as well as by deed) the place and fate of their silent partners in the colonial drama. The colonized are thus trapped by the colonial system and the colonialist maintains his prominent role."[21]

Xicanos and their Indigenous brethren are those silent partners. Condemned to be explained by the colonizer and maintained as a labor force ensuring our own imprisonment within the colonial system. We should study the fears of settlers closely and see if there is a way to bring them to fruition. They are very clearly outlining the blueprint of the most potentially dangerous Indian rebellion in the last 500 years. We who have married the daughters and sons of white America, who have lived and continue to live next door to white America, attended school, lived and died, fought wars with—we constitute the ultimate threat to the hegemony of this country. We, who reside in the belly of the beast and our cousins who join us every day must determine whether life is worth living or not and if it is then do we live in submission or resistance? Black Panther, organic intellectual and revolutionary anarchist Lorenzo Kom'boa Ervin wrote in his pamphlet "Anarchism and the Black Revolution" about the US, "America is a mother country with an internal colony... Ours is a captive, oppressed colonial status that must be overthrown, not just smashing ideological racism or denial of civil rights."[22]

It is impossible to increase the power of the Xicano nation with an army of social workers[23] who address, within the confines of the colonial system, the very problems and conditions that are created by the poverty of culture and economics that is fundamental to the capitalist colonial system. Their job is to help colonial unfortunates unable to adapt learn how to fit into this society in the hopes they will become assimilated productive workers diligently striving to maintain the crushing economic hegemony of this system. There is evidence that business degrees are on the rise with the idea that we must make money in order to empower ourselves but in reality there isn't much difference in the political uses

---

21    Memmi, Albert. *The Colonizer and the Colonized.*
22    Ervin, Lorenzo Kom'boa. "Anarchism and the Black Revolution."
23    I have an MSW. It is a noble profession, and mostly well meaning.

between a MSW and MBA. Both deal with poverty, one to alleviate the symptoms and the other to create them, both offering the same colonial solution, total compliance with their oppressors to oppressed Indigenous people around the globe.

Third World revolutionary thought when examined as a whole shows Xicana/o/x people we must seek answers outside of the framework of the colonial system and in fact must begin to work toward new ways of understanding contested Indigenous and settler identities.

Xicano Indigenous peoples must then commit to building structures here and now that emphasize centralization and cultural-politico behavior within a democratic framework. Communities must begin to form that will practice the fundamentals of this idea. Xicana/o/x have to see if this change is possible on a small scale before we can try and convince people it is possible on a large scale.

Xicana/o/x can have a society based on mutual respect and trust. Not on the exploitation and robbery of labor and land. This is the real revolution: the war on capital. In reality all revolutions to this point have been fought to replace one boss with another. Led mostly by the bourgeois, these revolutions fail to address the issues of economic exploitation in part because they can't and in part because many of them failed to do so in their own organizations before the period of overthrow.

Some may argue there will always be poor people—and they may be right in saying so, however, the difference between starving to death and simply owning less than your neighbor is significant. The whole of society must produce for the whole of society. The Xicano nation in its currently fragmented form must prioritize Indigenous education and political empowerment. If we spent less time in the accumulation of personal goods as a society and took that energy and rerouted it into the pursuit of knowledge, how fast would we move forward? Why would the colonizer support and educate the descendants of conquered people past primary education?

We don't need PhDs to run their machines, we could use PhDs to invent and manufacture our own return to history as a distinct nation. That the return to history is the basic fear of the colonizer and one that is articulated over and over by systemic inequalities within settler colonialism. Many people call it xenophobic behavior but in reality it is white patriotism at its finest.

# ILLEGAL LETTERS

## PATRICK FONTES

Boisterous laughter rose up from a dozen kids as a brilliant orange sky cast festive, glowing hues down onto the party. Lupita's cousin Mari twirled her around in circles attempting to disorientate her—both laughed with their hearts. Lupita stopped, her legs firm but her body felt like it was still moving. Dizzied, she flexed her calves, stood her ground, and raised her face towards the warmth of the hidden sun. Giggles, coughs and throat whistles from her cousins and close friends echoed around the enclosed patio.

All her life she dreamed of this day, of becoming a state licensed Cuerpo, strong, fit—respected by both La Gente and El Gentry for contributing to a working society. "Your body is the temple," since birth, Lupita heard from the Ministry broadcast every morning.

She didn't want to be like her Tio Jesse who failed to receive certification, and who now lived in a Wastelands shack in the Firebaugh sector. Her mom once took her to visit Tio Jesse. The Ministry didn't place air purifiers in that sector. Lupita remembered the atmosphere so thick that she used up one "breather" that day—breathers lasted at least a month. Jesse lived in a community of makeshift wooden shacks. Inside his small home Lupita recalled a fire pit and a bed made out of discarded Ministry cardboard. A plastic crate with a few tattered books contained all that he owned. Sandra, her mother, said Jesse was a poet, a crazy rebel who played with useless words that only brought misery to his life. To society, and his family, Uncle Jesse was a wheezer, an outcast, unfit to serve the Ministry as one of the respected Cuerpos.

"Mija, come here," Jesse motioned to nine-year-old Lupita. His raspy voice muffled beneath a set of soiled rags tied about his lower face. Even though only in his late 30s, Jesse's skin was weathered like an old boot, his reddish eyes with hints of yellow at the edges testified to a couple decades in the Wastelands.

"Look at this, Lupita, open it," Tio Jesse handed her a tattered book.

"Don't go filling her head with any of your nonsense Jesse, do you want her to end up like you, pendejo? Living here alone with nothing but wheezers for friends?"

Jesse looked away with a pained expression.

"Here, I brought a breather for you," Sandra handed him a device.

"What, no flavors?" he tried to joke as he coughed. Sandra laughed, the plastic mouthpiece fogged up.

"Does she know her letters?" he forced words out through a bloodied throat, then coughed. His face turned red. He spat blood onto the dusty floor.

Lupita gasped.

"No! I'm raising my kids the right way. One day she'll be a Cuerpo, like me, like Pop and Ma—letters are not for our people," Sandra pleaded with her brother, recalling their youth when she attempted to sway him to reason. "Jesse, remember, the nursery song Ma sang to us at night?" Sandra's muffled voice fluttered in eerie motherly fashion. Broken slats in the walls let in rays of red light illuminating dusty air, "My children, mis hijos, tools for la gente, and books for el gentry. Strong eyes, strong arms, strong hearts. We are all a part."

Sandra had taken Lupita to visit Jesse in order to make an impression on her, and it did. Ever since that day, Lupita's sole goal was to receive Cuerpo certification and live a respectable life in the East Quadrant, Fresno Sector.

For the last few years Lupita kept a disciplined daily routine, as suggested by the Ministry of Duo-Freedoms. Every morning on the screen her workout regimen appeared for her to follow. Laying on her weight bench, building biceps and forearms for lifting, she would get lost in the colorful sky above her enclosed patio. Deep red, purple, yellow and green clouds swirled about, constantly painting the air in new color variations. The Ministry's air purifiers along the street allowed Gente to see as far away as a couple of blocks; without them each home would be lost in its own deep orange cloud. Lupita and all Gente knew how toxic the air was; each day brought about new deaths from the wheezer colonies, yet to Lupita, in those moments, the fatal air was something beautiful, a horizon reaching out to her with new possibilities and hopes.

Lupita stood firm, balanced, as the other kids yelled, "Hit that piñata!"

"Come on, Lupita!" and "Wow, look at those muscles!" a few teased. With biceps taut, a grin appeared on Lupita's face as she cocked back her arms and swung with all her might. She wanted to prove how strong she was on this special day, her Quinceañera. Blindfolded, with an old broom handle firmly gripped, she landed a blow to the piñata that sent candy flying in every direction, even bouncing off the ceiling of the hard plastic interior of their patio.

"Don't throw the stick, Mija!" Lupita's mom Sandra yelled.

While the candy was still flying about in midair Lupita hurriedly ripped away her blindfold and jumped into the mob of children greedily vying for candy and sweet air pills.

Sandra and the few other moms present tried to keep their children calm. Too much excitement might bring about uncontrollable coughing that lasted for hours, or even worse, wheezing that lasted for days, even weeks.

After the mad rush for candy the children sat down breathing heavily into their devices.

"Aw cool, look what I got!" shouted Louie, Lupita's stout ten-year old cousin.

A ring tone shot out from the living room. "Lupita! Lupe! Everyone," Sandra called, "the Ministry is calling, hurry." The kids grabbed their goodies and ran into the living room, surrounding the holographic projection stage atop a coffee table.

"OK, ma, answer the call," Lupita said nervously to her mom. The room was completely silent. Only the deep droning sound of the air purifiers in the street could be heard—their sound was constant. A Ministry spokeswoman appeared atop the hologram receiver plate. "Whoa, a Gentry," one of Lupita's younger cousins blurted out, much to her embarrassment. He'd seen Gentry only one other time in holographic form. Lupita nudged him to shut up. "Lupita, on behalf of the Ministry of Duo-Freedoms I would like to congratulate you on your Quinceañera celebration." Lupita and Sandra held their breath for more news. "I also bring great news to you. We recognize your hard work on developing a strong, fit body that will serve society well. You passed your test for Cuerpo certification. You are now an adult, with all the benefits the Ministry grants Cuerpos. We shall see you and your mother in San Francisco tomorrow. Travel well."

"How come she didn't have any muscles?" asked the younger cousin

"She is Gentry. Gentry are skinny and weak in the body," Lupita said, "Not like us, we are strong," she flexed her biceps.

"Without our strength Gentry couldn't survive." Lupita said to a captive audience.

Overcome with pride, Sandra stared at her grown daughter from the kitchen. Sandra looked down at her own forearms and biceps, flexing her muscles as hard as she could so that her veins popped out. At thirty-two years old, Sandra's biceps still measured at fifteen inches of hard muscle. She looked down over her shoulder to her calves, the size of footballs. Sandra looked back again at Lupita's young, fit body. She was relieved that Lupita was now carrying on the family legacy of hard-working, strong Cuerpos.

"Lupita, I forgot to get a candle for your cake. Go to the Ministry pantry and pick one up?" Sandra asked. "My ration card is in my worker's bag."

Lupita took off her indoor breathing unit and put on her outdoor air mask. The mask covered her whole face, from her eyes down to her chin. She placed a cherry flavored air pill into the mask receptacle. Lupita took a deep breath; she thought about San Francisco, the clean air she only had heard about. With eyes closed, Lupita imagined the sweet air of the city.

Lupita stepped outside. The painted atmosphere felt like a warm napkin caressing her skin. Looking back at her home, she wondered at her future. Her future was predictable, practical, yet there remained an inarticulate longing in her stomach for something more. Lupita could not describe the feeling in her gut. She tried to describe it to her mom recently, "It's like if you're caught outside without a breather on a toxic day, you keep gasping for more, deeper and harder, yet there's no oxygen to satisfy you. Then fear hits. That's how I feel, Mom, inside. I don't know why I feel this way." Lupita hung her head. Sandra made the sign of the cross, said a quick prayer to St. Chavez and hoped Lupita's feeling would quickly leave.

Her single-family unit, built for one parent and one child, was twenty feet wide and twenty feet from the street to the back. Within that small space was a kitchen, a living room that served mostly as a Ministry hologram space, and a bedroom that she and Sandra shared. The concrete floor of the enclosed patio made the space an unbearable, toxic oven during the summer heat waves from February to October, when temperatures outside rose to 125 Fahrenheit by late March, dropping down to the 80s only in late October.

Lupita walked past several identical dwelling units. The streets were barren—the Ministry issued a warning alert for the Central Valley atmosphere that morning. Gente stayed inside, behind sealed doors, watching Ministry hologram documentaries on the history of workers' rights or the benevolence of Ministry paternalism toward Cuerpos. Lupita tired of those documentaries long ago. She wanted to know more about society, but she didn't know what questions to ask—she had a constant blunt pain in her stomach, like the sensation of homesickness.

After a minute of walking, Lupita's summer jumpsuit was covered in fine, orange dust. She clapped her hands, sending a cloud of luminescent particles back into the atmosphere. The silhouettes of two towering, neighborhood air purifiers came into view; approaching, the air became clearer, their humming, sonorous. Four, large vacuum ducts on each machine sucked in grimy air, letting out purified oxygen through massive wind turbines fifty feet above. Lupita stood in front of the machines, letting the deep humming vibrate her body as she watched in wonder at the swirling colors where the fresh air was released back into the environment. On the underside of the machines red letters said something, Lupita didn't know what—she was bothered by not knowing. When she was a little girl she would lie on her back and stare at the letters. She never told her mom. It was forbidden for Gente to know the letters. Punishment for understanding letters meant banishment to the Wastelands without any Ministry aid: no unit, no food, no breathers, no Ministry credits, nothing but a savage existence, short lived.

A group of wheezers sprawled out in front of the Ministry pantry begging for credits and breathers. In their mid to late twenties, living such a harsh life made them appear to be in their forties. Dressed in shredded clothes and rags, only their hands and faces were visible. Their skin had deep furrows, bleeding in parts where the skin became so dried, it cracked open, like the parched ground Lupita once saw around her uncle's shack in the Firebaugh Wastelands. As Lupita passed the group one of the men called out in a rough voice, "Ah, a Quinceañera, wow," he spat out blood onto the pavement, "happy adulthood." How did he know? Lupita thought to herself. The man could see the confusion in Lupita's face. "Don't worry, I'm not a mind reader, I'm not that far gone yet," he laughed, then gagged for several seconds, "You're Lupita, right? You're pretty famous in the East quadrant, your strength is legendary already," he let out a raspy guffaw along with the other wheezers. They all began to gasp for air, a couple clasping their throats, with faces turned red. Lupita hurried into the Ministry Pantry, once inside she could still hear them choking outside.

While she was paying for her candle, Ministry sirens screamed across Fresno's smog-kissed landscape. The noise warned of life-threatening air levels. The sirens came alive several times a year, while acid rains killed off sickly, homeless wheezers. Anyone outside quickly made his or her way home, lest their skin burn within the poisonous environment. The sirens didn't bother Lupita. She remained overjoyed at passing her qualifications for Cuerpo certification.

"Lupita, you better run home, Mija, the blood rains come." Old Manuel, the Ministry attendant warned Lupita, his wizened white hair shrouding a weather-beaten face. He still wore the old-style metal breathers from half a century ago. "This was my mom's breather, it's all I have left of her, I just clip off a bit of the new filters and it's just as good as new," he would say to kids who saw him for the first time. "Of course, I ain't got no sweet air pill slots but I'm old school, I don't need none of that, just fresh air for me, Ma'am." He handed Lupita her candle, "Now hurry home, Lupita, and Happy Quinceañera! Say hi to Frisco for me, I once left my heart there." As Lupita left into a darkening neighborhood, Old Manuel took out an ancient record, placed it on a turntable and began to dance in place." The twentieth-century hit "My Girl" followed Lupita out the door.

Outside, Lupita noticed the group of homeless wheezers had turned their cart upside down and placed it against the pantry wall, then erected acid-rain-proof plastic tarps over their makeshift frame. She felt a bit of pity for them and wondered at their silhouettes surrounded a single light inside. The storm was approaching at a dangerous distance now, but her curiosity compelled her to step next to the makeshift tent and listen. The young man who had talked to her was talking aloud yet his words seemed off, as if he were not talking to anyone directly but into the air.

"Hey, someone is out there," one of the young women inside the enclosure said.

Lupita screamed and jumped back as the young man quickly pulled open the tarp, startling her. "I, I, um," Lupita stumbled.

Lupita stared inside. They all sat in a circle. One flickering candle lit up their faces in eerie fashion. The young man held a book in his hand.

"We're reading, care to join us?" He said, with a coy yet sincere gesture.

"Uh, no, no, thanks, I've got to run now, the acid storm is coming." Only a few miles away, the massive black cloud rolled towards Fresno, a giant tsunami of acid rain. Lupita made it back home just in time. "Traviesa! Didn't you hear the sirens, Lupita!?" Sandra yelled, then wiped her tears from her cheeks.

"Yea, I heard, then came right home, here's the candle," Lupita said as she washed fine, orange particles from her arms and face at the kitchen sink.

Lupita then joined her mother and the rest of the partygoers at their living room window as all looked out at the ominous acid rain cloud overtaking Fresno. A couple of the smaller cousins pressed their awe-struck faces against the window, where only inches away polluted rain missiles sent out miniscule mushroom clouds on impact. On the other side of the window smoke arose from the ground, creating an eerie scene with a black sky as a backdrop.

The next morning Sandra and Lupita stood at the train station awaiting their ride to San Francisco. The morning after an acid rain downpour a heavy smell of sulfur filled the air. Even the strongest sweet air pills hardly masked the smell and taste. Mr. Chester's Saltwater Taffy came close, but still not quite. Cuerpo workers scoured the streets spraying a new layer of plastic asphalt where rains had left pockmarks throughout the city's infrastructure.

Sandra took the train to the City every morning since she had turned fifteen, so many years ago. "I remember when I was standing just about here with my mom when I turned fifteen. I remember how excited I was," Sandra exclaimed as she looked into Lupita's eyes. "Are you excited, Mija?" Sandra asked her daughter.

"Yea, yea, I am," Lupita grinned beneath her breather.

"Don't be nervous, don't be afraid, I am going to be at your side the whole day,"

Sandra said reassuringly, stroking Lupita's long braid. "You are going to see Frisco, Gentry, a blue sky, and be able to see miles in any direction. The air is that clean." Sandra beamed.

"No way, a blue sky!" Lupita raised her voice in feigned awe.

Lupita already knew all this info from watching documentaries created by the Ministry of Duo-Freedoms.

"Don't be a smart ass, Mija," said Sandra. Both women laughed, fogging up their breathers.

"I'm kidding, Mom, I can't wait to see a blue sky, and I try to imagine what it will be like but it's hard. And Gentry, too, I've only seen them in holograms, but never in person, not like you, you work for Gentry every day. What was it like to see them for the first time?" Lupita asked her mom.

"Oh, Lupita, I wasn't like you. You are so strong, and brave, and well, I was more naive than you." Lupita wondered at what her mom meant.

"I was scared to be around Gentry at first, they are so tall and beautiful, I mean, you are beautiful, Mija, but they are different, they are beautiful like the mountains with a large blue sky beautiful. The top of my head barely comes to their waist. For the first five years I couldn't look at them in the eye, even my boss lady who was so nice to me, sometimes giving me food they had left over from dinner. I was very strong, yes, like you, but they scared me. They are so intense. You can sense how smarter they are, way smarter than us, but were stronger—we need each other, we balance." Lupita sensed an uneasy, disingenuous tone in her mom's recollection, as if she were trying to convince Lupita. She couldn't explain exactly this thought or feeling, she did not have the words to describe it, but she felt dishonesty in her mom that was foreign to her character. Lupita felt sad for her mom. Her sadness was a fleeting thought, as the two watched their train pull up to the station. "Oh, I'm so excited," Lupita said squeezing her mom's hands.

"Wow, watch that grip, Superwoman," Sandra laughed as she shook the pain off.

"Train to San Francisco now boarding," a Cuerpo attendant walked up and down the waiting corridor. He was thin for Cuerpo standards, his job did not entail the heavy lifting and manual labor most Cuerpos undertook. Yet, his muscular chest stood out like two cinderblock bricks, his right forearm as large as a grapefruit, swung a bell up and down as he yelled out, "Now boarding train to San Francisco. ¡Ándale Gente!"

Lupita rushed aboard to get a window seat, she wanted to see as much as she could. To this point she had never ventured out of the East Quadrant, Fresno, not even to the other Fresno sections. Her whole life was spent in a four-mile radius from her home, and most of that within her own housing block near familia, except the time she visited her Uncle Jesse out in the Firebaugh Wastelands. Lupita could never see past her block, even on the clearest of days, and most often she was content with that. Now, excitement filled her gut as the train left the station in amazing speed.

"We will be in Frisco in one hour, Mija, just sit back and enjoy the ride." Sandra said.

For the first half hour, Lupita could not see more than a hundred feet or so past the rail tracks, the swift train disturbed the air, causing unique color formations that played on Lupita's imagination. In those curious swirls of toxic air, she imagined her new job as a Cuerpo. Where would she work? Would her co-workers be nice? Would the Gentry be nice to her? Would she see the world? Would she learn to...

As she was thinking to herself, wondering about the many possibilities for her life, the train began to ascend a hill. The reddish, orange smogscape soon gave way to an amazing vista as far as her eyes could see. Giant wind turbines pointed toward the Valley, her home, kept the toxic air at bay, separating the clean air Gentry breathed and the air Gente lived in. Lupita's mouth dropped. She gasped. Sandra bit her lip and grasped her knees as she saw the wonder on her daughter's face. Lupita began to cry, as if all her life she were blind and saw the world for the first time. She wept, pointing outside, "This, this, this is what I haven't seen all my life? Why, why? Why, Mom?" she cried aloud. In her train carriage other Quinceañera girls were also taking their first trip to the City. A group cry rose up, as wonder overcame them all.

In no time, the train approached San Francisco. A new amazement hit Lupita as the city rose higher and higher up to the wondrous, beautiful blue sky. She had never seen a building higher than two stories. Ministry air purifiers were the tallest things she had ever seen. Now, she was looking at hundreds of buildings rising like metal monsters up to heaven.

"How far does the city go, Mom?" she asked Sandra.

"Well, that part there is San Francisco," Sandra pointed to an identifiable center where the buildings were highest. "But the Gentry live continuously from this point all the way to the Mexican Republic sector. One long, unbroken city along the California Republic coast."

"And only Gentry, right, no Gente?" Lupita asked.

Sandra felt uneasy about answering her questions.

"Arriving at Jack London Square. Arriving at Jack London Square, San Francisco." A Cuerpo called out. A dozen Quinceañera birthday girls exited the train with their mothers. A Gentry woman appeared on the platform to meet them. She was nearly seven feet tall, slender, poised, dressed in a dark blue skirt suit. Her blonde hair held up in a bun underneath a blue cap. She was pale, even translucent compared to Lupita and the rest of the Gente who arrived in her coach. Her nametag read "Agent Hanson." Lupita marveled at the woman, twice as tall as her or her mother. Lupita looked back at the women who had also arrived from Fresno, then looked at the Gentry agent, then back at her Gente. Lupita suddenly felt inadequate, even ugly. She looked down at her forearm and flexed, then looked at the Gentry's body, sleek, smooth, defined but not bulging like her body. The woman stood erect with back straight, so straight it looked weird to Lupita, as if the woman were to tip backwards. Then, Lupita looked at the Gente. She never noticed their slouch before, as if their arm muscles were so large, pulling their shoulders downward. Lupita felt embarrassment. Lupita felt the urge to cover up and hide. Yet, she stood still, and listened.

"On behalf of the Ministry of Duo-Freedoms I welcome you Quinceañera girls to the beautiful city of San Francisco, capital of our beloved California Republic," she said with professional poise, "Please, you may remove your breathing devices, you do not need them anywhere in the Plutocity. So, remember, no matter where you are assigned to work, from Frisco to San Diego, you may remove your breathers, as you call them," she smiled at her attempt to connect with the Cuerpos by using their slang, she winked at Lupita. She went on, "...as soon as you enter the Plutocity." Then she waved her arm and shouted, "Let your party begin!" Her white teeth sparkled beneath a brilliant sun.

Out of nowhere, a mariachi band appeared blasting their instruments. Sandra and many other Cuerpo mothers began to cry, because all Gente cry when they hear mariachis, but also because they were reliving their party celebrations so many years past.

A couple other Gentry appeared, this time young women, the same age as Lupita. Lupita once more stood in amazement. Standing at least six feet tall, a young woman with a wide smile, red, flushed cheeks, red lips and long, blonde hair, approached her with a traditional Quinceañera dress. The dress was powder blue, tight at the waist, spreading out with multiple layers of lace. It was the most gorgeous dress Lupita had ever seen or worn. All the Gente were ushered into a shuttle and taken to a reception hall.

Once dressed, the Fresno Gente group sat at a few round tables with placards that read "Fresno Quinceañera Cuerpos—Welcome." Lupita guessed what the placards might have said and thought it was ridiculous since none of them could read.

Lupita leaned over to the table behind hers and asked another young Cuerpo, "Where are you from?" The young woman answered back excitedly, "Hey, I'm Missy, from the Bakersfield sector, and see that group? That's the Sac sector. Did you know Sac used to be the capital of California before the Great Woes? And over there, you see them, very dark girls?" The girl said a little too loud, "Well, they are from the West Hills sector, a lot like the Wastelands but still Ministry regulated, Mom says stay away from them, they're like wheezers." The girl talked too fast for Lupita, yet she was fascinated that she knew so much.

"And do you know where we are from?" Lupita asked the girl.

"Hmm, let me see, the girl said staring at the placard on Lupita's table. The girl made an F sound, then made it again. Ah, OK, Fresno! You're from the Fresno sector but I don't know which quadrant."

"Oh!" Lupita exclaimed, "Did you just read that sign? I mean, you can read?" Lupita asked.

Another girl at the Bakersfield table jumped up and yelled at the top of her voice, while pointing to the girl Lupita was talking to, "She can read! She reads! Maria knows how to read!" Her voice carried throughout the auditorium hall. Everyone went silent. Then, two Gentry men with blue jump suits and long, flowing, blond hair walked up to the Bakersfield table. The girl's mother cried aloud, "No, no, this is a mistake, I swear, she doesn't know how to read! She was pretending," she begged.

"Liar!" the accusative Bakersfield girl protested, "She's lying, I knew she was teaching Maria the letters, I knew it! So gross, ew!" The girl gyrated in place as if shaking off worms.

"Did you read our letters?" One of the Gentry agents asked Missy. Missy held back tears, but held a defiant look in her eyes, a look more mature than fifteen years of age. Lupita felt a connection with her, as if she wanted to side with her, but didn't know why. Missy looked around the auditorium. All eyes were upon her. All remained silent.

"Your letters?" Missy said aloud.

"No baby, no baby, please don't do this, my god," Missy's mom said, pleading with her daughter to stop.

"Come with us, please," one of the agents grabbed Missy's arm. Even though they were seven feet tall, Missy was twice their strength. She pulled away from his grasped and yelled out to all the Quinceañera birthday girls in the hall, "They are not their letters! Letters are for all! Strength is for all." At that, they sprayed her face. Missy immediately slumped over, hitting her head on the table. A communal gasp went up from everyone in the hall. All the women at the Bakersfield table began to cough and wheeze; those closest to Missy passed out. Lupita buried her nose and mouth into her dress as a filter. Missy's sobbing mother followed the two agents as they carried Missy's limp body out of the auditorium.

After a minute went by, Gentry agents appeared at each exit doorway. Ms. Hanson entered the hall, her feet clacking loudly through the silence, as she walked toward the stage.

Agent Hanson raised both her arms over the crowd. She slowly lowered her arms, at the same time the lights in the hall were dimmed. A musical tune rose steadily, one everyone in the hall knew so well. Hanson and all the Cuerpos present sang together: "My children, mis hijos, tools for la gente, books for el gentry. Strong eyes, strong arms, strong hearts. We are all a part."

"Let's sing it together standing, holding hands," Hanson exclaimed.

Lupita told her mother she had to use the restroom.

"Hurry back," Sandra replied. Sandra held hands with a Quinceañera and another mother. She closed her eyes and sang along, repeating the nursery rhyme five more times.

"Now everyone hug your neighbor, then hug your other neighbor." Hanson asked.

After twenty minutes Lupita had not returned. Sandra began to worry. She asked one of the Gentry officers to look for her. After an hour went by, Sandra feared the worst, that the Gentry also took her daughter as they had taken Missy. Lupita never returned.

Two weeks later, in a small shack in the Firebaugh Wastelands, Tio Jesse looked up as an intruder entered his home without notice, "Hey, hey!" his raspy voice called out, startled. He grabbed his protection stick, pointing it at the stranger.

Lupita unwrapped her face. Dirtied, desiccated, thirsty, she said, "Tio, please, teach me my letters."

# QUANTUM LOVE STORY

## JOE MENCHACA

**Part I**

There is no death...only a change of worlds.

*—Chief Seattle*

Baltimore Reynolds was about to address his ex-wife Carmelita's request when three sicarios with tattooed faces slithered into the bar and opened fire.

An hour earlier, Baltimore agreed to meet her at The Silver Bullet Saloon, thinking it an opportunity to exact a megaton of revenge for the humiliating way she dumped him in this reality. They met in a Physics for Non-Science Majors class that Baltimore, a research physicist, taught. Carmelita SpeaksToOwls Ruiz was a graduate Cultural Anthropology major, and to Baltimore, the most beautiful woman in nine dimensions: Straight black hair that fell to her waist and moved like whispers when she tossed her head back and laughed, skin like liquid caramel, and eyes as dark and infinite as a black hole. But an aura of danger emanated from her like radiation from plutonium fuel rods. It should have been a warning.

The Silver Bullet was in a part of Old Twosuns where desperation and hopelessness were the dominant social currencies, and even with VR Maps and the DARPA-issued Global Navigation System, it had taken him the better part of that hour to find the place. Baltimore opened the door, and the stench of stale beer and vomit whooshed passed him like a drunk frat boy's breath at a pledge party. Already peeved that meeting Carmelita might cause him to miss a consultation with his business partner, he nearly turned around and walked away. Reluctantly, he stepped in, paused to let nausea fade and for his eyes to adjust, and scanned the room.

A dark, dingy blind made of partially rusted metal slats covering the front window sliced thin, horizontal bars of sunlight through clouds of cigarette smoke, and a mournful wail rose from a smudged and dusty jukebox slumped against the wall next to the window. Feeble light from several randomly placed fixtures with beer logo shades shined through the thickening haze through which Baltimore discerned vague shapes of tables and booths. Carmelita sat in a booth in a dimly lit corner at the back of the room. She waved him over.

About a dozen early morning patrons slouched on backless stools or leaned on a wooden bar, scarred by initials and obscenities carved into its surface. All of them were smoking. All of them turned to inspect Baltimore. Thin, pale, button-up shirt, slacks, and a backpack—not at all intimidating, *which in this place could be a favorable characteristic or a major liability,* he thought. Baltimore grew up in a white middle-class suburb and was, thus, unsure how to comport himself as he walked past the patrons. He decided on a confident but not haughty posture, even though he thought he'd need a tetanus shot after leaving the place.

He stepped up to the booth and was startled by her appearance. Carmelita's skin had tightened around her face like Saran Wrap on a hambone, and several red angry sores marred her once flawless complexion. The ravages of 'cide. Her appearance sapped most of the energy out of his hunger for revenge, so rather than berate her looks, he said, "Geez, Carmelita, you couldn't find a more lowlife dive?"

"This is the only place where nobody knows me," she said.

"And that's good because...?"

"I got a real problem, Baltimore, and only you can help me."

"What, Ninja Boy ran off with someone else's wife?"

"Shit, I dumped that fool a long time ago. No, I got real problems, Baltimore." Carmelita lowered her head, casting suspicious glances around the room, and whispered, "I crossed El Ojo, and now they're out to kill me."

"El who?" Baltimore said a bit too loudly. A few barflies glanced in their direction— their moist, filmy eyes betraying little.

"Shh, keep your voice down, pendejo," Carmelita said. "El Ojo de Oro. If they find me, they're gonna cut my fucking head off." Lips quivering, eyes moistening, she was on the brink of losing her composure. She paused to regain control and said, "Please, Baltimore, you've got to get me out of here!"

"Why would I want to do that?" he said.

"You're not still pissed about Alex, are you?" Carmelita said.

"No, why would I be? I mean, the woman of my dreams—my wife—hooks up with a cretin on a Kowalski Ninja and says, 'adiós, cabrón' while the newlywed glow is still luminous and warm—for me, that is. And now, after I've finally moved on, she calls and says she needs my help. Why would I be 'pissed' about that?"

A slight smile curled her lips.

"You find that humorous?" Baltimore said. He was on the verge of losing his cool.

"No," she said sweetly, "'Adiós, cabrón?' Is that the Carmelita effect? 'Cause you know I didn't say that to you."

"You didn't have to. And your diversionary tactics won't work, Carmelita. Yes, I'm still pissed about Alex."

"Come on, Baltimore, don't be like that." She couldn't look at him and instead cast her gaze down at the dingy table. "I'm sorry I hurt you, Baltimore—"

"That's it? 'I'm sorry I hurt you?' You shattered my heart like a chem lab beaker. And if that wasn't enough, you shamed and embarrassed me in front of my friends and colleagues."

"What else do you want me to say, Baltimore? Besides, it's not like it's all on me. You claim the 'newlywed glow was still luminous and warm,' but that's not what it looked like from my perspective. Remember that hateful shit you said to me about believing in spirits?"

They had been talking about the Native practice of infusing the natural world with spirit, and when she had tried to explain that Natives believe all things, sentient or insentient, possess a spirit force, he had dismissed it as superstition and ignorance.

"Many things scientists dismiss do exist in the natural world," Carmelita had said.

"Like what?"

"Well, like spirits."

"I'm sorry," said Baltimore. "But I can't accept ethereal entities of myths and legends as being real. And I'm finding it difficult to reconcile how you, an otherwise intelligent individual, can believe as real a paganistic, primitive belief with no basis in scientific fact."

"I understand your dilemma, Baltimore, I really do, and I empathize with you because I face a similar dilemma: How can you, an otherwise intelligent individual, believe in a branch of physics that promotes theories like matter exists as probabilities, objective reality may be an illusion, and the universe might be a hologram?"

Baltimore nodded. "Great counterpoint." His upper lip curled up on one side, and anger swept across his eyes like light from a passing car's headlights. "One big difference: Quantum phenomena have been observed in laboratory experiments. Can't say that about spirits."

"Have they? Didn't you once say that scientists haven't actually seen particles, that proof of their existence occurs when particles collide or pass through film?"

"Well...yes, but—"

"Please, let me finish. My interpretation of 'quantum phenomena' is that a particle reveals itself under specific conditions and chooses the form—particle or wave. Unscientific phrasing, but generally speaking, true, right?"

"Generally speaking, yes."

"Revealing itself under specific conditions—like rituals—and in what form is what a spirit does."

He had turned away, his face reddening, and said, "Still superstitious pagan bullshit."

The Silver Bullet's gloomy environment hid the shame in Baltimore's eyes. The self-reproach he'd felt at having once said such degrading and disrespectful things to Carmelita hadn't diminished; he was about to apologize again, but Carmelita held up a gaunt hand to quiet him.

"Still, leaving you the way I did was a fucked-up thing to do, I know that," she said, "like I know there's no way I can ever make it right. But, please, Baltimore, you've got to help me; you gotta get me out of here."

"I don't understand why you called me. If you need to leave that badly, you could buy a plane ticket, a bus ticket—whatever mode of transportation suits you. Surely there must be many places where you could hide from El Ojo."

"No." Carmelita looked at him with an intensity that caught him by surprise. "El Ojo's tentacles run far and deep. I mean, where're you going to run from an organization whose motto is, 'No hay dónde esconderse'? And it's not just a motto; it's a code of honor members live by and are willing to die for."

"Well, they can't be that widespread. I haven't ever heard or read anything about El Ojo de Oro."

"Are you so sure?" Carmelita raised an eyebrow and smirked.

*What did she mean by that?* Baltimore wondered. Carmelita's smirk, a sort of I-know-something-you-don't-know sneer, fueled the ominous dread growing in his unconscious mind since he established a business partnership with Curtis Latrans. "Of course, I'm sure," he said. "It's not like I socialize with gangsters."

"El Ojo's not a gang, Baltimore; they're a criminal enterprise. They're the country's largest manufacturer and distributor of 'cide, and they prefer to operate in the shadows. But the organization doesn't concern me as much as the assassins who work for them." Fear accompanied intensity in her eyes. This troubled Baltimore, for Carmelita did not frighten easily. She was born on the Chalk Mountain Kai-yen-ta Indian Reserve and lived there until middle school when her parents divorced. Her mom then moved them to Phoenix, where Carmelita began running with gangbangers, and smoking and selling 'cide. Baltimore learned from her that showing fear in either environment made you a target or a victim.

"I'm telling you, Baltimore," Carmelita said, her voice wavering in tone and volume, "those guys are death walking—it's like they aren't even human. And they absolutely will not stop until they give their boss my head." She took a drink of beer and drew a long, slow breath as if preparing to dive into deep water. "No, Baltimore. There's only one place they won't find me. I want you to hide me wherever it is you go when you're in your lab."

"What?" Baltimore hoped his face didn't lose color and betray his shock. He focused on assuming a façade of nonchalance and said, "I go to my lab when I'm in my lab."

"Come on, Baltimore. You know what I'm talking about." She dialed up the intensity—Baltimore was sure he squirmed. "My father says you can walk between worlds."

"I have no idea what you or he is talking about."

Baltimore's attempted nonchalance was interrupted by the bartender—a large, bald man whose sneer exposed an abstract landscape of rotting and missing teeth—who bellowed, "Hey, college boy. You drink, or you walk."

*Ah, this is what "saved by the bell" feels like,* thought Baltimore. He hoped the interruption would divert the conversation. He smiled sweetly and asked, "Would you like another beer?"

"No, I don't want another fucking beer."

"Well, Shrek says I need to buy something." Baltimore hoped the bartender didn't hear that and considered what to order. Given the less-than-sanitary conditions, he ruled out anything in a glass. He turned, smiled at the bartender, and said, "I'll have a bottle of India Pale Ale, please."

"Ain't got none of that yuppie shit here, dufus. All we got's Budtz, Koors, and Meiller."

"A Budtzveiser it is, then." Baltimore turned to speak to Carmelita.

The bartender opened a bottle and plunked it on the bar. "That'll be three bucks." Baltimore placed money on the table. "And I ain't no fucking waitress," Shrek thundered, causing the jagged, crescent-shaped scar on the left side of his face to flare a demonic reddish glow. *Should I be surprised the bartender's disposition matches his appearance,* thought Baltimore; nonetheless, he was thankful for the distraction and the opportunity to regain his composure.

Baltimore put a five-dollar bill on the bar and said, "Keep the change."

Shrek caught Baltimore's wrist as he reached for the beer. "That ain't enough," he said. Before Baltimore could respond, the bartender added, "'Cause you said you were buying a round for the bar, didn't he, fellahs?" Shouts of "Hell, yeah," and "Fucken' A," along with snickers and guffaws, erupted from the patrons. Baltimore stammered what could have been an objection as Shrek and the "fellahs" laughed.

"No, he didn't," Carmelita said. She must have moved like a wraith because no one, including Shrek, noticed her until she was standing a few feet behind Baltimore. Her tone—loud, clear, and unmistakably menacing—had the same effect as pressing a mute button: Shrek froze in mid-ridicule, and the barflies stopped laughing.

"Ha, ha." Shrek tried and failed at levity. "We was just fuckin' with him, ya know?"

Carmelita didn't respond to Shrek but didn't take her eyes off him. "Grab your beer," she said to Baltimore.

As they walked to the booth, Baltimore said, "I noticed the bulge under your hoodie." *Ugh, that sounded awkward,* he thought. "I mean, given your emaciated condition, it is quite prominent."

"Gee, thanks, Baltimore. You look like a million fucking bucks yourself."

"I-I'm sorry. I didn't mean that as an insult, but the bulge—it's a gun, isn't it?"

Carmelita flashed a look a mother gives a kid pestering for another cookie. "Shut up and sit down."

They sat, and a strange, contradictory impulse swept over Baltimore. Though grateful Carmelita intervened at the bar, he was nearly overpowered by an urge to unleash the total verbal hell on her that he had intended but decided against when he saw her. *Perhaps because I'm feeling totally emasculated,* thought Baltimore. Nevertheless, the unexpectedly intense desire to inflict emotional pain on an addict seeking help somewhat mystified and shamed him. The retaliatory gesture, however justified, felt like an irresistible biological imperative to kick someone while they're down—an impulse Baltimore considered himself much too evolved even to entertain. He chose to dial it down.

"So," he said, "what happened to the young woman who wanted to heal the earth and bring joy and enlightenment to its people through Native rituals?" Although he toned down the vehemence, sarcasm twisted his lips into a curvature of cruelty as he spoke.

"So, what happened to the young man who thought quantum physics would rescue humanity from its path of self-destruction?" She didn't return the cruelty; instead, the icy intensity of her glare frosted him down to the testicles. She answered for him: "The idealistic young man became just another greedy, punk-ass science pimp."

Silence.

"Checkmate," said Baltimore, after a few tense moments.

"Right," said Carmelita. "And now, who's guilty of diversionary tactics?"

Silence.

Carmelita broke the silence this time: "Are you done?" she said. Baltimore nodded sheepishly. Her voice and eyes softened as she resumed at the point where the bartender had interrupted. "My father said that the first time he shook your hand, he sensed an energy in your spirit he hadn't encountered before."

"Your father was probably high on peyote."

"Don't be an asshole, Baltimore. My father holds you in high regard."

"Sorry. I think highly of him as well."

"Father said he prayed for months for a vision to help him understand." She paused and again switched on her probing gaze. "And when a vision finally came to him, he said... he said you came to him in the vision."

Baltimore was stunned. *Holy crap! That was real?* He thought he had dreamed it.

"Except it wasn't a vision," said Carmelita.

"Then it was probably a dream," Baltimore said.

"No! It wasn't. Father said it started as his vision until it began to feel like he was being drawn into someone else's." Her eyes locked onto his. "And then he realized it was no vision. He was in another realm, a realm you drew him into. Father asked how you made that possible. He said you tried to explain—stuff about decoherence, non-locality—things he couldn't understand." She sipped her beer. "But he didn't need scientific explanations to understand that you could walk between worlds."

Knowing you're about to fall off a cliff doesn't make the landing any softer. Baltimore had anticipated Carmelita would eventually find out about his multiverse tripping because they'd had conversations about parallel worlds since their first date.

Baltimore chose La Casa Mestizo, a restaurant owned by a renowned Navajo-Mexican gourmet chef, for their first date. About half an hour into their dinner, Carmelita said, "You know, it was obvious you glossed over the topic of parallel worlds in class. It seemed as if there was something you didn't want us to know."

Baltimore couldn't stop fidgeting. "Well, concepts of multiverses and parallel worlds are speculations, unproven theories some consider outlandish."

"That sounds like modern science denial orthodoxy. I want to know what *you* think."

"Do I believe in alternate realities in which we exist as discrete yet somehow connected entities?" Baltimore paused as though pondering an answer, though he was really trying his best to conjure a non-committal response. "Mathematics does say the existence of parallel worlds is possible. If you recall, we studied the Many-Worlds Interpretation."

"Yeah, I remember. We were completely lost when you tossed around jargon like locality, uncertainty principle, wave function collapse—words and concepts we didn't understand, and which you didn't seem too eager to take the time to explain."

"Those are challenging concepts to explain to a layperson; indeed, one of the greatest theoretical physicists once said, 'I think that I can safely say that nobody understands quantum mechanics.' The most common barrier is the limitation of language. English or any language doesn't have the linguistic capacity to describe quantum phenomena adequately; thus, terms like the examples you used are simply approximations."

"Yeah, that's what you said in class. Still sounds evasive to me—although the 'limitation of language' makes sense; it reminds me of Edward Abbey."

"You've read Abbey?"

"Of course. Abbey's one of the few white men who spoke like an Indian about the land and humanity's connection to it. He said that language is like fishing for simple facts with a loose net."

"I remember that line. It's as apt a metaphor for language's limitations as I've ever read, except 'simple' and quantum phenomena don't belong in the same context. Realistically, developing a functional understanding would take several years of math and physics."

Carmelita nodded. "That sounds reasonable," she said. "And what about the math? We studied the quantum wave function, but what do you mean math says a multiverse is possible? In regular English, please, if that's possible."

"Mathematically, every single point in the wave function represents a quantum state, which physics currently defines as existing simultaneously as a particle and a wave—a definition of superposition you so eloquently pointed out is our feeble attempt to explain what we don't fully understand." She executed a seated curtsy; he bowed and continued, "Some physicists define a quantum state as a sum or superposition of all possible states, states they claim we can't detect because they exist in parallel worlds. Furthermore, they argue that our world, our reality, and even our universe exist in a quantum state; hence, we exist in superposition with thus far undetectable parallel worlds."

"Wow. We didn't study that theory in class."

"No, we didn't. It's the simplified version you requested, and it illustrates the limitation of language, for what words do we have to define states of existence beyond particles and waves, heck, even beyond solids, fluids, and gasses? Can we even conceive of what those states might look like? Moreover, do we assume parallel worlds are three-dimensional and, therefore, the same laws of physics apply, including our concepts of space and time? Should we assume parallel worlds are completely different versions of this one or only slightly different worlds in which we live out choices we didn't make in this world, as some multiverse theories propose?"

"Damn, Baltimore."

"Indeed. So that's the dilemma: One can choose the conventionally accepted binary interpretation of quantum states, or one can accept that all states are possible and, therefore, that one exists simultaneously in an infinite number of discrete alternate realities."

"So, does that mean you believe in the Many-Worlds Interpretation?"

"The math says it's possible; it doesn't show us how to make it possible."

"So, either you do, or you don't. Which is it?"

"Hmm. You've effectively backed me into a metaphorical corner with only two options for escape: either I believe or don't believe." Contemplative pause, and then an aha moment. "However, quantum mechanics offers a third option: Why can't I believe and disbelieve simultaneously? A superposition of beliefs, as it were."

Carmelita regarded him with a raised eyebrow and a smile that seemed more inspired by revelation than mirth. She shook an index finger at him and said, "You're a tricky one, Dr. Reynolds. I'm going to have to keep an eye on you."

"I'm hoping," he muttered.

"Oh, you are, are you?" She flashed a radiant smile.

Various shades of red washed over his face. He stammered through an attempted apology before saying, "You weren't supposed to hear that."

"More tricks? Are you a trickster?"

"No. I—"

"You know, in our folklore, Coyote is a trickster," Carmelita said. "Are you a Coyote, Dr. Reynolds?"

"No. No, I-I, I don't indulge in subterfuge," he replied.

In the dingy Silver Bullet booth, Baltimore avoided Carmelita's gaze by trying to peel off the beer bottle's label and said, "Well, 'walking between worlds' would be quite a scientific achievement, wouldn't it?" He laughed weakly, knowing the attempted denial was unconvincing.

"That's why I finally snuck into your lab—or should I say labs? I wanted to find out exactly what you were up to."

"You could have asked. I would have shown you my lab."

"You wouldn't have shown me what I saw behind the door with the digital lock."

He shrugged, dismissing her last comment. "There's no way you could have snuck into either lab; they're highly secure areas."

"Please. It was easy. I found a janitor—a horny bastard who undressed me with his eyes. He unlocked the front door."

Baltimore was beginning to get nervous. He tried not to show it. "And then?"

"I saw the door with the high-tech lock, figured it was another lab, and went in."

"Not possible. That's a state-of-the-art, password-secured digital lock." Baltimore shot her a raised eyebrow look. "There's no way you or a horny janitor could have unlocked it."

She smirked and said, "Really? You think you're that hard to figure out?" She described how she had entered the names of physicists she'd heard him and his friends talk about, but none unlocked the door. She then recalled advice he'd repeatedly told his team: Keep it simple, stupid. She asked herself: What's the simplest answer?

Baltimore couldn't keep his leg still and fussed with his shirt's buttons. He knew where this was going.

"'He's a nerd in love,' I told myself, 'what else would he use?' I typed in my name and"—Carmelita snapped her fingers—"open sesame."

Baltimore shifted in his seat. He could no longer hide his concern. "What'd you do then?"

"I saw you in a round, steel chamber. I waved but thought you didn't see me, so I got closer. I looked you straight in the eyes and waved. You were looking right at me, but it was like you were looking through me, at something far away. I got scared. I was worried something awful was happening to you." She scrutinized him with the intensity of a detective who had just found the suspect's fingerprints on the murder weapon. "I opened the hatch, wiggled into the chamber, and reached out to touch you. My hand went right through yours."

*Crap!* Now, what was he going to do? "You must have been smoking 'cide that day."

"Don't say that, Baltimore. That's just mean." The icy glare returned. "Besides, I wasn't doing 'cide back then, fucker," she said in a whisper that sounded like a snake flicking its tongue. She paused, possibly for effect, perhaps to allow the icy glare to thaw before continuing: "Anyway, when my hand passed through yours, these, uh...these images, no, more like scenes from a movie, flashed through my mind. But..." Carmelita shook her head and looked down. "You'll probably think I'm crazy, but...," she hesitated, seemingly gathering the courage to say it. She looked up at Baltimore and said, "It was like watching a movie through a kaleidoscope—images of people sliced into irregular shapes and reassembled in unnatural forms."

Baltimore just nodded, his mind racing through analyses of the implications of what he was hearing and formulating statistical probability models for possible outcomes.

"I freaked out and started to back out of the chamber, and then you...you just...you just disappeared." Tears highlighted the red in her bloodshot eyes. "I got so scared, Baltimore. I didn't know what to do, so I went to see my father—I hoped he'd help me understand."

"What did he say?'

Carmelita regarded Baltimore; awe and suspicion framed her expression. "Father is convinced you and he met on another plane of existence. He believes you somehow found a way to walk in other realms, even realms where only the most devout, experienced seers can go."

"Many-Worlds," he said as if thinking aloud.

"What?"

"The Many-Worlds Interpretation. The Native concept of other planes of existence is similar to the Many-Worlds Interpretation. Their similarity is what I tried to explain to your father the day he took me for a walk in the desert, and when I...." Baltimore let the words drift to silence, relieved he'd caught himself before admitting he had appeared in...in what? He was still shaken by the possibility he and Carmelita's father had not met in a dream or a vision but had likely met in another realm—a realm Baltimore might have drawn him into.

Carmelita shook her head and stared at Baltimore—wonder and puzzlement seemed to illuminate her gaze. "I didn't—I couldn't believe it back then, and I'm still having trouble wrapping my mind around it. But I had to know for sure because it's my last hope."

Baltimore was beginning to calm down and simultaneously was relieved to finally share the secret he'd kept from her since the day of his breakthrough experiment. Maintaining DARPA-mandated secrecy meant he couldn't acknowledge to Carmelita and her father that parallels he had drawn between quantum mechanics and their spiritual beliefs had inspired the paradigm shift that resulted in the experiment's success. Especially influential was their conversation about the Ghost Dance.

That conversation had begun with him insulting her by insinuating that Natives ate peyote just to get high.

"I'm—I apologize. I did not intend to offend," Baltimore had said.

"I know you weren't being malicious," Carmelita had said, "but it still pisses me off that white people think Natives ingest hallucinogens just to get fucked up. My father and I practice a sacred ritual called the Ghost Dance. I won't go into specifics, but it's a ceremony in which peyote plays an important role."

"Just curious, so please don't be offended, but what is the purpose of this ritual?"

Carmelita's eyes bored into Baltimore's. He felt himself wilting like lettuce under a heat lamp. "The Ghost Dance lifts the veil between this world and the spirit world." She maintained the uncomfortable gaze. "And don't give me that, 'Oh, no wonder they need entheogens,' look."

"I, I...," Baltimore's cheeks felt like they were on fire. *How did she know that's what I was thinking?* he wondered.

"Peyote doesn't help us see our ancestors in the spirit world; peyote frees the shackles the mind places on the spirit that bind it to this reality."

Baltimore perked up. "Yeah, I thought that would get your attention," Carmelita said. "In one of your lectures, you said some physicists speculate that objective reality doesn't exist and that we live in a hologram. Some Natives believe this reality is a dream and real life is lived in the dream world."

Baltimore's mind had roiled with the practical implications of what Carmelita had just said. One thought, however, had risen above the analytical din: How this ritual aligned so closely with the theories of alternate realities and those questioning the existence of objective reality.

But a new problem now presented itself: What to do about Carmelita. In her present state, no one would believe what she witnessed in his lab. Still, he didn't want his discovery to go viral until his business partner completed the market potential research. He scoured his memory for the day Carmelita might have walked in on the experiment.

Baltimore stiffened. Several alarming thoughts poked his brain like thorns piercing eyeballs: *Carmelita said, "greedy science pimp," does that mean she knows about my intent to market my discovery? Does she know my business partner, Mr. Latrans? More pressing, what if she's told someone in El Ojo about what she'd seen?* "Have you told anyone besides your father what you saw in the lab that day?"

"Are you kidding? If I told anyone else what I saw, they'd have me tossed into a padded cell faster than you could say, 'Large Hadron Collider.'"

"What else did your dad say?" Baltimore wanted to ask whether her father had shared their conversation with anyone but calculated the probability was high she would intuit his motive if he asked the question directly.

"He said that only someone with great power could pull a man like him out of his vision." She paused to sip the beer she'd been nursing. "There's something else I need to tell you. During certain rituals, I've walked in other realms with my father. Those realms felt peaceful and benign, and the beings inhabiting them were gentle and welcoming. What I saw and felt in your lab that day was the exact opposite. The beings seemed so full of hatred and anger and fear, but the worst part was the vibe: I felt malevolence so overpowering that it seemed to suck the oxygen out of my lungs. The whole experience felt like...like some evil brujo magic, Baltimore, and it terrified me. That's when all I wanted was to get the fuck away from you." She shuddered and said, "That's some seriously spooky shit you're messing with, Baltimore."

"So, you ran off with Alex and his *Clockwork Orange* scumbag buddies. That's how you dealt with your fears?"

"I told you I was sorry."

"Sure, and now you want me to take you to a parallel world and hide you." Baltimore nodded, and his speech slowed as he spoke the last few words. It was like finding the solution to a frustrating equation. He was about to address her request when the tattoo-faced sicarios opened fire. In the half-dozen heartbeats between the thugs entering, locating them, and aiming their weapons, Carmelita grabbed Baltimore's wrist and yanked him to the floor with her.

"Stay low, and stay on my ass," she said as gunfire jack-hammered their eardrums. The shower of particles that seemed to leap in slow motion from the surfaces of tabletops, chairs, and the wall entranced Baltimore. It was as if patches of molecules rebelled against their atomic bonds and burst free in a dance of wood, vinyl, and gypsum debris.

"Hurry up!" The sound of Carmelita's voice broke the spell. She led them through a nearby doorway and into a hall where the bathrooms were. At the end of the hall was a door leading to an alley. Outside on one side of the door was a dumpster.

"Help me roll this," Baltimore said.

"That's not going to stop them."

"No," he said, grunting, "but it will slow them down."

With the dumpster in place, Baltimore began tapping on the screen of what looked like a wristwatch.

"You're checking the time?" Her facial expression seemed to question his intelligence. "It's time to get the fuck out of here, Baltimore. Now!"

"I'm working on it."

"What? How?"

Baltimore didn't answer; he continued tapping on the screen. "There," he said. He pointed at a metal box about the size of a laundromat dryer some twenty yards away. "Let's go—and stay on my ass."

"What is that?" She asked, as they ran toward the box.

"An electrical transformer."

"Not that. The thing on your wrist."

Baltimore didn't answer. The thugs trying to shoot through the door tabled any further discussion. They ran faster. One of the thugs screamed, and the shooting stopped. Baltimore deduced that a bullet ricocheted off the dumpster and wounded him. Good, thought Baltimore, *that buys us a few more seconds.* They were near the transformer when the shooting resumed briefly and then stopped.

At the box, Baltimore once again tapped on the watch's screen.

"Baltimore, we—"

"Shut up for a second," he said, keeping his eyes on the screen. The entire time they'd known one another, Baltimore hadn't ever spoken to Carmelita so assertively. She was momentarily stunned into silence.

The lull in gunfire exploded into thudding of rifle butts striking the door, followed by the crackling and splintering of wood—sounds that echoed down the alley as the thugs broke through the door's bullet-riddled top half.

"How the hell did they find me so fast?" Carmelita muttered to herself.

Without looking up from the screen, Baltimore said, "The logical conclusion is El Ojo offered a reward and—"

"Oh goddamnit! One of those fucking lowlifes in the bar snitched me out."

"Exactly." He looked up from the watch and said, "Okay, hold on to me." She complied. "With both hands. And get closer."

Carmelita wrapped her arms around Baltimore's waist. He tapped the screen, and instantly, waves of nausea washed over them as a field of electromagnetic energy enveloped their bodies and began to rotate. "Damn, Baltimore!" she said. "From a steel shell to a wristwatch in three years?"

The gunmen grunted and cursed in English and Spanish as they pushed the dumpster aside. The air around Carmelita and Baltimore pulsated. In microseconds, the vortex's rotational velocity reached dizzying speeds, and Carmelita had to close her eyes to keep from falling. A dark cloud formed above the vortex as the two remaining thugs shouldered their weapons and prepared to fire. Bolts of black lightning sizzled from the cloud as an aperture of blackness opened in its center and expanded. Powerful vibrations passed through Baltimore's and Carmelita's bodies like fast, amplified shudders. The vortex then shot upward into the blackness, and the aperture slammed shut with a thunderclap that sounded like the end of the world, leaving nothing to indicate Baltimore and Carmelita had ever existed in this reality.

*Note: "Quantum Love Story" continues in Part II in* Xicanxfuturism: Gritos for Tomorrow, Codex II.

# BORDER-TOWN

## NATALIA RIVAS

border-town

clamor ascends
into the sky
the scent of shipyards
swallowing
the air
leaving eroding chemicals

brown skinned and boisterous
busy streets
shopping bags filled with
tamarindo, mango y verduras
magic and sage

mariachis
serenading
sturdy flowers pushing through cement
displaying strength and beauty

a mother sitting on a chair
with the cosmos
in her eyes
tenderly stroking her child's face
sleeping on her chest

cantinas boozy and loud
blasting sordid tales
of raunchy nights

with pleasant kisses
tasting like beer and mint gum

thundering beastly cars
riding low
riding slow
tres flores air freshener
and pachuco swagger growling

as finely clad compas
narrate the cost of extraterrestrial travel
while discussing ancestral rules and regulations

y los vatos that hang at the park
nod in unison
acknowledge
the pleasant taste of a cool chela
chiflando at the fine ruckas passing by
the chavalas glance back
and said "chale
we have no time for locos"

amate colorfully displaying
piñata's swing above sight
slightly sway awaiting final blows
striking abundance showering

border-town - part 2

the voice of the people marching
waving righteous flags to protect
humanity from being destroyed
pain dragged through centuries
in perpetual grief

dismay greets
truth to poverty
vulgar in its displays
random violence patient
sucking the life source
leaving poisoned imprints
stop signs at every corner

vulgarity dresses up
cheerful in its appearance
but deadly in its blow
by dead beat politicians
slowly grinding their teeth
into false smiles

reminding us to pay our taxes
do our time
die on the installment plan
as they dine on the future

with
perpetual ads
blasting our brains
into submission
so we forget

border-town - part 3

so there it is
all the ingredients mixed
sweet, bitter, sour and salty
the pot stirred
ready
with cosmic

memories wrapped
in surprise and intention
ready
for the drums to start
the sage to burn
ready
for the next indicated
evolution

revolution
indigenous whimsy
tribal roots
weaving our journey
with poetry and art

can you feel the ancestors
can you hear the ancestors
call out in timeless urgency

calling out from
the place where logic is astral

calling to us
calling to us
to stand
to stand like warriors
stand like warriors
warriors stand

# OBSIDIAN VISIONS: YES, WE WILL

1. How does the "The Many-Worlds Interpretation" from "Quantum Love Story Part I" meet the concept of Yes, We Will and the "pot stirred" of "border-town"?

2. Considering the last line in "Illegal Letters" by Patrick Fontes of, "Tio, please, teach me my letters," how is education resistance? What is education resisting?

3. How do the ideas of "bone dust" being fuel in Osmani Ochoa's "Drag queen 3004" and "warriors stand" in Natalia Rivas's "border-town" meet? Are they similar notions? What other pieces in this section express these ideas?

4. How does the image of Joaquin Murrieta riding a rocket in space ("#00202" by elindiocopyright1985), as part of a famous image of the 19th century folk hero, figure in this section, on overcoming inherent in "Yes, We Will"? How does the tongue-in-cheek imagery mix with empowerment?

5. What kind of future does "Section One: Dispatch from an Aztlan Insurgent" by Ernesto Mireles advocate for? What needs to happen to make it happen?

# CONTRIBUTOR BIOS

**Angela Acosta, Ph.D.** is an Assistant Professor of Spanish at the University of South Carolina. Her Rhysling and Utopia Award-nominated writing has appeared in *Somos en escrito, Apparition Lit, Radon Journal,* and *Space & Time.* She is the author of *A Belief in Cosmic Dailiness* (Red Ogre Review).

**Frederick Luis Aldama,** also known as Professor Latinx, is the Jacob & Frances Sanger Mossiker Chair in the Humanities and Affiliate Faculty in the Department of Radio-Television-Film at the University of Texas at Austin, as well as Adjunct Professor and Distinguished University Professor at The Ohio State University. He is the award-winning author of more than forty-eight books, including the bilingual children's books *The Adventures of Chupacabra Charlie* and *With Papá.* He is editor or co-editor of nine academic press book series, including Latinographix, which publishes Latinx comics. He is the creator of the first documentary on the history of Latinx superheroes and the founder and director of UT Austin's Latinx Pop Lab.

**Gerardo Aldana y Villalobos** is a professor of Chicana/o Studies at UC Santa Barbara. His work focuses on non-fiction, including *Calculating Brilliance: An Intellectual History of Mayan Astronomy at Chich'en Itza* (University of Arizona Press), but he recently ventured into speculative fiction with *Citlalli in the Sky with Cnidaria* for the Berggruen Institute.

**Rocio Anica** is a former lecturer at Cornell University where she garnered the Martin Sampson teaching distinction. Her work has appeared in various literary publications, including *Driftwood Press, Acentos Review, Woven Tale Press, Review: Literature and Arts of the Americas,* and *Chiricú Journal.* She has written and collaborated on several theatrical works, including a one-act debut at Casa 0101 in Boyle Heights. Her awards include first place in *Juxtaprose Magazine's* 2016 Short Fiction Contest and *Wigleaf's* Top 50 (Very) Short Fictions 2017. She now fully devotes herself to writing, teaching, and traveling between upstate New York, Northeast Pennsylvania, and the Florida panhandle with her husband,

Mike, and their two dogs, Corrido and Cajita. Cajita, naturally, is her mejor amiga. Find out more at rocioanica.com.

**Ernesto Ayala** is a lifelong member of el Partido Nacional de La Raza Unida, a proud Chicano father to a 17-year-old Chicanita and a 17-month-old Chicanito. He is an organizer and a future educator. In late 2019, Ernesto co-founded Telejaguar and in 2020 joined MeXicanos 2070. He and his family proudly reside in Pacoima, CaliAztlan.

**Colton "Cuca" Campbell** is a PhD. student in Chicana/o Studies at the University of New Mexico. His research is mix of history, cultural studies, and fiction. His art deals with topics surrounding ecology, surveillance, the mysterious, and Xicanxfuturism. Instagram: @ camel_campbell_camel. Email: coal10tx@gmail.com.

**Dr. E.C.-Dukes** is a Xicana award-winning multi-genre writer and entrepreneur from southern New Mexico, U.S.A. E.C. earned a Doctor of Philosophy degree in Rhetoric and Composition from the University of Texas at El Paso, a Master of Fine Arts degree in Film from Columbia University in the City of New York, and a Bachelor of Arts degree from the University of Minnesota-Twin Cities in Journalism and Chicano Studies and a minor in Theatre Arts. She is the author of two graphic novels, *Daizee & the DUKES of Chuco: Chuco- Juárez World Rally* and *A.W.O.L.: Cruz Ochoa.* To learn more about her work, visit: www.drecdukes.wordpress.com.

**Ronnie Dukes** is a Black artist with Latino and Indigenous heritage from South Shore Chicago. His first professional artist experience began at Gallery 37 while in high school. Ronnie earned a degree in computer animation in Minneapolis before relocating to Harlem in New York City where he began to paint and exhibit work. Ronnie created his publishing company DUKEScomics with his wife, partner Elvira Carrizal-Dukes, featuring their first major print project *A.W.O.L.: CRUZ OCHOA,* a full -color graphic novel available in English, Japanese and Spanish. Ronnie's second graphic novel as the artist is *Daizee & the DUKES of Chuco: Chuco- Juárez World Rally* available in English, German, and soon Spanish and Japanese. To learn more, visit DUKEScomics.com.

**Scótt Russell Dúncan,** a Xicano writer, edited the first Chicano sci-fi anthology, *El Porvenir, ¡Ya!* He is director of Palabras del Pueblo writing workshop and co-creator of Maíz Poppin'

Press. His novel, *Old California Strikes Back,* a magic memoir and meta-novel, is published through FlowerSong Press. www.scottrussellduncan.com.

**elindiocopyright1985's** work is mostly a digital mix and mash or cut and paste of historical and popular images, with a concentration in Mexican/Chican@ iconography. Just imagine Andy Warhol meets Emiliano Zapata, with a sprinkle of Frida and a dash of Banksy. He works with serious subject matter, but tries to present it in a "pop" or light-hearted manner. His debut poetry book, *Once Upon a Time in... Occupied Aztlán,* is soon to be published through Maíz Poppin' Press.

**Dr. Patrick Fontes** grew up in Fresno, where he lives and teaches today. He received an MA in history from CSUF, and a PhD in American History from Stanford University. Patrick's poetry has appeared in multiple journals, including *La Bloga, The Mas Tequila Review,* and *The Acentos Review.* Patrick is also an avid and published photographer: www.patfontesart.com Floricanto Press published Patrick's first novel *Maria's Purgatorio,* in 2017. Bone & Ink Press published his first poetry collection in 2019, titled *Mountains of Rust. Blood Set,* Patrick's second novel, is first in a series. Patrick is Professor of US History at Clovis Community College and teaches Chicano Studies at Fresno State.

**Martin Hill Ortiz** is a professor of Pharmacology at Ponce Health Sciences University in Puerto Rico. Over fifty of his stories have appeared in print. Author of six mystery thrillers, the most recent, *The Missing Floor* from Oliver-Heber Books, he is an active member of Mystery Writers of America.

**Pedro Iniguez** is a horror and science-fiction writer from Los Angeles, California. He is a Rhysling Award finalist and a Best of the Net and Pushcart Prize nominee. He is the author of *Mexicans on the Moon: Speculative Poetry From a Possible Future* and *Fever Dreams of a Parasite.*

**Jenny Irizary** co-edited *El Porvenir, ¡Ya! - Citlalzazanilli Mexicatl - Chicano Science Fiction Anthology, Our Creative Realidades,* along with other books published by Somos en escrito Press and served as an assistant editor on *Somos Xicanas* (Riot of Roses Publishing House, 2024). Their work has been published in *CERASUS, Squalorly, Hinchas de Poesía, Communion, Snapping Twig,* and other journals. Jenny's poem "Good Samaritan Church" placed in Litquake San Francisco's 2018 writing contest, and their poem "If You Want More Proof She's Not Puerto Rican" won first place for poetry in *Green Briar Review's* 2016 genre contest.

**Erika Said Izaguirre** is based in Houston. She holds a BA in Hispanic Studies from Universidad de Chihuahua and a MFA in Spanish from UTSA. She is currently a candidate for the PhD. in Spanish Creative Writing and the author of the poetry collections *Postcards From The Border* (Mouthfeel) and *iPoems: Poemas En Shuffle* (El Humo). She is also the author of two bilingual children's books with Arte Público Press.

**Samantha "Eggsy" J.** is a digital artist from Texas. Instagram: @eggmil.k. Email: SammieJo. Harbaugh@gmail.com.

**Joe Menchaca** is an emerging Latino/Native writer of fiction, poetry, and nonfiction with a Master's in Creative Writing from the University of Denver. Joe's writing is marked by an unpretentious and gritty, yet lyrical style. Unflinching in his examination of self, literature, and culture, his distilled style reflects a sensitive and perceptive exploration of life. His poetry can be found in *Dissident Voice* and *Somos en escrito*. Joe currently lives in Fort Collins, Colorado, with his lovely wife of nearly forty years and Tiny, their Chihuahua.

**Ernesto Todd Mireles,** MSW. PhD. is a filmmaker and award-winning author, a three-decade student, community, union, and electoral organizer. Mireles has been a professor of Xicano Studies for the last 17 years. When he rocks on the mic, he rocks the mic right. He holds an MSW in organizational and community practice and a PhD. in American Studies from Michigan State University. His book *Insurgent Aztlan* was awarded a 2020 International Latino Book Award in the Best Political/Current Affairs category. Mireles does a podcast called *The Reality Dysfunction* and has completed his first documentary about Xicana/o/x student organizing titled *War of the Flea: Fight for Xicano Studies*. He has recently started writing short screenplays and filming them.

**Osmani Ochoa** (he/él/they) is a queer Mexican-Xicano poet, co-editor at Maíz Poppin' Press, and long-time national organizer for immigrant and worker rights based in San Antonio, Texas. Their migrant futurist work has been accepted for publication in *Space & Time Magazine, Star*Line Magazine, Windward Review, La Raíz Magazine,* and *VOICES* *de La Luna.* They won the 2025-2026 Abode Press chapbook prize for their forthcoming *How to Survive an Asthma Attack in a Climate Apocalypse.* For more information: www.osmaniochoa.com.

**Dante Olivas** is a graduate student in a Master's Program in Chicanx Studies at the University of New Mexico. He has always been interested in writing poetry, fiction, and nonfiction. From the beginning of his academic career, he has wanted to be published academically and in passion projects like this, where he can flex his creativity on the page.

**Juan Manuel Pérez,** a Mexican-American poet of Indigenous descent and the Poet Laureate for Corpus Christi, Texas (2019-2020), is the author of numerous poetry books including the newly published poetry-memoir, *Thirty Years Ago: Life and the First Gulf War* (2023). Juan, a former migrant worker, is also the 2021 Horror Authors Guild's Inaugural Lifetime Achievement Award winner and a recipient of a 2021 Horror Writers Association Diversity Grant. To learn more about this award-winning Chicano poet, combat vet, and gourd dancer, check out his official website at: www.juanmperez.com.

**Natalia Rivas** is a 73-year-old survivor of revolutionary jargon and a retired substance abuse counselor, who found her voice again after retiring. Her style is surrealistic storytelling, and she loves the idea of weaving together her journey with myth and ancestral magic. She has been active in the poetry and art scene in San Francisco in the 70s when the murals were going up in the Mission district and started reading again two years ago in San Diego.

**Catrióna Rueda Esquíbel** (1965–2024) was a professor of Race and Resistance Studies at San Francisco State University. She published extensively in the field of queer Chicanx studies and was a devotee of Octavia Butler. Along with Luz Calvo, she co-authored *Decolonize Your Diet: Plant-Based Mexican-American Recipes for Health and Healing* (2015).

**Ricardo Tavarez** is a Bay Area educator and arts organizer. Most recently, Ricardo co-edited *Después del Aguacero: A Pan Dulce Poet Anthology* on Pochino Press and is a member of the International SF Flor y Canto Festival. His short stories use historical narratives and geopolitics to explore dilemmas. Ricardo holds an MFA from San Francisco State, his writing appears in publications online and in print.

**Luis Valderas** has taught art in Texas Public Schools for 29 years. In 2005 Valderas co-founded and produced Project:MASA I, II, and III—a national group exhibit featuring Latino artists and focusing on Chican@ identities. He co-founded A3—Agents of Change LLC, a large-scale printmaking community engagement collaborative. Valderas is a mentor and board member for the New York Foundation for the Arts. He has exhibited at the Medellin Museum of Art-Colombia, the Queens Museum-NYC and the URC ArtsBlock-Riverside CA, The Museum of Anthropology at UBC-British Columbia, Canada. His work is featured in books such as: *Altermundos-Latin@ Speculative Literature, Film and Popular Culture, Mundos Alternos-Art and Science Fiction in the Americas, Chicano Art for Our Millennium-2004* and *Triumph in Our Communities: Four Decades of Mexican American Art-2005*. He is in the permanent collections of UTSA, Arizona St. University, Art Museum of South Texas and the San Antonio Museum of Art.

# ABOUT THE EDITORS

**Scótt Russell Dúncan,** a Xicano writer, edited the first Xicano sci-fi anthology, *El Porvenir, ¡Ya!: Citlalzazanilli Mexicatl* and is creator and editor of the *Xicanxfuturism: Gritos for Tomorrow* codices. He is director of Palabras del Pueblo writing workshop and co-creator of Maíz Poppin' Press. His novel, *Old California Strikes Back,* a magic memoir and meta-novel described as *Fear and Loathing in Las Vegas* meets *Yo Soy Joaquin,* is published through FlowerSong Press. www.scottrussellduncan.com. Find & follow @scottrussellduncanfernandez & @chicanofuturism.

**Jenny Irizary** co-edited *El Porvenir, ¡Ya! - Citlalzazanilli Mexicatl - Chicano Science Fiction Anthology, Our Creative Realidades,* along with other books published by Somos en escrito Press, and served as an assistant editor on *Somos Xicanas* (Riot of Roses Publishing House, 2024). Their work has been published in *CERASUS, Squalorly, Hinchas de Poesía, Communion, Snapping Twig,* and other journals. Jenny's poem "Good Samaritan Church" placed in Litquake San Francisco's 2018 writing contest, and their poem "If You Want More Proof She's Not Puerto Rican" won first place for poetry in *Green Briar Review's* 2016 genre contest. Find & follow @irizaryjenny.

# ABOUT THE PUBLISHER

Riot of Roses Publishing House was founded in 2021 specifically to amplify the stories of historically silenced voices and narratives.

Xicana owned. Mujerista focused. For the people.

We publish books that heal and liberate.

Read our rebellion.

Find & follow us @riotofrosespublishing
Visit us at www.riotofrosespublishinghouse.com